CHASING cowboys

MICHAEL LITTLE

To Peggy –
Best wishes to a Calgary cowgirl!
Chase your dreams, always.

Aloha,

Michael Little

Honolulu
October 2009

An *Aloha Romance Writers* Publication
3116 Mokihana Street
Honolulu, Hawai'i

Book design: Stephanie Chang Design Ink

Printed in the United States of America
1 2 3 4 5 6 7 8 9

For Stephanie

IOWA

1,545 mi   *"Adios to the dark side..."*

RENO

"I see by your outfit that you are a cowboy..."

ALASKA

1,969 mi

"North to Alaska..."

VIRGINIA CITY
"Take me to the green valley..." 23 mi

CARSON CITY
"A little starlight ranching..." 38 mi

"Cody and the cable cars..."
SAN FRANCISCO
217 mi

1 Charley

"I see by your outfit that you are a cowboy...."

You should have been there the day Lacey Anderson walked into Parker's hunting for some cowgirl clothes because someone at her new law firm had told her she wasn't in San Francisco any more and she would need some Western wear if she wanted to be a Reno lawyer. She looked lost. And mad at someone, probably the person who had thrown her into this alien cowboy world.

I watched her from behind the counter. At Parker's we generally let folks browse a while before we offer to help. I couldn't keep my eyes off her. Something about her was so familiar, but what it was had me stumped. She was a city girl all right, probably right at home at Macy's and those fancy downtown emporiums, but I doubt she had ever set foot in a big Western store.

Then she spotted Cody, the new kid who sure looked like a cowboy and would be able to help her, but what she didn't know was Cody had just arrived a few weeks before from some town in Iowa. He knew a lot about corn and pigs but not much about horses, except that he wanted to be a cowboy in the worst way and he already had his cowboy clothes, but of course Lacey thought he was a real cowboy and that's where all the trouble began.

I studied Lacey from the moment she entered the store, but then Donna Cooper walked in, her big blonde curly hair lighting up the place, and she began showing me her new rodeo wave, the one she had been perfecting for months so she could become the next Miss Reno Rodeo. Typical. All day nothing happening and then bang, we had two shows going on at once.

"Charley Meyers," Donna said, looking so serious, "you've seen lots of rodeo queens, tell me if you've ever seen one wave like this." Donna thinks I'm an expert at anything to do with cowboys and rodeo. It's true I've worked on ranches most of my forty-five years, and done my share of rodeo. Now I'm just a part-time or seasonal cowboy, like a lot of folks, and working at Parker's gives me a steady income and a chance to observe people.

"Never saw that wave before," I said. "I like the way you put your whole body into it." Donna flashed me that megabucks smile of hers. Then she said something about the Queen of England needing to work on her wave, and I told her to try on a new white hat that had just come in and practice in front of a full-length mirror. Any other day I could have stayed there and talked to Donna for hours. Just then, however, the San Francisco lawyer lady was walking up to Cody and I didn't want to miss anything.

I hustled over near the aisle where Cody was straightening some shirts, pretending I was looking for something. I got there just in time and didn't miss a word. The only problem I had was trying not to laugh at those two youngsters.

"Excuse me, do you work here?" Lacey said to Cody. Her voice would have melted the butter you just pulled out of the freezer, even with the edge on it from wanting to be somewhere else. I liked the way her big city perfume mixed with the leather and hardwood smells of Parker's.

Cody stopped fussing with the shirts and turned around. There in front of him, close enough to reach out and touch, stood a young woman with long legs, straight dark hair of medium length, and green eyes. She wore a navy business suit and would have been properly dressed for an appointment with a very conservative, very important client. She looked so out of place, Cody must have thought she was looking for something for a friend, or maybe had wandered into the wrong store.

"Yes, ma'am," he said, in that flat Midwestern voice that was all heartland and good manners. Somebody had raised him right.

"They told me I need some Western clothes," she began.

"Yes, ma'am?" he encouraged her, aware now that she was not in the wrong establishment.

"Well," she continued, "you see, I need everything."

"Yes, ma'am," he agreed with her, not knowing what to say to this intriguing customer. Cody had settled into his new job and surroundings, and now, after a month in Reno, he felt like one of the townspeople, if not a real cowboy yet. He had waited on some cowboys, and lots of folks dressed like cowboys, but never before today someone in such total need of help.

"I don't know where to start," she said.

"Yes, ma'am," he said without thinking. Face to face with a vision, the kid was suffering from a bad case of brain lock.

"Is 'Yes, ma'am' all you can say?" she asked, raising her voice a bit.

"No, ma'am," he said. They both laughed. This broke the ice.

"Okay," she said, "I'll tell you the whole sad story. I'm not a cowgirl."

This almost cracked him up, but he managed to keep it down to a big grin. The young woman grinned back. She had begun her confession, there was no escape now, and so she pushed on, hoping that the young cowboy would keep grinning and not laugh at her.

"You see, I'm from San Francisco and the law firm I work for there has opened a new office in Reno, and they made me transfer here, even though I wanted to stay in San Francisco, and I've been here just a couple of days and they say I will need to wear Western clothes for some occasions, everybody does, even lawyers, but they promised that I won't have to ride a horse if I don't want to." She stopped, out of breath and doubtless feeling more than a little foolish.

"No problem, ma'am," Cody said to make her feel at ease. The people at Parker's, as Cody had learned the first day, never rushed a customer or made them feel unimportant. In fact, Cody was enjoying this moment and wanted it to last. The next thing the customer said was music to his ears.

"You're a cowboy," she said, as if stating the obvious, "so I guess I need all the stuff you're wearing, only in a smaller size and more feminine." Her eyes pleaded for understanding. The words had come out a little strange. Cody was so impressed by the first part of her statement that he hardly noticed the rest of it. He gave the attractive young city lady his best cowboy grin and decided to take charge.

"Well, ma'am, let's move over to the ladies' side of the store and see what we can find. Let's look for a hat first. If you get the right one, everything else will kind of follow naturally. By the way, my name is Cody West, in case you need to visit us again." The cowboy name would close the deal, Cody knew, and she would never guess he was only a month out of the Iowa cornfields.

I didn't want to miss a word of this, so I followed Cody and Lacey over to the other side. By now Donna Cooper had moved on to the big three-way mirror and was practicing her rodeo queen wave again and checking out the profiles. Donna was missing the Cody and Lacey show, but when she was practicing her wave she could shut out the whole world. The girl knew all about focus.

Lacey smiled when she heard Cody's name. "Thanks, Cody," she said, visibly relieved that he would satisfy her Western clothing needs and she could end her embarrassing confession. "My name is Lacey Anderson. Pleased to meet you." The damsel in distress offered her hand to this polite young knight of the high desert.

"Lacey," he said as he shook her hand, "nice name. Sounds like a genuine cowgirl name. Are you sure you're a San Francisco lawyer?"

"Oh yes, two years out of law school and never been close to a horse. My mother wanted a feminine name for me, but I was a real tomboy as a kid. I never thought of my name as a cowgirl name."

"Well," Cody said as he began to show her some Western hats, "I think that names are mighty important." Cody had picked up the "mighty" part watching too many cowboy movies. "I believe you can discover someone's destiny just by knowing their name."

"Could be," Lacey offered. How could she argue with this tall cowboy who was going to get her outfitted and share some authentic cowboy wisdom at the same time?

"Sure," Cody continued, "take my name, for instance. With a name like mine, I couldn't be anything but a cowboy, could I?" He knew she could never forget this talkative cowboy with the genuine cowboy name.

"I guess not," said Lacey. "So I would bet you're working here to get a discount on the cowboy stuff."

"Well yes, and helping out the fellows here. Most of the year I work with horses and cattle outside town." Where did he come up with that lie?

"Oh," she asked, "do you have your own ranch?"

"No, I work with some friends, do whatever needs doing," he replied vaguely, then quickly changed the subject. "Let's try this black hat on you." He must have thought his cowboy inventions would be harmless, but now they were making him nervous. He looked down at his boots for a moment, as if he'd been careless and just stepped in a big cow pie.

Before long, Lacey Anderson the San Francisco lawyer had been transformed into Lacey Anderson the Reno lawyer, ready for any Western social occasion. She had the black hat with the thin silver band, the calfskin Justin boots, the dress jeans, a couple of sharp cowgirl shirts, and a cowgirl belt with a shiny silver buckle. Not bad for a city girl who didn't want to be in Reno in the first place.

And that's when it hit me. I looked at cowgirl Lacey and I was seeing someone else. Someone from twenty years earlier. Someone who had kidnapped my heart and ridden out of town, never to return. I was staring at Lacey, but I was seeing Angel. I'm single, never did get married. I should have asked Angel to marry me, but I was slow and stupid. I have no ex's down in Texas, or anywhere else. I have no heart to give to another woman. It's gone way the hell up the trail with Angel, wherever she may be, probably married now and with a mess of kids.

I blinked and then I was seeing Lacey again. Inspecting her transformation in a full-length mirror that stood against the wall next to the ladies' hats, she appeared to struggle to recognize herself.

"What would my friends in San Francisco say if they could see me now?" she chuckled.

At the same time Cody West was admiring his cowgirl creation. "Well, Lacey, I guess you're living up to your name."

"Not so fast," she said, pointing a finger at Cody. "I have the clothes but that doesn't make me a cowgirl. I bet you could teach me a lot about horses and cattle, maybe show me how to ride."

"Yes, ma'am," Cody said slowly, retreating suddenly to his polite manner. Too much talking had quickly landed him in a ticklish position. Was it too late to escape? Was she serious about the riding lessons, or just playing with him? A young lady that beautiful had to have a boyfriend back in San Francisco.

Lacey stepped closer. "Well, Mr. Cody West, I know your name and I know where you work. And you think I'm destined to be a cowgirl. I'm going to make you prove it to me one of these days."

"Yes, ma'am." Cody's voice was barely audible.

Lacey paid for her cowgirl duds, deciding to keep them on rather than change again, then marched proudly to the front door of Parker's famous Western store. Before she disappeared, though, she turned and waved at her new cowboy acquaintance. It was a big day for waves at Parker's. Lacey's own wave was like the friendly salute of a rodeo queen as she rides her horse at full gallop into the arena, looking her best and knowing it. Cody waved back, but his wave was more like that of the dude in the stands who waves at the rodeo queen but wonders to himself, "Who is this amazing creature, and why is she going so fast?"

Once Lacey disappeared I was able to turn my full attention back to Donna Cooper. She was still at the three-way mirror, but she had stopped working on the wave. Now it was the smile. She faced the mirror, pulled her hat low, and looked down at the floor. There she stood, hands on hips, and paused for one dramatic moment before slowly raising her head and flashing that smile of hers. God help the judges at the rodeo queen pageant. They'd be wise to whip out their sunglasses before Donna made her entrance.

2 Charley

"It's your misfortune and none of my own...."

As Cody turned away from the door he saw me behind the counter, shaking my head and trying not to laugh. From the day I hired him, I felt like a big brother toward the kid, or maybe a protective uncle. I had suggested a good apartment building for Cody, had given him tips on what to wear and how to help the customers, where to go for the best eating, and even when to take off his hat and when to keep it on. But I realized now that I hadn't got around to educating him about women. This was going to be some kind of deal.

Now he walked up to me, grinning like a sheep. "Did you see that?" he asked.

"Oh yeah," I answered, "I saw everything. You know, pardner, you've got your rope around a strong one there. You'd better be careful or you'll find yourself being dragged across the desert at the end of that rope, bumping into every rock and rattlesnake along the way. Sometimes it's hard to say who's branding who!"

"She thinks I'm a cowboy," Cody said.

"Yep, and I bet you didn't set her straight about it either."

Cody let out a big sigh. He needed help and I was his only real friend in town.

"Charley, you've been a working cowboy most of your life. Do you think you could give me a quick education before she comes back?"

"A quick education? When's she coming back?"

"She didn't say."

"How do you know she's coming back?" I asked, not wanting to tease the kid but anxious to find out more about this situation before I got involved in it myself.

"She said she knew my name and where I worked, and I think she wants me to teach her about horses and cattle."

"Boy, you're in a heap of manure there. Tell me something. How long do you think it takes to become a cowboy?"

"I know it's not easy," Cody answered, "but maybe you could teach me enough so she wouldn't find out."

"Cody, this is not pig farming, where you don't have to ride a horse to round 'em up. You know, critters out here don't stay in one place like a field of corn. I could teach you some things, but it takes a long time to become a real cowboy. And besides, she's probably got a boyfriend already. They always do."

"Then why was she flirting with me?"

"Women like to flirt," I said. "Don't you know that? That's how they test if they're attractive. If you go chasing every woman who flirts with you, you're sure to get your heart broken."

That made Cody stop. I could see the wheels turning. Perhaps someone had broken his heart before.

"Maybe," he said at last. "But maybe not. Come on, Charley, give me some help here." I think he didn't want to pester me, but Lacey was worth it. And he had told me he wanted to become a real cowboy anyway because his mom must have had that in mind when she named him or else she could have named him Dexter or Max after his uncles.

"Well, okay," I said. "I guess we can give it a shot. I like a good challenge now and then." I thought back to times when I had taken on some impossible challenges. "But no guarantees. And you have to listen to me and do what I say."

"Sure," Cody said, "you're the boss. What do I do first?"

"Learning to ride and work cattle's important," I began, thinking out loud, "but it's gonna take a while, so I think we need to stall her." And just then it came to me. It was so obvious. "Kid, what does a cowboy have that you don't have?"

Cody realized that his teacher was waiting for an answer, so he ventured a guess. "A ranch?"

"Well, we're not going to buy a ranch today. What else?"

"Chewing tobacco?"

That made me chuckle. "No, you'll scare her away, and you might choke to death. Then she'd lose interest fast. Guess again."

Cody tried to think of the John Wayne movies. "A colorful vocabulary?"

"Well, that helps," I said, "but I was thinking of something else. What you need is a truck. You can't be a Reno cowboy without a truck."

And so we would reverse history. Before the horse would come the horseless carriage, in this case a used Dodge pickup, purchased from Bob Morgan, one of my old friends. Bob had just bought a fancy new cowboy Cadillac, a big pickup loaded with everything a cowboy could imagine, as well as some features he didn't know he needed until he saw them.

From the first moment he laid eyes on the used truck, Cody was in love. He told me later that driving it home from Bob Morgan's place, shifting gears and checking the mirrors, he took a curious pride in the Dodge's battered appearance. Each dent and scrape bore witness to some cowboy adventure, and he felt less like a dude as he guided it down the road on a bright May morning. I had advised him that the scars in the pickup's hide would make the city lady think he was indeed a real working cowboy. I had also told him not to sweep out the leftover hay in the back, since it added to the Western ambience of the vehicle. Ambience? Cody looked surprised to find that my vocabulary was not limited to words like "rattlesnake" and "manure."

I also loaned him some CDs to play in the truck—a Willie Nelson, a Michael Martin Murphey collection of old cowboy songs, and a handful of others that I certified as appropriate for him and his pickup.

So Cody was ready for the next test. I assured him that since Lacey already believed him to be a real cowboy, the pickup was sure to pass inspection. When Cody opened the glove compartment and found a half empty can of Copenhagen chewing tobacco, I told him he could keep it there as long as he promised not to use the stuff. If the lady discovered the can and showed her disapproval, Cody could simply say that another cowboy had left it there, which was the truth anyway.

When we went to buy the truck, Bob Morgan took a photograph of the historic occasion, with Cody and me standing in front of the beat up blue pickup, both with rather somber expressions befitting the seriousness of this rite of passage. We held our Lone Star longnecks straight as my friend snapped the picture. It was the kind of picture most folks would keep for years afterward and take out now and then to reflect on a time when they were younger and full of frijoles. Cody said he planned to frame his copy and give it a place of honor.

Cody pulled into the parking lot in front of his apartment building, looked around to see if anyone was noticing his fine new acquisition, and was disappointed that no witnesses were around. "Oh well," he thought, "I didn't buy it to impress the neighbors." And as he stepped out, closed the solid driver's door, and locked it, he saw that half the vehicles in the lot were pickups. Two of them even bore a striking resemblance to his own battered Dodge. At first this discovery caused his spirits to drop, but then he realized that the whole idea was to fit in, and if his truck fit in then maybe he did too.

"Am I a cowboy yet?" he asked himself the question from his first day in Reno. The answer this time was "maybe half a cowboy." And there was no doubt that his pickup was a one hundred percent cowboy truck. Cody told me that before he fell asleep that night, he got out of bed twice to go out and check on his truck. He said it looked real pretty in the moonlight.

3 Charley

"First to the card house and then to the dram house...."

The next morning, with the sunlight on it, the pickup still looked pretty good to Cody. He climbed inside and headed for work. From this perch, he saw the world as a friendlier place, and on this cool morning, without a cloud in the sky, all things were possible.

Sure, the beautiful lady he had his eye on could have just been having some fun with him. Or she might go out with him and then break his heart in two on the second or third date, or maybe later on, when it would shatter into a thousand tiny pieces. Maybe she did have a boyfriend back in San Francisco, someone with lots of money and a fancy new car, someone she wanted to marry and she was just waiting for him to ask. Cody tried to shoo those doubts out the window of his new truck.

"Hey, cowboy, the junkyard's back the other way!" a loud voice interrupted. Cody looked to his left to see a pickup driven by a man who resembled the famous cowboy actor Ben Johnson, or as much as anyone could without being related. That was me, of course, not the movie star.

Cody used to needle me about the resemblance. "Hey, Charley," he asked once, when business was slow, "are you sure you're not related to that Hollywood cowboy Ben Johnson?"

"Sure, why?" I took the bait.

"Well," Cody began to reel me in, "you're just so danged handsome, in a beat up kind of way. I bet the ladies can't resist your cragginess."

"Keep it up and I'll show you a beat up face," I said, pretending to be angry. Later Cody caught me studying my face in the mirror when I thought nobody was watching.

Now we were driving into work and having a good time yelling at each other.

"Oh yeah?" Cody yelled back at me, "why don't you stop looking at yourself in the mirror and drive? The light's turned green." The driver of the car behind us, thinking that a serious traffic fight was about to break out, quickly drove onto the shoulder and around the two cowboys who were yelling at each other. If he had looked back he would have seen the two crazy cowboys laughing wildly.

Later that day, with paychecks cashed and settled at the bar of a local saloon where just about everyone knew me, we drank Lone Star from the bottle and continued Cody's education.

"Kid," I began in a deadly serious voice, "let me tell you about women."

Cody, who smiled easily, tried to make his face match the tone of my lecture. When the subject was cowboys or pickups, he had accepted my words as scripture. Now that his mentor was about to impart advice about women, however, Cody seemed hesitant to follow me blindly. True, I had many years of experience in the subject, as I had often assured him, but I think Cody usually followed his own advice in matters of the heart.

I paused, took a healthy pull on the beer, looked slowly to one side of the bar and then the other, and then, with the suspense just about right, began in a conspiratorial voice. "You see, son, women are different from men."

Cody somehow suppressed a smile, probably thinking to himself that I would have to do better than state the obvious. Instead he nodded thoughtfully and waited for more.

"They look different," I continued, "they smell different, they act different. You know that already, or else you wouldn't be interested in the subject. But the thing you can never forget is that they think different. Their minds just don't work the same as ours."

Cody said he had to agree with this, based on his own more limited experience. He began to listen more seriously.

"Think about it," I went on, my eyes growing larger as I contemplated the enormity of this difference between the sexes, "I know how your brain works and you know how mine works, am I right?"

Cody had to agree that was a true statement. He drank some more beer to prepare for the rest of this formal argument.

"And we've only known each other a few weeks," I pointed out. "But with women . . ." I stopped to look for the words. "But with women, you can know a woman for ten years, you can close your eyes and know how she looks and how she smells and all of that, but you will still not know how her mind works."

Cody was silent, studying my words as if they might be the genuine article as advertised.

"And here's the kicker, so listen carefully," I continued in a lower, more intense voice. "Just when you've got it all figured out, when you think you know a woman and how her mind works, that's the most dangerous time for you."

"Why is that?" Cody asked, leaning closer to catch every word.

"That's the most dangerous time because you've deluded yourself. You think you know her, but you don't have the smallest clue. It's like riding broncs."

"Like riding broncs?" Cody looked unsure he had heard this right.

"Exactly."

"Why is that?"

"Because," I said patiently, "each time with a bronc is different. Each bronc is different, and even with the same bronc, why each ride is different.

And if the cowboy in the chute thinks he knows what's going to happen in the next eight seconds he's sadly mistaken."

"So one woman is different from another?"

"Kid, you're a fast learner."

"And with the same woman, each day is different?"

"Bingo!"

Cody paused. This was getting too serious. "So, Charley, tell me just one more thing."

"What's that?"

"How do you get the woman into the chute?"

I must have looked like a teacher whose student has just cracked a joke in the middle of his most serious lecture. I tried to picture the scene that Cody had just suggested, which started me laughing, then I took off my hat and started swatting at the young rascal, and then I concluded by ordering another round of Lone Stars.

Cody and I spent a while trying to apply the bronc rider philosophy to our misadventures with women. Somewhere in there the conversation turned to current events and women that we knew at the moment. I invited Cody to drive down to Carson City with me Sunday evening to visit a lady friend who had a small ranch there. Cody said he had planned on washing his truck that day but that he could always wash it on Saturday.

Then I suggested a way that Cody could spend some time with the lawyer lady that didn't involve horses and cattle. I advised him to take her for a ride in his pickup, to escort her to the old mining town of Virginia City. This way he could get to know her better and could play her some cowboy songs in the pickup to get her into the mood. Cody had asked, which mood was that? I replied, the cemetery mood, of course, and went on to explain that the old cemetery set on a hill just outside of Virginia City was the most romantic place I knew. All the history of the region came to rest there. It was usually deserted, the view of the old town and the desert mountains was unparalleled there, and the odds were usually good that the lady had never been taken on a cemetery date before.

Cody had some misgivings but agreed to give it a try, partly because he was impressed by my bronc rider philosophy of women, and partly because he lost a bet when I beat him at arm wrestling so he had to take Lacey to the cemetery.

I left the saloon to attend to some business, and Cody told me later that he strolled into the nearest casino. It was a busy Thursday evening and he walked around the tables for a while. The payday cash in his wallet was screaming to get out, but he wanted to hang onto it for a while. He planned to watch for a while and then go for some dinner, but then something happened to change his plans. There in front of his eyes, at one of the two-dollar blackjack tables, was Lacey. She was alone. No rich guy feeding her chips and drooling over her. She had a short drink and a shorter stack of chips in front of her and was studying her hole card when she heard a familiar voice say, "You might want to double down, ma'am."

She turned to see the young cowboy who had helped her at Parker's. "Okay, I'll try anything," she said as she doubled her bet. When the dealer gave her the face card she needed, she almost shouted in relief, like someone waiting for a train that has finally arrived at the station. "Well, cowboy, you brought me luck."

"No, ma'am, just playing the odds. Mind if I join you?"

"Sure, just bring your luck right over here," she said, patting the chair to her left.

"New deck. Put down a dollar in case you get a blackjack," Cody advised her.

"I thought that was just a gimmick to attract business," she told him.

"No, you get 17 dollars if you get a blackjack. If you're a pessimist you can bet a dollar that the dealer will get a blackjack, but I don't recommend it. It's bad luck."

She smiled at Cody. "I thought you didn't believe in luck, just odds."

"Never said that, ma'am. I thought you lawyers knew all the angles."

"I thought you cowboys all hung out down at the saloon."

The repartee was interrupted by a bored dealer, a glum middle-aged man who advised them to place their bets. Lacey placed an extra chip on the table as Cody had advised. As it turned out, Lacey was dealt a blackjack and fairly beamed when the bored dealer moved a small mountain of chips her way. Cody had to work just to push and win back his two bucks.

"Ma'am," Cody said, "it seems you are blessed with sudden wealth this evening."

"You know, I feel rich. And please don't call me ma'am."

"All right there, missy," Cody replied in his best John Wayne voice. Unfortunately, it always came out sounding more like Fred Flintstone.

For a while the luck held out, but when they both lost three straight hands, Cody touched her arm and said they should leave while they were ahead. Lacey thanked him for bringing her luck and offered to buy him dinner with the winnings, if he hadn't eaten yet. They decided that they had won enough to visit the seafood buffet at the Eldorado, which came highly recommended by me.

Walking down Virginia Street, Cody remembered just how tall she was, about five-seven, even without boots. Tonight she had come from work and was dressed in a black skirt and white blouse. Cody, who had worn only cowboy clothes since arriving in Reno, felt as if he were escorting the pretty new schoolmarm down the street, or maybe a visiting opera singer from back east. They talked easily as they crossed the railroad tracks that marked the end of Alan Cody West's western trail, the same tracks that had brought him to Reno just a month earlier, the day he had dropped the Alan from his name and declared himself a cowboy.

Over dinner, Cody was grateful that Lacey did most of the talking, some of it about the attractions of San Francisco and some of it about being a lawyer. She seemed to welcome the challenge, and she talked about making partner as fast she could. She said she had a mentor in the firm back in San Francisco who had promised to put her on the fast track.

As they began on their gourmet dessert—chocolate suicide cake—Lacey suddenly stopped talking about her work and apologized for going on about it.

"No problem," Cody assured her, "I can see how all that legal stuff could weigh on your mind."

"Not as much as this cake is going to weigh on my hips," she joked. Cody was amused, but his amusement didn't last long, because Lacey had just remembered something.

"So when are you going to teach me to be a cowgirl?" she asked.

"I'm glad you asked," Cody lied. "I wanted to talk to you about that. You're a city girl and I don't think you should jump into this all at once. You need to learn some of the history of this region first." Cody said a silent thank-you to his friend Charley. He was a good student.

"What did you have in mind?" Lacey asked, relieved that she could stall him for a while on the four-legged critter stuff.

"I think you ought to see what was happening here over a hundred years ago. The treasure then was in the silver mines, not in the casinos. If you want, I could drive you up to Virginia City and show you what it was like."

Lacey quickly accepted and said she was free Saturday. Cody told her that he had planned to wash his truck but that it could wait. He realized, even as he said it, that a dusty truck might look more genuine. They agreed to meet at nine o'clock Saturday morning. Lacey gave him her address and telephone number, if not quite her heart, and they parted on Virginia Street to rest up for the historical junket. Her last words were more sweet music to Cody's ears.

"Goodnight, cowboy," she said, "sleep well."

4 Donna

"Anything you can I do I can do better..."

You're probably wondering what I'm doing here, so I'll tell you. My name is Donna Cooper and this whole writing thing started early on a Friday morning when I stopped by Celia Moon's new coffee shop, the Stella by Starlight Bakery and Gourmet Coffee Emporium. I just call it Stella's. That's where I caught Charley Meyers writing in one of those little black composition books. He tried to hide it when he saw me, but I was too quick for him. I sat right down next to him and made him show it to me. Turns out he'd started writing about Cody West, the new guy at Parker's, the one who's really cute but not for me because I'm going with Darryl King and have my hands full at the moment.

"Oh look," I said, "you've got me in the first chapter."

"You weren't supposed to see that part," Charley said, but it was too late.

"Seems pretty accurate, I can't complain." I read some more. "Oh, here you are spying on Cody in the store. Did that really happen, when he met that Lacey person?"

"Every bit of it," Charley said. "You were there, didn't you notice?"

"Well, I wasn't putting my nose in everybody else's business. I did see her, but I was busy trying on hats and practicing my rodeo queen wave."

"How's that wave coming?"

"I'm almost there," I said. "I'll be ready for the pageant."

"Good luck, I hope you win," Charley said.

"Thanks, me too, but if I don't I'll just try again next year. It's hard to win on the first try. But I want to win. But it's hard. But I want to win *so bad*." I looked through Charley's writing book some more, then Celia brought me coffee and I asked her to surprise me with a pastry, something rich and sweet but not too fattening.

"The shop's looking great," I told her.

"Thanks," Celia said. "How do you like the new sign? It cost a lot because the name's so long."

"Don't change a thing," Charley said.

Celia smiled. "Can't afford to," she said. Then she left to get the pastry. I went back to reading what Charley had written about Cody and Lacey.

"So," I said, "what is this going to be, some kind of novel?"

"Yep, something I've wanted to do for a long time, ever since college."

"I thought you went to college on a rodeo scholarship," I said.

"True, but I took a lot of English classes."

"Well, why don't you write about rodeo? You must have lots of good stories from all those years you were riding broncs."

"Maybe I will," Charley said. "I'll tell you what, if you make rodeo queen maybe I'll write a book just about you."

"Would you?" I said. "Like a big photo album, only with words?"

"Sure, and you can add the pictures. There should be one with you smiling, and one with you waving."

"Heck," I said, "that's only one picture. I can smile and wave at the same time." Charley laughed. I could always make him laugh.

"So tell me, Charley Meyers, what are you going to name this novel, the Cody one?"

"Been thinking about that," Charley said, scratching his chin. "I think

I'll call it *Chasing Cowgirls*."

"Not bad. How about *Chasing Cowboys* instead?"

"Depends on who's chasing who," Charley said.

"Whom," I corrected him.

"Say what?"

"Who's chasing *whom*," I said, slower this time.

"Thank you very much." He said it in a sarcastic way, but he was only teasing. Then he said, "Who's the writer here anyway, me or you?"

Well, that's exactly the moment that I got this big idea to write a book myself. Not that I have a lot of free time, what with running for rodeo queen and taking classes at UNR and keeping Darryl happy when he's not working at his dad's hardware store. But I thought I could squeeze in a couple pages here and there in my busy schedule. I've always kept a journal, ever since high school when Mrs. James had us all keeping journals. My journal is mostly full of rodeo queen stuff you wouldn't be interested in. I think writing a novel must be a whole lot different though, but I wanted to do it anyway, partly because I'm very competitive and I wanted to show Charley that I could do just as well, or better than him, if I really focused on it. Mrs. James was big on focusing. I've been focusing mostly on making rodeo queen lately, but it's good to take on new challenges in life.

"Okay, Charley," I said, "you go ahead and write your *Chasing Cowgirls* book. Just promise me one thing."

"What's that?" He looked a little worried.

"No big thing, just let me peek at it now and then. That's all."

"Sure, why not?" Charley appeared relieved. "You'll be my first reader. You can correct all the grammar too."

"Be glad to," I said. "Hey, Charley, do you think Lacey has a boyfriend already?"

"I'd bet on it. Lacey's a city girl, so she probably has a city boyfriend. Hard for a cowboy to compete, especially if he's not a real cowboy."

"Poor Cody," I said, "going to all that trouble. I'd hate to see him get shot down."

"Let's just see what we can do," Charley said. "Maybe Cody will have better luck than I've had."

"I'm not feeling sorry for you, Charley Meyers," I said, waving my index finger back and forth at him. "Don't even try it. You told me you've known lots of women."

"Well, there are different prizes in life. Some are better than others."

"No, no, no," I said, waving my finger again. "Don't go feeling sorry for yourself. You'll give yourself more wrinkles. And you have enough already."

That shut him up. When we finished our coffee and pastry I said goodbye to Celia and gave Charley a peck on the cheek. Then I got in my truck and drove straight to the nearest store that had composition books. I bought half a dozen, for a start. I figured it would take one or two just to catch up with Charley, and the rest to pass him in the book writing competition.

After my classes were over I went home. It's a cute little apartment, my first place. My dad just got a job in Las Vegas and he and my mom helped me find this apartment before they left because I wanted to stay in Reno and so did my older brother, Rooster. Rooster's rooming with one of his friends, so I'm in this nice apartment building, which was a lucky thing for my new novel because of what happened that Friday after I got home.

I had some laundry to do, so I thought I'd take care of it right after dinner. I made myself a ham and cheese sandwich, with only three potato chips, honest. But you probably don't want to hear about that so I'll try to leave out the food parts of the story from now on, unless it's something really special. Anyway, I walked into my building's laundry room, and guess who was there. Lacey! The woman from Parker's that Charley spied on and wrote about in his story. I recognized her right away.

She was reading something that looked like legal stuff, like one of those lawyer interviews when they question a witness. I forget what you call them. So there I was with a whole basket full of jeans and a week's worth of Western shirts and socks and underwear.

"Howdy," I said to her. "My name's Donna Cooper."

"Lacey Anderson. Pleased to meet you. I just moved here from San Francisco and I've been kind of tied up with work." She held up the legal stuff to show me.

"So what are you reading there?"

"Just a deposition."

"Oh, right," I said. Deposition. I would have remembered the word if I'd had more time. "Well, work is important, but it won't keep you warm on a winter night."

"That's true," Lacey said. "I hear the winter nights are colder here than in San Francisco."

"They are, but the men are warmer. So you're a lawyer?"

"Yep, that's why I'm reading this exciting deposition while my jeans are drying."

"Well, I bet you bring home lots of money."

"That's a good one," Lacey said. "I can pay my bills and have a little left over, but I won't make a lot unless I make partner some day. That's my big goal, and the sooner the better."

"But at least you're helping people."

"I guess I help them move the money from one pocket to another, until another lawyer comes along and moves it somewhere else. It's a game, but it is fun to win."

"And you make lots of friends," I said.

"I have friends in San Francisco," Lacey admitted, "but I've only made one friend here in Reno, and I just met him. He's a cowboy I met at Parker's."

"Hold on there," I said, "that's where you're wrong. You've got two friends in Reno."

"What?"

"Sure. I'll be your friend." I gave her my rodeo queen smile.

Lacey smiled back.

"So you like that Cody guy?" I asked her.

"Sure, he seems real nice."

"You don't have a boyfriend back in San Francisco?"

"Not really," Lacey said.

"Not really?"

"Well, before I left I had a few dates with one of the lawyers at the firm where I worked. Nothing really serious."

"So you broke it off?"

"Not really."

"Uh oh. There's that 'not really' again. Tell me about him, the guy in San Francisco."

"He's just a guy, somebody to go out with. He taught me a lot about the firm. He's going to help me make partner."

"What's his name?"

Lacey paused, then she made a funny face.

"You forgot his name? Can't be too serious."

"No, I remember his name. It's hard to forget actually, once you've heard it."

"Tell me then," I said.

"Promise me you won't laugh." Before I could promise she said, "His name is Victor Kleindich."

"Nothing funny about that name," I said. "Sounds German."

"The last name's German. You ever study German in school?"

"Just Spanish."

"Well, it's German, and don't ever call him Vic, unless you want him to correct you. It's Victor. He's from old San Francisco money. Went to prep school in New England, then Yale, then Harvard Law. The whole deal."

"That's some kind of deal, all right. Does he talk funny?"

"Talk funny?"

"You know, funny, like he went to Hahvahd and you didn't."

Lacey laughed. "No, he's pretty normal when he talks. Very intelligent though. Uses lots of big words. Lots."

"A plethora?" I asked.

"Excuse me?"

"A plethora," I repeated. Mrs. James had given us a large vocabulary in that high school English class, although you didn't often have the chance to use them. She would have been proud of me right about now.

"A plethora of big words," I said.

"Oh yeah," Lacey said. "Definitely a plethora."

"Is he perspicacious?" I asked. There's a word I hadn't used since Mrs. James's class.

"Absolutely," Lacey said. "You know, Donna, you could probably understand him when he talks."

"So when do I get to meet him?"

"I don't know, he wants to come visit me, but I've been busy getting settled."

"So you don't miss Victor?" I asked. "You don't miss his plethora?"

Lacey smiled. "I guess I do. He's very good to me. I'd be lost in the firm without him. Right now, though, I'm kind of interested in that cowboy. Tomorrow he's going to drive me to Virginia City and show me the old town."

"Lucky you," I said. "Say, Lacey, you want to know something about men?"

"Sure," Lacey said.

"Well, here goes. Listen up. A man is like a horse you've had for ten years." I waited for this to sink in before continuing. "Do you follow me so far?"

"Yes, a man is like a horse."

"No, that's not what I said. A man is like a horse you've had for ten years."

"Oh, the ten years part is important," Lacey said.

"Exactly, and I'll tell you why. Have you ever had a horse for ten years? No, I guess not. Well, when you've had the same horse for ten years you know what they're thinking. You just know. The reason you've had the horse for ten years is that you can depend on it. It's not going to gallop off or do something out of character. You catch my drift?"

Lacey pondered this new comparison. "I think so. You mean that if I can keep the same man for ten years, I will know what he's thinking and I can depend on him, that he won't gallop off?"

"Well, it's even better than that," I said. "You see, with a good horse you don't have to wait ten years to know what they're thinking. You know right away. You can look that animal in the eye and see right into his mind. You can size him up the first day. Then you just take him for a ride and see how he handles."

Lacey laughed. "You may have something there," she said. "What are those mythical creatures that are half man and half horse? I forget the word."

"Me too."

"But," Lacey said, "I always thought that two-legged animals were more complex than the four-legged ones."

"Are you serious? When it comes to men, we just make it all more complex than it really is. Take my boyfriend, for example, Darryl. At any given moment, I can tell what he's thinking. I always could. But I don't think he has the first clue about me."

Lacey didn't say anything, so I went on. "Take that cowboy friend of yours, Cody. I know what he's thinking about you."

"What's that?"

"He's thinking that he'd like to know you better."

Lacey smiled. "Tell me more. Are men really that easy to read?"

"Well, yes and no," I said. "Men are simple, and you can figure out what they're thinking most of the time, but you still have to find yourself a good one. That's the hard part. But it's like horses again. When you find a good one, hang onto him."

By then Lacey's jeans had stopped dancing in the dryer and my clothes were ready to dry.

"That's an interesting cowgirl wardrobe you have there," Lacey said. "I feel kind of under stocked with my single Western outfit."

"Well, you just moved here. I had a big head start on you."

"You know," Lacey said, "I never realized that cowgirls' panties could be so colorful."

"You like my collection?" I said. I held them up so Lacey could get a better look. One pair had wild horses pictured galloping across them. Another pair had little red hearts.

"The one with the hearts, are those a gift from a cowboy admirer?"

I just smiled. Another pair featured a rodeo queen racing into an arena on a beautiful black horse and waving to her many admirers.

"That must be your favorite," Lacey said.

"You bet," I said.

Before Lacey left, we exchanged apartment numbers and telephone numbers. Lacey walked out of the room with her basket, then turned and glanced back just in time to see me waving at her. I gave her my latest genuine, authentic rodeo queen wave.

5 Donna

"Take me to the green valley…"

There's magic in a rodeo queen wave. At least there is in mine. I know because that wave in the laundry room cast a spell over Lacey Anderson that carried her like a princess through her date with Cody. She told me all about it later. For one day, at least, she had forgotten about being in a rush to make partner, and about her San Francisco boyfriend who was going to help make it happen.

So anyway, here comes a really romantic part of this story. I doubt that Charley Meyers could tell it as well as me, even if Cody tells him much about what happened. You ladies will enjoy it, I'm sure. You gentlemen may be tempted to skip over this part because there's more action in some of the later chapters. Not so fast, guys. You would be well advised to stick with this. You just might learn something.

Saturday morning found a battered Dodge pickup heading south out of Reno and towards the mountains southeast of town. Behind the wheel, Cody pretended that he had been on this road many times. Seated to his right was a young lady in new cowgirl clothes looking over some CDs. She popped the Michael Martin Murphey CD into the stereo and settled back for the 40-minute ride to Virginia City.

Cody was glad he had been reading about the history of this region even before he had stepped off the train from Iowa in April. Charley Meyers told me that part. I could tell right away that Cody was a dude, but what did a city girl like Lacey know about cowboys? I thought it was cute that she had mistaken him for a real cowboy, and I wasn't about to tell her the truth and spoil her fantasy. Let Cupid have his fun, that's what I say.

For every acre of sagebrush that they passed, Cody had a bit of history to relate. The region was once known as the Truckee Meadows, Cody informed his passenger. We still call it that, of course. It's a local thing. Cody said the action started when silver was discovered in the Comstock Mines in 1859. People poured into Virginia City by the thousands, seeking to get rich quick, and some did. In those days Virginia City was the richest city in the country. The money from the silver mining helped to finance the Civil War. President Lincoln pushed for statehood for Nevada, and Nevada's vote was the difference in getting the 13th Amendment ratified, abolishing slavery.

Lacey sat back and enjoyed the history lesson, then she turned up the music because one of her favorite songs was beginning, "The Streets of Laredo." She began humming along, then sang softly:

"As I walked out on the streets of Laredo,
As I walked out in Laredo one day,
I spied a young cowboy wrapped up in white linen,
Wrapped up in white linen and cold as the clay."

Cody's history lesson was over, and he joined in singing:

"I see by your outfit that you are a cowboy,
These words he did say as I boldly walked by,
Come sit down beside me and hear my sad story,
I'm shot in the breast and I know I must die.

Oh, beat the drum slowly and play the fife lowly,
Play the dead march as you carry me along,
Take me to the green valley and lay the sod o'er me,
For I'm a young cowboy and I know I done wrong."

The old Dodge pickup was the only vehicle on this stretch of the road to Virginia City, and the only sounds were the truck's steady engine and the bittersweet music of The Cowboy's Lament:

"It was once in the saddle I used to go dashing,
It was once in the saddle I used to go gay,
First to the dram house, and then to the card house,
Got shot in the breast and I'm dying today."

After the song ended, the two were silent for quite a while. When the road began to climb into the mountains, and Cody remembered their destination, he broke the silence.

"There's a place I would like you to see when we get to Virginia City."

"What did you say, cowboy?" Lacey's thoughts had been far away.

"I just mentioned that when we get to Virginia City, I would like to show you a special place," Cody said.

"Okay, don't tell me now, let it be a surprise." Lacey returned to her private thoughts.

Cody agreed, and they continued on to Virginia City, as more old cowboy songs filled the truck with the sweet sounds of an acoustic guitar, fiddle, steel guitar, and an occasional harmonica.

They arrived rather abruptly in the old mining town, because Virginia City was not big enough to have suburbs. One moment they were going around a bend in the road, and the next they were in the middle of the main street, with raised wooden sidewalks on either side and a series of small tourist shops of various kinds. They parked across from the wooden building that had housed the *Territorial Enterprise*, where Samuel Clemens had worked and made the name Mark Twain famous. They walked up one side of the street and down the other, buying post cards and ice cream along the way. Back in the truck,

Cody drove along side streets, past the old wooden churches, the opera house, and one house where Marilyn Monroe had stayed during the filming of *The Misfits*.

Cody was enjoying playing tour guide, and was doing quite well, considering that he had never been in Virginia City before, only read everything he could about it.

"Close your eyes now," he told Lacey.

"Why?"

"Just do it, as a favor to me."

She decided to go along with this. If it was some kind of cowboy trick, she sensed it would not be a mean one. They drove like this for a couple of minutes until Cody stopped the truck and told her she could open her eyes.

Lacey saw the old cemetery on the small hill in front of her, with the desert mountains stretching for countless miles toward the eastern horizon, and she knew that this was the special place Cody had mentioned before. Nobody else was around. They got down from the truck and began to walk up the dirt road that was bordered by sagebrush and short pines. Lacey glanced back and saw a small whirlwind stirring up the dust near where Cody had parked the truck. She told Cody to look and they watched as the little twister played out and vanished as if it had never been.

"Wind's playing tricks," Cody remarked.

"Or the spirits," Lacey said. She put her hand in his and they walked slowly to the entrance to the old graveyard. A train whistle blew in the distance, off to the south of town.

"More spirits?" Lacey asked.

"No, just the Virginia & Truckee," Cody said. "They run it for the visitors."

The cemetery was brown and dry, and many of the burial sites looked as if they had not been touched for more than a century. Cody and Lacey walked carefully past the plots and old headstones, stopping to read many of them, calculating from the dates on the markers the various ages of those who had been laid to rest high in these desert mountains. Many had died in their 20s and 30s, and a few graves were those of children. One large stone angel looked down on them, and they circled it to study its benevolent gaze.

Occasionally they saw a recent grave. One, that of a young girl with a small wooden cross to mark it, stood out because of the bright colors of the many flowers placed there.

"Cody, look at this one." Lacey had discovered the grave of three children from the same family. The children shared a common marker that recorded the dates of their deaths in the 1870s and 1880s—a two-year-old girl, an eleven-year-old boy, and a nine-month-old girl. Lacey read aloud the inscription under the names:

"Why should our tears in sorrow flow
When God recalls his own.
And bids them leave a world of woe
For an immortal crown."

"Look, Cody, they recorded their ages at death, down to the number of months and days. They counted each and every day of their lives. Every day was treasured."

The two visitors continued on, saying little, occasionally pointing, stopping at a grave, nodding to each other, and then moving on. A strong wind blew through the cemetery, and once a tumbleweed bounced soundlessly across their path, like a restless spirit that had somewhere to go and couldn't stick around another minute.

When they reached the farthest point, Cody and Lacey turned back and saw, for the first time, the town spread out against the mountain, much as it must have appeared in the 1860s. From this perspective, they could see none of the tourist shop signs.

Lacey looked into Cody's blue eyes and said simply, "You're right, it is a special place. Thanks for bringing me here." She smiled at Cody, then kissed him on the cheek. He took her hand and they began the short journey back to the truck.

"You know," Lacey said, "this is one of the most romantic places I've ever been." Cody just smiled and held her hand more tightly.

On the drive back down the mountain, the cowboy songs went on and on, telling of lives that had been lived out more than a hundred years before, but the two young travelers felt that they had touched some of those lives today. The skies began to cloud up as they reached the bottom of the mountain, and they sang once more:

"O bury me not on the lone prairie,
These words came sad and mournfully
From the pallid lips of a youth who lay
On his dying bed at the close of day."

The drive back into Reno was too short, but they spent the rest of the day exploring the town, growing closer, unable to say goodbye. They ate a late lunch at the Coyote Bar & Grill and then walked along the Truckee River, stopping now and then to watch the ducks. Cody drove Lacey to Virginia Lake, where Canada geese ate bread from their hands.

Back in the truck, parked alongside the lake, Lacey took the key from the ignition and sat closer to the cowboy.

"What's up?" Cody said.

"You want the key?" Lacey asked.

"Sure, unless you aim to walk back to town."

"Okay, but you have to have dinner with me this evening," Lacey said. "My treat. There's another coffee I want to try at the Eldorado."

"It's a deal. Can I have the key now?"

"Just one more condition," Lacey said, moving even closer.

"Anything," Cody said. "As long it doesn't involve a lot of walking. A cowboy never walks when he can ride, you know."

"All right, cowboy, the key is yours for a kiss."

"A kiss?"

Lacey tilted her head. "You do know what that is, don't you? Or do you only kiss your horse?"

"Somebody might see us," Cody said.

"Just hush up and do it," Lacey said.

Now talking about a kiss beforehand can produce different results. The talking can kill the spontaneity, or it can heighten the tension and excitement. In this case, in an old Dodge pickup parked in the shade alongside a city lake, what was lost in spontaneity was more than matched by the increased tension and excitement. Cody and Lacey joined in a sweet, rather long kiss. Afterwards Lacey touched his cheek and spoke first.

"That wasn't so bad now, was it?"

Cody grinned. "No, ma'am. I just hope I can drive with the windshield all steamed up."

"Maybe I should hang on to the key for while then," Lacey said, and returned for another kiss. She could have waited a while for the second kiss, negotiating another deal with Cody, but she wasn't feeling patient just then.

After the second kiss, which served to confirm a few things in their minds, Lacey handed Cody the key.

"Are you sure you can drive?" she asked.

"I'll try," Cody said. "You can keep your hand on the back of my neck like that, but just don't massage it. It wouldn't be safe."

Lacey chuckled and stopped stroking the back of Cody's neck. "It's a deal."

Dinner at the Eldorado was delicious, as usual, and Lacey was somehow able to resist ordering the chocolate cake this time. When Cody finally drove her home, Lacey invited him in for apple pie, suggested he take off his boots and make himself comfortable, and later invited him to spend the night. Cody forgot all about washing his truck.

6 Charley

"Bacon in the pan, coffee in the pot...."

Cody told me he awoke the next morning to the smell of bacon cooking and coffee brewing. He opened his eyes to find himself in the bed of a certain lady lawyer, who had arisen before the young cowboy in hopes that a hot breakfast would restore his energy. He thought back to the events of the previous day and decided that he was one lucky cowboy. He had a friend in me who knew all the important things about horses and women, and now he had a lady friend who, among her many desirable qualities, knew all the words to "Streets of Laredo." Cody put on his Wranglers, ran a hand through his hair, and walked quietly toward the kitchen.

"Now there's a pretty sight," he drawled in one of those movie cowboy voices, "barefoot in the kitchen and rustlin' up some grub for the men folks!"

"Hush up," she gave it right back to him. "Get your butt in here before your eggs get cold."

"Such language from a lady," he said. "I don't suppose you know what happened to the sweet young thing who was here last night."

"I'm not sweet. You don't know me very well, Cody. And don't get any nearer or I'll put a hot strip of bacon down your jeans."

Cody sized up the situation. Maybe he was remembering what I had said about broncs, that they're different from one day to the next. What now? Invite her to visit the cemetery again? He decided to try another approach.

"Excuse me, miss, is there any room in that cold heart of yours for a lonesome cowboy?"

Lacey stopped what she was doing and walked up to Cody. She looked fiercely into his eyes. Cody could not help noticing that she still held a sharp kitchen fork in one hand. I guess I'll die happy, he thought to himself. Then Lacey put her arms around him and just held him for a long time. When she finally let go she went back to the bacon and Cody sat down at the breakfast table. I had been right again—sometimes you can't tell who's branding who.

During breakfast Lacey asked if she could ask him a personal question. Cody feared that it would involve his having to confess that he was not a real cowboy, or lie some more, but the question was whether Cody had ever been in love before. Cody said he thought so, but it had been years ago, so long that it felt as if it had happened to someone else. Lacey then said she had never been in love. She had always been too busy with school or work, and she always found herself with the wrong type. Cody asked her what her type was, and Lacey said she wished she knew.

She went to the refrigerator and brought out another slice of apple pie for Cody, who didn't object. She brushed her hand against the back of his neck as she placed the dish in front of him. Just then the phone on the kitchen wall rang. As Cody took large bites of the pie, he heard one side of the conversation.

"Hello . . . Oh hi, Mom, how's everything? . . . It's about 8:30 here . . . I know, same time zone, isn't that comforting? How's Dad, did you get him to take some time off work? . . . He took you where? . . . And you didn't have to bribe him? . . . Oh, you know me, I'm always fine . . . No, really . . . I worked hard this week but the weekend's been relaxing . . . Well, I was up at Virginia City yesterday and . . . No, not by myself, I went with a friend . . . Well, no, it was my cowboy friend." Lacey made a face at Cody, who had been grinning at her, and mouthed the words "Stop it!"

"I thought I told you about him. He helped me pick out some Western clothes the other day, and he brought me luck at the blackjack table, and then yesterday he drove me up to Virginia City to show me some history . . . No, Mom, he's a real gentleman." Lacey knew that these words would have a magical effect on her anxious mother.

"No, I can't tell you everything about him, I just met him myself . . . They're blue . . . No, he's taller than me, about six feet . . . Of course he has a job, in fact he has two, he works as a cowboy and helps out his friends at the big Western store downtown. He's a regular working fool, like the man you married!" Lacey looked around for something to throw at Cody, who was grinning again. All she could find was the telephone book, which would have to do.

"No, Mom, I'm okay, I just dropped something . . . What's that? . . . Oh, he drives a pickup, of course, I told you he was a cowboy . . . No, I haven't talked to Victor for a couple of days . . . Yes, he plans to visit Reno as soon as he can. . . Mom, I've got to run, I've got something on the stove . . . I love you, too. Say hi to Dad for me . . . Bye." She hung up the phone and sat down at the table.

"Don't tell me," Cody ventured, "that must have been your mother. Why didn't you let me talk to her?"

"I ought to give you a good kick in the shins," Lacey answered. "I'm sorry I missed with the phone book."

"Well, you kind of telegraphed it, so I had time to duck. Say, do you have any more of that apple pie?"

"No," Lacey said, "that was the last piece, and I wouldn't give you another slice if I had it."

"Well, it was wonderful. Your mom's recipe?"

"My mom taught me how to pick out a good bakery," Lacey confessed. "When would I have time to bake? They keep me busy at the firm. And tonight I have to go to a barbecue they're having for our clients. Would you like to go and keep me company? I'm afraid it's going to be a lot of shop talk, but the food should be good."

"Well, missy," Cody slipped into his Hollywood cowboy voice, "that sounds mighty invitin', with the barbecue and all, and gettin' to meet all them important folks, but I think I'm gonna have to be helpin' a friend tonight."

Lacey was disappointed. "I'll be stuck there on my own. Will you miss me?"

Cody took her hand. "Shucks, ma'am, I'll be thinkin' about you the whole time. I'll be howlin' at the moon, just like a lonesome coyote."

"I give up. You're incorrigible."

"Why, thank you," Cody smiled. "I'll take that as a compliment. I'm sorry, I'd really like to see you tonight, but I promised Charley, my friend at the store, that I'd go with him to a ranch down at Carson City."

"Just like my dad. He's always running off from my mom to the produce. He runs a wholesale place in San Francisco. I can get you some wonderful artichokes. Do cowboys eat artichokes?"

"Do lawyers eat beef jerky? You might be surprised what cowboys know about. You know, my friend Charley used the word 'ambience' the other day. What do you think of that?"

"Charley must not be a real cowboy," Lacey said.

"Oh, he's real, all right. You ought to meet him some day, then you can tell me if he's real or not. He's been around. He's got this theory about . . ." Cody stopped himself before he got himself in trouble with Charley's bronc theory about women.

"What theory is that?" Lacey wouldn't let him off the hook.

"Oh, nothing," Cody tried to wiggle off. "Just some theory about horses. I don't even remember it all."

"So," Lacey continued, apparently willing to leave Charley's theory alone for now, "I guess you'll be wanting to wash your truck now."

Cody thought she was politely asking him to leave so she could do whatever women do on a Sunday morning. "I do have some chores to attend to," he replied.

At the front door, before he left, Cody hesitated as if he had something difficult to say. "Lacey," he began, "you're a real lady and all, and I just want you to know I don't make a habit of sleeping with every woman on the first date, but one thing led to another last night, and . . ."

"I know," she said, helping him out. "I'm the same way, but once we took our boots off I knew we were goners."

She told him to be careful in Carson City, not to get thrown or stepped on by anything. He laughed and promised he would. He told her to watch herself at the barbecue, not to get roped by any dangerous lawyers. A passerby on the street, if there had been one, would have thought this was a routine domestic ritual, with the wife sending the husband off to work, except that the kiss she sent him off with lasted about 30 seconds longer than the passerby would have expected. When Cody climbed into his truck he was whistling "The Streets of Laredo."

7 Donna

"Make 'em be doctors and lawyers and such..."

Lacey studied her plate full of barbecue beef, potato salad, corn on the cob, and corn bread. She thought it looked good, but could be improved with some of her father's fresh vegetables. In this new town, surrounded now by a bunch of strangers talking about business and legal matters, she felt homesick for the first time. Until now she had been busy absorbing her new environment, and spending long hours becoming familiar with the case files on her desk. Then her two new friends had taken up her free time this weekend.

She felt somewhat overwhelmed by the cowboy and rodeo queen who had entered her life. One moment you're doing your laundry and in blows this blonde tornado with a big smile and you're listening to her theory about men. One moment you're sitting at a blackjack table by yourself, quietly losing some money, and the next you're up in the mountains at an old cemetery holding hands with a cowboy. And before you know it, you're cooking him breakfast.

Now, in the large back yard of one of the attorneys at Peterman, Biggen

& Kleindich, the excitement had passed and she found herself bored. She felt obliged to talk shop with the other lawyers, and to listen to the clients talk business. Everyone was nice to her, but she couldn't help wondering what Cody was doing at this moment, and what cowgirl adventure I was up to.

She found a small bench under a tall pine tree in one corner of the yard, where she sat and ate her dinner. Occasionally someone would walk up and make small talk and then return to the center of the party. Once a young lawyer from the firm brought her a beer and a glass. He reminded her of Victor, back in San Francisco, handsome and smooth and about thirty, same as Victor. What was Victor doing tonight? What would she and Victor be doing if she were back in San Francisco? She thanked the young lawyer for the beer but gave him back the glass, and took a long drink from the bottle. When she lowered the bottle she saw that the young lawyer had left to talk with a client.

After the second beer she was feeling more comfortable, giving everyone who passed by a nice smile and a "howdy." No one bothered her much and she continued to sit under the tall pine and let her mind drift where it would in the cool evening breeze.

After the third beer her thoughts drifted right over the fence and down the street, and then towards the mountains, until they floated down in Virginia City. She closed her eyes and imagined herself in the cemetery. It would be dark now, lit only by the moon and stars. The tumbleweeds would roll across the graves like silver ghosts, barely visible.

Lacey thought of her grandmother, who had passed away the year before, the one who always told her to be a lady and warned her not to let the fellows kiss her on a first date. Oh Grandma, she thought, I hope you weren't looking down on me this weekend. Grandma always made her laugh, even now when she was one of those tumbleweeds. Then Lacey remembered how Cody had taken her hand in the cemetery, how his hand had been smoother than she would have expected from a cowboy, but then she guessed they must wear gloves when they're working.

A familiar voice brought her back from her reverie. "What's a nice girl like you doing in a place like this?" Lacey looked up to see my rodeo queen smile. "Mind if I join you," I asked as I sat down on the wooden bench.

"Donna, I didn't expect to see you here."

"Well, I didn't crash this deal, one of the lawyers is an old friend of my parents. Why, did you think I was a waitress?"

"No," Lacey said, but she didn't fool me.

"Oh, that's all right, some people think that when they meet me. I have worked in restaurants before. It's a good place to meet cowboys, you know. Say, what do you have to do to get a soda around here?"

Lacey said she had to visit the bathroom and offered to bring me a Coke on the way back.

"Thanks, honey," I said. "I'll just sit here and check out the beef." Lacey was halfway to the house before she turned and looked back at me with a funny little grin. I think she had just realized that I was not referring to the food.

When Lacey returned with my Coke, I asked her a question I'd been dying to ask. "So tell me, how was your date with Cody yesterday?"

"It went very well."

"Details, details," I said, "don't stop there."

"Virginia City is an amazing little town. That cemetery is a time machine too, and so romantic."

"I knew that. Tell me about Cody."

"He was romantic too."

"So you're falling for the guy?"

"Maybe," Lacey said.

"How does he kiss?"

"What makes you think he kissed me?"

"Don't play innocent with me," I said. I was having none of that.

"He's a good kisser."

"So you spent the whole day together?"

Lacey paused, gave me a little smile, and then said, "I cooked him breakfast."

"Breakfast? Saturday morning?"

"No, Sunday morning. He slept over."

"Oh," I said, "this is serious." Now I didn't want to pry too much. Okay, I did want to pry, but I resisted being too nosy.

"So tell me," I said, "how does he like your . . ."

"My what?" Lacey said.

"Your cooking, your cooking."

Lacey laughed. "He likes it fine."

"Okay, we'll leave it at that. Just let me know if you need any help roping that cowboy. Although it seems you're doing just fine on your own."

"Thanks," Lacey said. "I'm sure you know a lot more about cowboys than I do."

"They can be a challenge," I said.

"Donna, not to change the subject, but there's something I have to know. What was that wave you gave me this afternoon in the laundry room?"

"Well," I said, "do you want the short answer or the long answer?"

"How about both."

"Okay, the short answer is, that's my rodeo queen wave. I'm one of the contestants this year for Miss Reno Rodeo."

"Cool. So that's the way rodeo queens wave?"

"No," I said, "that's not the only way they wave. Listen carefully. This is important. If you want to be a rodeo queen, you need three things. Number one, you need to know how to make yourself pretty."

"Come on, you're naturally pretty," Lacey interrupted.

"Right, and you think this is how my hair looks when I wake up in the morning? This is what they call 'queen hair.' On some girls it looks like a curly umbrella covering their shoulders. It's like, Dolly Parton eat your heart out."

"So the first thing is appearance," Lacey said.

"That's number one, appearance. And personality, of course. You have to be able to talk."

Lacey smiled. "You seem to have no problem with personality," she said.

"Or talking," I said. "Number two, you've got to be real good on a horse, because if you fall off the horse, looks and personality won't help you. Nobody wants to see a rodeo queen with dirt all over her in the middle of the arena and her hair ruined."

"I see your point," Lacey nodded.

"Okay, are you ready for number three? This is the best. When you've made yourself pretty, and you look good in the saddle instead of falling off, you're ready for the finishing touch. That's the wave. You've got the reins in one hand, and your other hand is free to wave at the crowd, including all those cowboys sitting on the fence and in the stands. This is where you get to express yourself. Your horse is looking good and riding strong, and you take your free hand and, well, you wave it."

"That number three sounds like the easiest part," Lacey said.

"Well, there are different kinds of waves, and you have to decide which one to use, then kind of make it your own, and then there's all that practice."

"Practice?"

"That's right. If you don't practice it till it's part of you, then it won't look natural when you ride into the arena."

"So what are the different waves?" Lacey asked, totally absorbed by this new knowledge.

"Well, first, the one wave you never want to use is the 'bye-bye' wave. You know, the one you give to babies and small kids." I demonstrated, holding my hand up and repeatedly moving my fingers down to touch my palm.

"I can see how you would want too avoid that one," Lacey said, warming to the subject.

"Then a lot of the rodeo queens like to do this one. You hold your hand up and then kind of wiggle it back and forth at the wrist. Like this. You get your horse going fast, and your hand going fast, and you race around the arena. Now you try it."

"This is fun," Lacey said, as she tried the wiggle wave.

"Not bad," I commented. "You may want to practice that one till you get it just right. It's a very popular wave. Another wave was big a number of years ago. You point your index and middle finger and kind of fling them out quickly, the way a cowboy gives an informal salute, only faster."

"Like this?" Lacey asked, demonstrating the two-fingered salute wave.

"That's it. You know what they call that one, don't you?"

Lacey paused. "I give up."

"They call that one the booger flick!"

Lacey laughed. "That's about what it looks like, all right."

"Another wave is this one, where you use the whole forearm and wave from the elbow kind of fast and let your hand kind of relax and fly around." I demonstrated the fast elbow wave.

"That looks like when you're waving at someone you haven't seen for a long time," Lacey said, "like at the airport. Or when you're trying to get someone's attention from a distance, and you may be yelling at them at the same time. I've been practicing this one all my life."

"Very good," I said, "you may have a natural talent for this. All these waves say something about the person who's waving. This fast elbow wave, for instance, is very friendly. In fact, it used to be the only wave that rodeo queens used years ago. But now we have modern advancements everywhere, and everything's more sophisticated. That includes rodeo queen waves."

"So tell me about your wave," Lacey said.

"Well, it's a little something I've worked on for a long time. You saw it Friday in the laundry room. Was it like any wave you ever saw before?" I knew the answer to this question already, but I wanted to hear it anyway.

"No, it was unique," Lacey had to admit. I smiled proudly.

"My wave is a combination of every wave rodeo queens use. This way I please everyone's expectations but also give them something new. I have the elbow movement, only a bit slower, the wrist movement, the relaxed hand, everything. People love it."

"Why don't all the rodeo queens use it?" Lacey asked.

"Glad you asked. Now I'm going to get you to answer your own question. Watch the wave one more time." I demonstrated my special wave. "Now, you try it, Lacey."

Lacey started to imitate my wave, then stopped, then tried again, then stopped again. She had found the answer to her question. "It's not so easy," she said.

"That's right, it's not easy at all. And I'll tell you something else. I could teach you the mechanics of it some day and you could practice until you could do a decent imitation. But it would still be just an imitation. If you bring me another Coke I'll tell you my secret." I had only told one or two people my secret before.

Lacey returned with the soda, ready to hear the secret of my rodeo queen wave. I looked around to see if anyone was listening, then moved a little closer and spoke more softly.

"You can't tell anyone this. Here's the secret. It's what I'm thinking and feeling when I do the wave," she said. "The thoughts and feelings I have are unique, nobody else has the same mixture. The way I feel about the crowd, and those cowboys, and about myself, I concentrate on that as I'm racing along. All the rest is just mechanics, it's second nature." I took a deep breath. It was good to share this secret now and then, and it had been a while since I had told anyone.

"Thanks for sharing that, Donna. I feel flattered. I guess we've really bonded now." We laughed and Lacey put her arm around me. Then we got interrupted. One of the older lawyers from Lacey's firm walked up and asked her how she was doing. Then he said he had just heard that someone from the San Francisco office was going to be visiting that week.

"Which one?" Lacey asked.

"One of the partners. Kleindich."

"Oh," Lacey said.

"Yeah," the lawyer said, "he's going to be here all week. You know him very well?"

"He was my mentor there," Lacey said.

"Good," the lawyer said. "Maybe you can spend some time with him, show him around Reno." It sounded more like an order than a suggestion.

"Okay," Lacey said. Then the lawyer walked away and we were left to contemplate a week with Victor Kleindich.

"So," I said, "now we'll get to meet your San Francisco boyfriend. How are you going to see him and Cody at the same time?"

"It's not that serious."

"Lacey, Lacey," I said. Did I have to teach her everything about men? "If he likes you and took you out, and you never told him to get lost, it's serious enough. How many horses do you want in your corral?"

"One at a time is probably enough," Lacey said.

"You've got that right."

"It's just that I need Victor on my side to make partner. I owe him a lot."

"You're really serious about this making partner business," I said.

"Just as serious as you are about making rodeo queen."

"Well, just holler if Victor's too much trouble. Maybe I can distract him so you and Cody won't be bothered."

"Thanks," Lacey said. "I'll let you know, promise. Donna . . ."

"Yes?"

"Maybe I shouldn't be so easy for Cody. Maybe I should avoid him this week."

"Sure, you can try that, play hard to get. Then he'll be looking around and find some other filly to occupy his time. And then where are you?"

"Really?"

"Listen to me," I said, "that might work on some guys, but if you have a cowboy half roped and you let him go, heck you may never see him again. Trust me."

Lacey stopped and pondered a while. She had a lot to ponder. I just let my good advice sink in. She was lucky to have me for a friend.

"Where do you think Cody is right now?"

"You don't know?" I asked.

"He said he had some work to do with his friend Charley Meyers."

"Charley Meyers? Work? On a Sunday night?"

"I kind of miss Cody," Lacey said.

"You just saw him this morning."

"I know, but . . ."

"I know," I said. "Hey, I'm going to Parker's in the morning. I'll remind him to call you."

"Don't do that," Lacey said.

"Got to," I said. "If you let guys wander around on their own they'll get lost in the desert, and who knows what kind of cowgirl will find them and take them home."

Lacey laughed. "What do I owe you for all this advice?"

"It's free," I said. "Just let me meet Victor."

"I'm sure you will," Lacey said.

"Is he as handsome as you say? Like one of those soap stars?"

"Yeah, and he knows it."

We both laughed. I saw a lot of potential in my new friend. Sometimes you can tell right away.

8 Charley

"A little starlight ranching…"

Late that Sunday evening Cody and I were halfway to Carson City. The first half of the trip had been highlighted by a series of questions from me about Cody's visit to Virginia City the day before. All I could squeeze out of Cody were a few fragments of information.

Yes, Cody had taken Lacey on the trip. No, Cody hadn't got lost and ended up in Elko! Yes, she had seemed to like the pickup. No, she hadn't spotted the can of Copenhagen in the glove compartment. Yes, she did like the music I had provided and had even sung along. No, he couldn't say if she had a better singing voice than me, because he had never heard me sing. Yes, they had gone to the cemetery in Virginia City. No, there was nobody else there. Yes, I was right, it was a romantic place. Then he mentioned waking up the next morning in Lacey's bed, so I felt like a successful matchmaker.

Cody had insisted on driving his own truck, so for the second half of the drive to Carson City I sat in the passenger seat, alternately giving directions and singing along with the stereo.

Home, home on the range,
Where the deer and the antelope play,
Where seldom is heard a discouraging word,
And the skies are not cloudy all day.

"Your voice can't match Lacey's soprano for sweetness and light," Cody said.

"I don't aim to sing sweet," I said.

"But your gravelly bass does feature a certain earthy quality that's also pleasing to the ear," the kid said. I stared out the window.

"Don't pretend you're not listening," Cody continued. "I know you're proud of your singing." I leaned back and covered my eyes with my right hand, leaving my ears uncovered.

"I feel as if I'm hearing 'Home on the Range' for the first time," Cody went on. "I wish everyone could hear you sing it just once. Maybe it's all those years living on the range. I can see John Wayne up on the movie screen singing the same song, but with your ability to stay on key." I didn't say anything, but I didn't stop him either.

"I can picture you about fifteen years younger and singing this same song by yourself while riding fence or minding the critters."

I could picture that too. I knew all the verses.

How often at night when the heavens are bright,
I see the light of those flickering stars,
Have I laid there amazed, and asked as I gazed,
If their glory exceeds that of ours.

Cody stuck his head outside the window to get a better look at the stars. Then he slowed and pulled over to the shoulder.

"Why are we stopping?" I asked.

"I just want to see something," Cody answered. He stepped down from the truck and moved a few yards away from the highway. Seeing my young friend looking up at the sky, I stepped out and joined him, trying to aim at the same part of the sky where he was looking.

"So what are we looking at?" I finally asked.

"Stars," Cody answered. He said it with such reverence that he might as well have said "God."

"They don't have stars in Iowa?"

"Oh yes, but they're different out here. Bigger and closer somehow. And more of them."

Just then another truck pulled over behind us and the driver stepped out. Hands on hips, trying to see something, the stranger asked, "What are we looking at?"

"Stars," I answered.

"Oh," the stranger said, and he stayed there with his hands on his hips, studying the stars.

Soon a number of drivers had pulled over, most of them expecting to see a UFO, or at least a meteorite shower. The word was relayed down the line: "Stars." And the response was always the same: "Oh." No one thought the three men at the front of the line of people were crazy, but most took a brief look and then resumed their journeys. About fifteen minutes later, when only the original three men remained by the side of the highway, the stranger finally took his leave. "Thanks," he said.

"You bet," I said, and soon Cody and I returned to the truck without a word. Back on the highway, I looked at Cody and said "Thanks, that was nice."

"They're *your* stars," he said modestly.

"Well, kid, now they're yours too." What I didn't tell him was that I used to study the stars with Angel, years ago. We'd be out at night at someone's ranch, away from the city lights, and we'd spread a blanket on the ground and just lie there watching the stars, hardly saying a word. After a while she'd turn on her side and kiss me, then roll back and watch the sky some more. To this day I can't look at the night sky without thinking of Angel. She's probably still looking at the same stars, but I doubt she thinks about me when she does.

Soon we were near Carson City and I warned Cody to keep a lookout for my lady friend's ranch. Cody pointed out that he had never seen it before, so what was he looking for? I told him to watch for colored lights. Two minutes later Cody spotted some small colored lights to the left and well off the highway. I said "Good eyes, pardner!" and we turned into a gravel road that led to a handful of low buildings, like a minor roundup of trailer homes.

"Seems like she's got lots of company tonight," Cody said, noticing a group of pickups parked in front of the buildings, resembling a small herd of patient horses tied up at a hitching post.

"Sure does," I said, "and it looks like the girls have been real busy lately. They haven't had time to take down the Christmas lights." I never failed to chuckle at this old joke.

Now Cody is a little slow sometimes, but he's not dense. He turned his head slowly toward me and selected his words carefully before speaking.

"Charley, don't tell me this is one of those ranches that I've heard about."

"What kind is that, kid?"

"Hey, I thought we were coming down here to help your lady friend with something. I thought you wanted me to meet someone special."

"Cheryl *is* special." I came to the defense of my lady friend. "Otherwise I wouldn't have beaten such a path to Carson over the years. Why, that highway we just came down was nothing but a cow trail when I first started visiting the Starlight Ranch."

"The Starlight Ranch?" Cody repeated.

"Yeah, kind of romantic, ain't it? Cheryl wanted to change it to the Starlight and Sunbeam Ranch, so that folks would know it was open in the afternoons too, not just at night, but I told her everyone would just shorten it and call it the Starlight Ranch anyway, so she never did. What I was saying is that Cheryl is the only lady I spend time with when I visit, and she always was."

"So you're a one-woman man."

"At the Starlight I am," I said.

"Charley, you romantic devil. So go on in and visit your Cheryl."

"No, you come too, I want you to meet her. She's quite a lady, and I've told her all about you, so she's expecting you."

"Okay, I guess there's no harm in just saying hello," Cody said.

"I tell you what, my boy, this business is perfectly legal in this county, and we're outside the city limits of Carson, so you don't have anything to worry about. It's regulated, just like the casinos. Either here or in the casino, it's just about the same. You pay some money, you have a good time, and you get to meet some interesting people. What do you say?"

"What are you saying?" Cody asked.

"Oh hell, kid, I'll pay your way. That makes it even better than visiting the casino. This way you have nothing to lose, and a lot to gain. Consider it part of your cowboy education. And the girls are all real nice, not like those hookers you see in some cities."

"I don't know, Charley, you make it sound harmless enough, but how about Lacey?"

"Oh lordy." I sighed. "You won't find her at the Starlight Ranch, that's for damn sure. She's probably running around with one of those lawyer fellows tonight."

"Okay, let's go," Cody finally said, "but don't let Lacey find out."

"All right, cowboy, I won't tell her if you won't."

Inside the Starlight Ranch, in a room that featured a wagon wheel chandelier and red satin curtains, we were greeted by an attractive, buxom woman. She had fiery red hair and warm blue eyes that could take the chill off a large room in the middle of a blizzard. She was dressed comfortably, as a woman might dress at home if the hour was late and she didn't want to fuss with a lot of undressing at bedtime.

"Charley!" she greeted me. "I was afraid you wouldn't make it. And this must be Cody. My goodness, Charley's told me so much about you. Aren't you a handsome young buckaroo!"

"How do you do, ma'am," Cody said.

"And so polite," the woman commented, truly impressed with my friend. "You call me Cheryl, all right? I'm too young to be your mother." Cody nodded.

"Cody," Cheryl said, "there's a young lady I would like you to meet. She's a lot like you. Very polite and she's from the Midwest too. Wisconsin, in fact. "Annie," she called down the narrow hallway, "come on out here, I want you to meet someone."

Cody looked to where Cheryl had called out and there soon appeared a pretty young woman, no more than 24, dressed in navy blue shorts and a white, stretch knit tank top. She spotted the younger cowboy right away.

"Hi, you must be Cody," she said. Her Midwestern voice must have sounded good to the cowboy from Iowa. "I'm Annie. Cheryl told me you were coming. Why don't you follow me and we can sit down and get acquainted."

I gave my friend a little push to get his feet moving, and in a few seconds I was left alone with Cheryl.

"Wasn't that sweet?" Cheryl asked me.

I grinned. "They do make a handsome couple. So how have you been, darlin'?"

"You were just here last weekend, you old billygoat. I'm just the same. Do I ever change?" Cheryl waited for an answer.

"Of course not," I said. "Except that you seem to get more beautiful every time I see you."

"Charley, you rascal, you could charm the horns off a horned toad."

"Speakin' of horny toads," I said, "why are we standing here talking?" Cheryl couldn't come up with a good reason, so that was the end of that conversation.

An hour later I walked out of the Starlight Ranch, adjusted my hat, and took a deep breath of air. I thought how lucky I was to be able to visit a little acre of cowboy heaven and still return to earth when my hour was up. I looked up into the Nevada night, smiling at Cody's stars. When I returned to the truck, Cody was already there, waiting for me.

I climbed in. "How long have you been waiting for me, kid?"

"Oh, about half an hour. It's all right."

"You young guys act like it's some kind of convenience store," I said. "I hate to tell you this, but they don't give out prizes to the customers who get out of the store the fastest. So, how was it?"

Cody started the engine, backed up carefully, then headed toward the highway. "She's a nice girl," Cody said.

"Sure, anyone could see that. And?" I waited for the rest of the report. I was curious, and naturally I wanted a maximum return on my investment.

"Well, we talked about where we were from, and how we got here, that kind of stuff. She came out here from Wisconsin with her boyfriend, but they split up and she was stranded in Reno. Then she answered an ad, and Cheryl's taken care of her ever since. After that I guess we started talking about current events, how the weekend was going. Annie said that weekends were the hardest for the girls at the ranch because there were always more trucks parked out in front then.

"She asked me if I'd done anything interesting lately, so I told her about visiting Virginia City and the cemetery there and how the tumbleweeds rolled across the graves. Then, all of a sudden, she clouded up and started crying kind of softly. She told me about how she'd lost a close friend recently, and I told her about my parents dying when I was young, and then I started feeling sad too. I tried to comfort her but she kept on crying. She said she was sorry, it must have been the part about the tumbleweeds that got to her. I told her not to worry, that I understood." Cody stopped to catch his breath.

"So," I said, "then you gave her a hug to comfort her, and she hugged you back, and you both stopped being so sad, right?"

"Not exactly," Cody said as he drove up the highway towards Reno. "I did give her a hug, but she kept on crying a little, and I didn't feel like doing anything at that point anyway. When she seemed to be all right, I kissed her goodbye on the cheek and walked back to the truck. I'm all right."

I pondered all of this, wondering what I had missed in Cody's report. "Tell me, kid, did you tell her about your lawyer friend?"

"Why would I do that?" Cody asked.

"So you weren't thinking about Lacey."

"I didn't say that. I've been thinking about her, off and on, all day long. I just didn't tell Annie about her."

"So you were being faithful?" I was trying to get this straight in my mind.

"I never thought about it that way. Maybe. I just make it a rule never to discuss one woman when I'm with another one."

"Are you trying to teach *me* about women now?" I asked.

"No, I wouldn't presume to do that," Cody said. Then he stuck his head out the window and looked up at the sky. "That would be like trying to teach God about the stars."

I surrendered. The kid might be a cowboy poet someday. I put in a CD and we spent the rest of the trip singing familiar songs about cowboys who had stared at those same stars a hundred years ago, when the Starlight Ranch was just a fleeting midnight dream in the mind of some lonesome cowboy.

9 Donna

"Charley Meyers, what were you thinking…"

It's not easy being a matchmaker. Okay, I know what you're thinking. I had nothing to do with Lacey and Cody meeting that day at Parker's. True, I was there, but they just gravitated to each other without anybody's help. Once they met, however, there was no guarantee that things would go smooth for them. On the contrary, love has to overcome any number of obstacles. *Romeo and Juliet*, the play we read in Mrs. James's English class, is a perfect example of that. When the families are feuding, like those Capulets and Montagues, it's going to be tough on the kids.

What we had here in Reno, with Lacey and Cody, wasn't the parents interfering. I found out from Charley that Cody's parents had died when he was a boy. Lacey's folks were still very much alive, back in San Francisco, and they were the kind of parents who just wanted their daughter to be happy, so they wouldn't be a problem. It was other stuff I had to worry about. I always want the best for my friends, including my newest friend, Lacey. She seemed so lost in Reno, and in need of some good advice regarding men, that I just appointed myself love cop. Somebody had to direct the romantic traffic. Mrs. James would have called me a mentor, but that sounds like a kind of tutor. I had to do a lot more than tutoring if Lacey was going to get her degree in romance.

First, I had to worry about that lawyer guy back in San Francisco, Lacey's boyfriend or ex-boyfriend or whatever he was. He was coming to town like a coyote getting into a herd of cattle uninvited. I'd have to be the cowgirl who chases him away so the romantic trail drive can keep moving along in the right direction. Whatever it took, I was ready to make Victor Kleindich realize that Lacey was not born to make him happy, and he'd be much better off staying put back in San Francisco, where maybe you can tell folks not to call you Vic. I hadn't met the guy yet, but I saw him as some kind of sophisticated city slicker who was just fine for a big city. Once he strayed into Reno, however, he'd be a troublemaking coyote.

So that was one thing I had to worry about. Another was Cody. Sure, he was off to a good start with Lacey, but I've seen that before. Some guys are lacking in stamina, and love is a long trail drive, not a Sunday picnic. I aimed to be the cowgirl who rides drag, in back of the herd, to make sure the cattle keep moving in the right direction and don't change their minds.

That's exactly why I was in Parker's on Monday morning, the day after the lawyer barbecue where I taught Lacey a little about rodeo queen waves and a little about men. I walked into the store and there was Charley at the counter, and Cody over by the boots. The way Cody was checking out those boots he looked more like a shopper than an employee. It started out like a slow morning, but it was about to speed up.

Right after I walked in, a couple of senior lady tourists wandered in and started asking Charley a whole string of questions. Next thing you know he had to give them a tour of the store. That left me at the counter, and what do you think I saw there? Charley's composition book. He had promised I could read it, so I opened it up and found a new chapter. It was all about Charley and Cody going down to Carson. There was a pretty part about watching stars, and then there was a part that made me slam the book down on the counter.

"Charley Meyers!" I shouted. Charley excused himself from the two older ladies and came walking back to see what was wrong.

Before he could say a word, I just started in on him. "What were you thinking?" I said, not yelling this time but very intense, believe me.

"What was I thinking about what?"

I held up the composition book. Then I grabbed his arm and pulled him toward the front door. "You need a break," I said. He didn't argue and next thing you know we were out in front of the store. I didn't want Cody to hear any of this.

I opened the book to the part about the Starlight Ranch, where they never raise any cattle, but they do raise other things.

"You took Cody to a brothel?"

"Well, yeah, it's legal."

"I know it's legal," I said, "but it's not *right*. He's supposed to be falling in love with Lacey, not running off with you to some brothel."

"It's harmless," Charley said.

"Good," I said. I was trying to control my temper, but it wasn't easy. "Good, you just tell Lacey it's harmless."

"I'm not going to tell her anything." Charley appeared nervous, like a guilty criminal getting the third degree from the police. I had appointed myself love cop, and it was a job I took seriously.

"You'd better not." My face was about twelve inches from Charley's at this point and I had him backed into a corner.

"And don't you tell her either," Charley said.

"You can bet on that."

"Nothing happened anyway."

"What do you mean nothing happened? You two went to the brothel, didn't you?"

"You didn't read it all," Charley said. "Cody ended up just talking with this poor homesick girl. All they did was have a good cry together."

"Really? You're not lying?"

"Honest to God truth."

"Swear on your horse's head," I said.

"Swear on Buster?"

"You heard me. Swear on your horse's head that nothing happened."

"Buster isn't here, he's out at Bob Morgan's. How can I swear on his head?"

"Charley, stop stalling. Swear on your horse."

"Okay." He knew I wouldn't stop till he swore. "I swear on Buster's head that nothing happened."

"I believe you," I said. "One more thing. Promise me you won't do any more dang stupid things like that again."

"Do I have to swear on anything for that one?" Charley had this funny little smile that I always liked. It took all I had not to smile back. Instead I looked at him as serious as I could.

"Promise," I said.

"Okay, I promise. May I go back to work now?"

"Yes, you may."

"Thank you."

"You're welcome." He held the door open for me and I went to the counter to read some more about the Starlight ranching. Charley walked back to the two ladies to resume the guided tour of Parker's. Cody was still admiring the boots. I had calmed down by then. Being the love cop can take a lot out of you, believe me.

Later that day, after I'd gotten out of my last class at UNR, I stopped downtown to pay a call on my new friend Lacey. Her law firm overlooked the Truckee River, in one of those big old Victorians that they'd turned into offices. It had a nice wooden sign outside and a bunch of even nicer dressed legal staff and attorneys. I was the only one in jeans, but it didn't bother me. If you can't be comfortable wearing jeans in Reno, where can you be comfortable?

I had to sit in the reception area for a few minutes, waiting for Lacey. The receptionist said she was in a meeting but would be out soon. While I was waiting I looked through their copy of the *Gazette-Journal* to see what was new in town. No rodeo stories that day, but I did spot a big ad for King's Hardware. That's my boyfriend's daddy's store. I always read those ads because then I know what Darryl will be selling that week, and also what he'll be telling me about. That guy loves hardware as much as I love rodeo. He can talk about power tools the way I talk about horses and rodeo queen waves. Sometimes I think he's joking and he's going to start laughing, but he never does. He can start in about a new chain saw, for example, and he just goes on and on. I guess it's good for guys to be passionate about something. As long as he's passionate about me too, I'm not complaining.

"Donna, what a nice surprise."

I looked up and there was Lacey in her serious lawyer suit. It's a little more formal than I want to dress, but I guess she has to impress the clients and judges and other lawyers. In some jobs when you're a woman you have to work hard to be taken seriously. At least she wasn't a blonde, so she didn't have to overcome that stereotype.

"I thought you might want to join me for lunch," I said.

"Of course," she said. Lacey's dark eyes sparkled. When her face lit up like that I just knew that Cody's chances of escaping her charms were slim. Not that he wanted to escape them.

"Do you mind if Victor comes along. I agreed to have lunch with him."

"Victor? I get to meet him?"

"The one and only," Lacey said. "Let me see if he's ready and we can go."

A couple minutes later Lacey and Victor came out together. I didn't look at his face very long because I was dazzled by his suit. Lacey had told me that he was from old money, but she had neglected to tell me it was that much old money. And even though she had told me he was handsome, I wasn't prepared for Victor to be so good looking. He had good features, good bones, good hair. He wasn't a shrimp either. And with that suit he looked as if he had just walked off the pages of *GQ*. *GQ*, now there was a nickname I could give him.

Lacey introduced us. I shook his hand. It was very smooth, nothing like a cowboy's hand. The only manual work he did was shuffling legal papers. I wish I could tell you that Victor had pink hands and fair skin, but in fact he had this really good tan. Either he had been hitting the tanning salons in San Francisco or he played a lot of tennis when it wasn't foggy.

"Pleased to meet you," Victor said as he shook my hand. He didn't put much into the handshake, not the way cowboys do. I think I was squeezing harder than he was. He was giving more of his attention to checking out my figure, the way guys do and they think we don't notice where their eyes are traveling.

"Likewise, I'm sure," I said.

"Shall we embark?" Victor said. "I have to be back for a two o'clock appointment."

"Embark?" I said. Then I raised my nose a little and said, "Yes, we shall." Lacey was watching all of this and trying not to laugh.

Victor insisted on taking his car. I don't ride in a Mercedes every day, especially one that big and luxurious. Victor showed off the stereo with some classical music. Lacey sat up front while I had the whole back seat to myself. I was like a kid playing with the buttons, making the windows go up and down, pulling the arm rest down and then back up so I could spread out a bit and feel the leather. Lacey looked back at me once and grinned. I bet if it were my car, and I drove it every day, before long I'd be saying things like "Shall we embark?" I'm more of Dodge pickup girl, of course, as anybody who knows me will tell you.

We drove to the Eldorado because Lacey wanted to eat there. I think the night she had dinner there with Cody it became her favorite eating place. We ended up at the fancy coffee shop, where they have a big menu, American and ethnic foods, and all of it good. When you walk in you have to go right past the bakery part, where they have these huge cakes, include one called chocolate suicide. If you so much as glance at it you take on about a thousand calories, but I always do anyway. Sometimes I even order it.

So there we were in a booth, the three of us, and I was being quiet and proper. I wanted to find out more about this Victor guy. If you're always talking, and never listening, you'll never find out anything about other people.

Victor, as it turned out, was only too happy to talk about himself, so I sat there taking mental notes. I heard all about San Francisco and what a great place it was. Victor never said it, but I think he felt that when he visited Reno he was slumming. All he saw was a little oasis of casinos surrounded by sagebrush and cowboys. No cable cars, no society, none of the big city amenities. If he had looked a little longer he would have seen a little city with lots of arts and culture. But he didn't.

He probably felt the same way about Lacey, that she was slumming too, and he couldn't wait to get her back to San Francisco and civilization. So here was my challenge. If I was going to be a successful love cop I had to keep Victor from pulling her back. I suddenly got this picture in my head of Lacey in the middle of a tug of war, with Victor on the San Francisco end and me on the Reno end. It was reassuring to know that Cody would be pulling with me on the Reno end. Maybe I should enlist some more help. I thought of all my friends. Mel and Harm could teach her to ride out at the Lazy J. They could change her from a city girl to a cowgirl faster than I could. Teri Autrey could sing her some sweet songs like some kind of Western siren. Celia Moon could be her friend and get her addicted to that gourmet coffee and baked goods at Stella's. I could have lots of help on my end of the tug of war. Cody was my biggest ally, though. If Lacey totally lost her heart to him, and I think she'd already given him a chunk of it, she'd never go back to San Francisco.

"So Donna," Victor said, "Lacey informs me you're running for rodeo queen." He said it with this oily smile, as if I were competing for Queen of the Trailer Park instead of Miss Reno Rodeo.

"That's right," I said. "It's just my first try."

"Well, good luck, if that's what you want."

"Thanks," I said. *Creep.*

"Donna's taking some classes at the university too," Lacey said.

"Oh," Victor said, perking up a bit at the thought that there might be hope for me after all. "What's your major?"

"Undecided," I said.

"Well, I'm sure you'll find something suitable," Victor said. *Jerk.*

"Oh, I'm sure. Maybe they'll let me major in home economics."

"That could be useful," Victor said. I think he was relieved that I wasn't going to major in rocket science or brain surgery, although at the moment I would have liked to take a scalpel to his brain, or other bodily parts, just to be useful.

"Here's our food," Lacey said. The waiter arrived before the discussion of my education could turn ugly. I don't know if I gave Victor a fair chance, but it was fairly clear to me that he never gave me any chance. He took one look at my blonde hair and good figure and all he saw was Bimbo, with a capital B. Then there was the rodeo queen part. Rodeo to him had to be some kind of macho activity for uneducated redneck cowboys who couldn't get a real job like being a hotshot lawyer in some hotshot city like San Francisco. Rodeo queens to him must have seemed like those women in the motorcycle magazines who let just about everything hang out and appear to have an IQ of seven.

Not that I was surprised. I had expected Victor to be the way he was. It's true I hadn't expected him to look like a male model. Lacey seemed smarter than to fall for the GQ packaging, although she had been attracted to Cody's cowboy packaging.

We ate. I had a big corned beef sandwich. Victor and Lacey had salads. Victor was a picky eater. I suspected that he had a long list of things that he would never allow in his mouth. He spent half the lunch talking about some museum exhibit in San Francisco and the other half taking bits of bell peppers, onions, and sunflower seeds out of his salad. You'd have to say he was a delicate eater. Maybe from a long line of delicate eaters. I imagined him as a boy, and his mother leaning over to take out the salad stuff he wouldn't eat. Would he expect Lacey to do that for him some day? Maybe expect her to iron his underwear? I had all these awful pictures flashing in my mind. It almost spoiled my appetite for the corned beef sandwich. Almost. It takes a lot to ruin my appetite.

I took a big bite out of the kosher pickle on my plate and started talking and gesturing with the uneaten half of the pickle. Normally I never do that, eat with my mouth full, but I felt like having some fun, and also because if I heard one more word from Victor about that hot museum exhibit in San Francisco I was going to puke.

"Want some of my pickle?" I asked Victor. I held the uneaten half toward him. I don't think the words came out clearly, my mouth being full of pickle and all, but he seemed to understand.

"No, thank you."

"Sure?" I said, holding it closer.

"Very sure," Victor said. He pulled away from me. Maybe he thought I was going to stuff it in his mouth. Not a bad idea actually.

"Lacey, how about you?" I said. I turned the pickle on her.

"Sure, thanks," Lacey said. She took the pickle from me and promptly took a very large bite out of it. Now that surprised me. I was just having some fun and I expected her to decline, but instead she copied me. There we were, our mouths full of kosher pickle, chewing away, trying not to laugh. I glanced over at Victor, who looked disgusted by such behavior in public. Too bad we didn't have a camera. That's one I would have framed, Lacey and I with our mouths full of pickle, maybe holding up our iced tea glasses, our arms around each other and smiling for the camera so the pickles in our mouths got in the picture too.

Those are the moments in life that just sneak up on you. One second you're being bored by a snob who might steal your new friend away, and the next you're enjoying a special pickle moment with the new friend. Happiness is like that, hiding behind a tree and you don't know which one until you walk by it. I was thrilled that Lacey had accepted the pickle and imitated me rather than following Victor's lead. It's what you call your female bonding. There was no doubt about who had won the first round in the tug of war. Chalk one up for Reno.

10 Charley

"Take 'em to Missouri..."

After Donna chewed me out about taking Cody to the Starlight Ranch, I decided I'd better spend more time on Cody's cowboy education and less on his education about women. To be honest with you, I'd only taken him with me because I wanted some company on the drive to Carson and back. I guess I thought it would be educational too, something for him to remember when he was older. If I'd known that it was going to upset Donna like that, I probably would have thought twice about it. Another lesson I learned is that I have to be careful what I write in this composition book. I should never have promised Donna that she could read it. Maybe I should keep things like the starlight ranching in a separate book and hide it away.

Soon after Donna left, and the tourist ladies, the phone rang. It was Bob Morgan. Bob's a man of few words, so it was a short conversation. When I hung up I called to Cody. He was over with the boots again. That guy loves cowboy boots. He put down the pair he was fondling and walked over to the counter.

"Hey, kid, you still want to be a cowboy?"

"Sure," he said. "Heck, I already know how to drive a pickup and sing cowboy songs. Oh yeah, and comfort the ladies at the Starlight Ranch when they cry. It's not so hard."

"Okay, Mr. Top Hand, if you know so much, who was that on the phone just now?"

"I don't know, maybe someone asking for directions to Cheryl's ranch."

"No, Mr. Thirty Minutes, it was not," I said. He was easy to tease. "That was my friend Bob Morgan. He feels indebted to you for taking that old beat up Dodge off his hands. He just called to make you an offer. It seems that Bob has a horse that's so gentle nobody wants to ride him, and he thought you might want to saddle him up and go for a ride with us today. It looks like it's going to be a slow one here, and Andy can handle the store if we cut out early this afternoon. What do you say?"

"Sounds great!"

"There's more. If you like the horse, maybe you can use it to help Bob out at his spread. That is, if you don't mind riding fence and doing some odd jobs out there. Hell, he might even pay you. You don't want to spend all your time indoors anyway." In Cody's eyes I could see his cowboy dreams taking shape in a hurry.

"Thanks, Charley. I hope you didn't have to bribe Bob or anything."

"No, I guess he just liked the way you took to his old truck the other day. He said it reminded him of his first truck years ago. That's why he went to get his camera, to give you something to remember. Oh, there's just one more thing, I forgot to tell you the name of the horse Bob selected for you."

"Oh, what's his name?" Cody asked.

"Devil's Dance."

"Devil's Dance?" This made him stop. "This horse that's so gentle nobody wants to ride him, he's called Devil's Dance?"

"Well, we just call him Dancer for short. Don't worry, he got his name when he was younger, but he's slowed down a lot. But not too much. You wouldn't want to ride a point and shoot horse."

"A what?" Cody asked.

"That's what you call a push button horse, a horse with no spirit, one that's too easy to ride. With Dancer, the only dance he does now is a slow waltz, mostly." I tried to swallow the "mostly," but Cody heard it.

"Mostly? What is mostly?"

"Well, you know, sort of like...mostly."

"No, I don't know. Does this animal do a fast waltz? Does he like to two-step?"

"No." I tried to stall, still searching for a way to tell my student that he had to a take a pop quiz on the first day of class. "He's really gentle, but the thing is, you don't want to spook him."

"All right, now we're getting somewhere," Cody said, wanting to find out the bad news, whatever it was. "So I don't want to scare the horse?"

"That's right."

"So if I don't do anything spooky, he'll just do his slow waltz?"

"That's right, mostly."

Cody put his hand over his eyes. He didn't want to see what was coming next. "'Mostly' again?"

"Well, Cody, animals can get spooked by different things. They say that cats and dogs know when an earthquake's coming and start to act strange. Hey, riding's not so hard, it's roping and wrestling steers and riding bulls that's hard. Trust me."

Cody seemed to consider this for a minute. "Well, I've done fine so far by trusting you. And you have been a real cowboy for a long time."

"That's right. So it's time for you to cowboy up."

"Okay, Charley, let's do some waltzing."

"That's the spirit. I guess you're ready now for the rest of the good news."

"There's more?"

"You bet, kid, we're going for the whole deal—the Reno Rodeo. I mean right down there in the arena with the critters, and thousands of people watching and yelling. There's nothing like it."

"Hold on now," Cody said. "There's no way I'm climbing on 2,000 pounds of bull. One with a name like Nasty Temper. Then flying off and trying to scramble away from the horns. Or flying off the back of some bronc named

Twister. Or jumping onto a steer and trying to wrestle it down, but getting dragged across the arena instead. Worse yet, I might try to rope a calf and end up roping my own horse instead. And Lacey sitting in the front row witnessing my humiliation. Tell me you're kidding,"

"Oh no, dead serious."

Cody cringed. "Don't use that expression, please."

"Oh, sorry, I didn't mean to spook you. You couldn't get into any of those events anyway. You need a license and all kinds of experience. It's just the steer-decorating event. You and I can be a team. You know about steer decorating, don't you?"

"I've seen it once or twice," Cody said. "Not as easy as decorating a Christmas tree."

"Yeah, more like confronting a bully in a saloon and trying to put a ribbon in his hair."

"Let's do it," Cody said. He seemed relieved that he wouldn't have to compete in one of the more dangerous events.

"Hell, let's not just do it, let's win the damn thing!" I put my arm around my young partner as if we'd just won the event and were posing for pictures.

That evening Cody and I were at his apartment. We had worked up a good appetite at Bob Morgan's. So there we were devouring a couple of barbecue sandwiches and a large bag of potato chips.

I had seen in the paper that *Red River* was playing on TV that night and told Cody that this movie was an essential part of his cowboy education. Cody had said that he had seen it two or three times already, but I pointed out that he had never seen it with me. Sort of an "annotated version," I told him.

That afternoon, out at Bob Morgan's ranch, Cody's cowboy lesson had gone surprisingly well. No big mishaps. Cody had learned how to saddle a horse, how to mount, how to place his boots in the stirrups, how to hold the reins, and all the rest. Devil's Dance had turned out to be a fine animal, not too old but not too frisky. Bob had warned Cody to avoid spooking the Dancer, and had advised him not to make any sudden movements, and not even to talk. That was a good one. Cody had been forced to communicate with sign language and had found himself doing things like forming the words "Now what?" without actually saying them.

Bob and I, on the other hand, got to talk all we wanted to. Cody bought the idea that Devil's Dance could only be spooked by his own rider's talking. He managed to communicate well enough with the horse through the reins, and he must have felt like a real cowboy as he rode along with two old cowboys. Cody even got to see some cattle. I think he was grateful he hadn't been asked to try to rope one yet. One thing at a time.

And he saw some beautiful country. Cody told me later he realized why cowboys always liked to buy trucks. It wasn't just for hauling hay and saddles and girlfriends. It had to be the fact that the cowboy could sit up high in the truck, which afforded him a view like the one he got accustomed to while riding a horse. He said the view from Devil's Dance was outstanding.

Cody talked a lot as we drove back from Bob Morgan's. He had to make up for all the silent time on the Dancer. He said that riding on a horse was more primal than riding in a pickup. He said he enjoyed the cowboy songs that he and Lacey and I had sung along with in his truck that weekend. But they didn't sell horses equipped with stereos, at least not yet. Cody guessed that cowboys could take along a Walkman stereo, with earplugs and all, just as they might pack a cell phone, but the traditional cowboy would just provide his own music, singing the old cowboy songs accompanied only by the sounds of the cattle, the wind, and the rain. That's Cody for you. If he didn't make it as a cowboy the kid could always be a poet.

So Cody's cowboy lesson had been a success. The only drawback appeared to be the fact that he was saddle sore. Back at his apartment I kept teasing him by telling him to sit down and rest, but Cody kept saying that he preferred to stand, which gave me a good laugh. He kept finding excuses not to sit down. Once, when I commented on his reluctance to stay seated, the kid told me to turn on the television, since he didn't feel like being my only source of amusement.

While I searched for the remote control, Cody went to answer the phone. It was Lacey, who had just gotten home and had heard a message Cody had left on her machine. Cody said he had just called to say hello and see how she was doing. I heard Cody telling her he was about to see the annotated version of *Red River*, that famous cattle drive movie. Then Cody invited her over to watch with us and to bring Donna.

Not too long after Cody hung up the phone, somebody knocked on the front door. Cody ran a hand through his hair and went to answer the door.

"Hi there, come on in," Cody welcomed the two visitors.

"Howdy, cowboy," Lacey said, and gave him a kiss on the cheek. I stood up as the two ladies entered the room.

"Lacey," Cody said, "this is my friend Charley Meyers."

We were both pleased to meet each other. I told her I'd seen her shopping at Parker's.

"You look like somebody famous," Lacey said.

"Here we go," Cody said.

"Somebody in the movies."

"Western movies," Cody said.

"Thanks for the clue."

"I'll help you," I said. "Ben Johnson, right?"

"*The Last Picture Show*," Lacey said. "Am I right? You won an Oscar."

"Well, *he* did. The real Ben Johnson, I mean. He was a real cowboy, you know, before he was a movie star. He was wrangling horses for a movie company when he was discovered."

"I love that story," Cody said.

"Has Donna showed you her wave yet?" I asked. I was tired of being in the spotlight.

"More than that," Lacey said, "she gave me a lesson."

"Say, Donna," I said, "why don't you practice your wave on us." I was curious to see if she had made any changes.

"Okay," Donna said. It was an offer she could never refuse.

"Let's sit on the sofa and pretend we're at the rodeo," I said. Cody and Lacey joined me on the sofa.

"You're in for a treat," Lacey whispered to Cody.

Donna put her cowgirl hat on, stood in the living room about ten feet in front of us, then slowly lowered her head to concentrate, and for dramatic effect, of course. We held our breath as Donna slowly raised her head, tilted it slightly to one side, smiled her biggest smile, then raised her right hand and did her latest rodeo queen wave. It had become very elaborate, impossible to describe. You had to be there.

The reactions were immediate. Lacey smiled. Cody gasped, and his eyes got even bigger than they had been. I let out a whistle. We all clapped.

"They don't wave like that anymore," I said.

"They never did," Donna said, "only me." Which was only the truth.

Lacey brought out the cheeseburgers and Lone Star that she and Donna had brought with them, and we decided to eat in the living room because the movie was about to begin.

Red River started, and we all watched the opening credits. "It's in black and white," Lacey said.

"More authentic that way," I said.

"Oh that's right," Cody said, "life was in black and white in those days." We just ignored him.

I began my annotated version of the movie, offering all kinds of comments, everything from how the movie was made to the smallest detail of the cattle drive.

At one point Cody asked, "Is that you, Charley, the cowboy over there on the left?"

"No, but I wish I had been there. I was just a baby when they were filming this down in Tucson. Funny you should say that, though, because I've seen this movie so many times I feel as if I were on that cattle drive."

Lacey, who had felt the need to apologize for never having seen *Red River* before, had to hush me now and then because I would forget and start saying the words before the actors did. When the John Wayne character, Tom Dunston, was about to start the cattle drive, I leaned forward as the camera panned the thousands of cattle and then focused on the trail boss. When John Wayne told the Montgomery Clift character, "OK, Matt, take 'em to Missouri," Lacey noticed my lips moving with the words. Then, when all the cowboys were yelling "Yee-hah!" at the start of the drive, I let out my own "Yee-hah!" which was matched shortly thereafter by "yee-hahs" from Donna, Cody, and then Lacey. The cattle drive was officially underway.

"Hey, Cody, come sit down and watch the movie," Lacey said, wondering why Cody kept getting up and walking around.

"I am watching," Cody protested. Unable to sit comfortably for long, he kept looking for excuses to get up. Fetching food was a good one. Now he came up with a new excuse. "I'm just practicing my John Wayne walk," Cody told Lacey as he tried to walk like the Duke.

Lacey shook her head and tried to divide her attention between the real Duke on the screen and this comical imitation. "I hope you're not doing this for my benefit," Lacey told him.

"No, missy, don't worry your pretty little head," he said, trying again to sound like the Duke instead of Fred Flintstone. "This is the way I walk, and if some folks find it amusing, I can't help it. Just go on watchin' your movie there, and don't pay me no never mind."

"Cody, will you kindly shut up?" I said. "Some of us are trying to watch the movie, you know."

"Sorry there, Mr. Charley," Cody apologized, still working on his John Wayne voice. "I wouldn't want to spoil your evenin's entertainment. I'll just be over here in case you need some help with the critters."

"Co-dy!" This time it was Donna who was objecting. "Why don't you just cool your saddle and sit over here by the lawyer lady? She looks a little lonesome."

Cody didn't want to argue with Donna, and his John Wayne impression wasn't getting any better, so he sat down next to Lacey. Donna and I were sitting on the floor in front of the sofa, each of us holding a longneck and studying the movie to see if we could spot something we hadn't seen before.

During the stampede scene, Lacey tensed up and grabbed Cody's arm. When they were burying the cowboy killed in the stampede, I saw Lacey glance at Cody, perhaps wondering if he had ever been involved in a stampede. "Cowboying is dangerous work," I said, and Donna nodded in agreement.

I pointed out details to notice in scene after scene, how this cowboy dressed or rode a certain way, or how that one talked like a real cowboy, or how Walter Brennan made a great chuck wagon cook, or how that horse, that one right there, was a beauty. I talked about how big a man John Wayne was, and how the horses he rode in the movies always looked small but they weren't really. I talked about sleeping on the trail, the importance of having a good wrangler for the horses, and why the trail boss had to be tough.

I talked about things outside the movie, like the fact that Fort Worth had grown up as a cow town because it was on the Chisholm Trail. During the branding scene, I talked about different brands and what they meant. I mentioned that John Wayne often wore a buckle with the "Red River D" brand on it. I was right at home, passing on important oral history to a new group of cowboys gathered around the campfire. Never mind that the campfire was an electronic one. The television set would do just fine for now.

When they reached the scene where Joanne Dru flirts with Montgomery Clift while arrows and bullets are flying all around, Lacey inched a little closer to Cody. The scene was almost as romantic as the Virginia City cemetery.

As the movie ended, we all applauded, and Donna and I added some loud whistles of appreciation.

"Now that's what I call a movie," I said. "Did the lawyer lady enjoy it?"

Lacey laughed. "I enjoyed the hell out of it," she said, "except when the cowboy who's seen it a hundred times kept saying the lines along with the actors. And when the other cowboy wasn't practicing his John Wayne impression. Not that it wasn't cute, Cody, it was just a distraction."

"Shucks, ma'am," Cody said sheepishly, "I didn't mean no harm."

Donna shook her head. "There's just one thing wrong with this movie."

"Something wrong with *Red River?*" I asked in disbelief.

"Not exactly wrong," Donna said, "just something missing. There's no rodeo."

"But there's plenty of horses and cattle and roping and riding, what do you want?" I argued.

"Well, you know, a rodeo queen riding in and waving at the boys. That would have made it just about perfect."

"Oh, that's okay," I said, "we saw that earlier. Any rodeo queen in the movie would have been an anticlimax after watching you perform tonight."

Donna smiled. "You silver tongued devil, you always know what to say."

"Well," I said, "time for me to head home. Thanks for dinner."

"Thanks for the movie lesson," Cody said.

I drove away as Donna was getting into her truck. She gave me a good wave. I noticed that Lacey was staying behind. She and Cody stood and waved. They made a good couple. I guess that starlight ranching we did in Carson the night before wasn't going to be a problem. Not that I wanted to mention it to Donna. Not then or ever again.

11 Donna

"If you wanna be a cowgirl…"

It's me again, Donna the love cop. The week was going well, considering that Victor was in town and I had to focus on keeping him away from Lacey so she could spend more time with Cody. Watching cowboy movies with Charley and Cody had been a good idea. Cody acted as if he was saddle sore. I think Charley's been taking him riding. That's fine, as long as he doesn't take him down to see the working ladies in Carson City again.

The next afternoon I walked into Lacey's law office. Reporting for duty. Victor was in Lacey's office. I saw the two of them walking out together. The receptionist went to tell Lacey I was there.

"Donna," Lacey said, "you're too late for lunch. Come on into my office."

Lacey had an office with a view of the street. I guess she would have to be there longer to get a view of the river. She had nice chairs though. I settled into one of them and curled my legs up on it.

"Hey," I said, "you look like a real lawyer sitting behind that desk. Just like on TV."

"Give me a break," Lacey said. "Say, last night was a lot of fun."

"I know," I said. "You got a cowboy lesson from Charley. Now it's time for a cowgirl lesson from me."

"Cowgirl lesson? Are we going to watch another Western movie?"

"Nope, the real thing. I'm taking you riding. You've been on a horse before, right?"

"I was on a pony ride when I was a little girl. Does that count?"

"Well, today's your lucky day. Big horses this time," I said. "And you know why? Because you know me, and I know Mel and Harm, and they always have extra horses."

"Great, you know real cowboys with real horses." Lacey was so sweet, sitting there smiling at me. And so innocent. Should I tell her that Mel and Harm were cowgirls, not cowboys? Please forgive me, but I just couldn't resist.

"I've never ridden big horses," Lacey said.

"Riding's not that hard, and Mel will make sure you have a good horse. You'll be a cowgirl before you know it. It might be a good way to impress Cody."

"Okay," Lacey said, "you talked me into it. Who are Mel and Harm?"

"Only two of my oldest friends. The Johnson twins. We went to high school together. Their daddy has a big ranch east of here, and that's usually where I go to ride. Mel and Harm are just great. We've done everything together, the three of us. When we were in high school I used to sleep over with them just about every weekend. I was always closer to Mel, but Harm's a lot of fun too." I watched Lacey's face closely, waiting for an eyebrow to go up or a jaw to drop.

"You used to sleep over with both of them?" Lacey asked.

"Hey, it's a free country, as my daddy always says. What's wrong with that?"

"Oh, nothing, I guess," Lacey said. "If I go riding with them at their ranch, does that mean I have to sleep over too?"

I tried hard to keep a straight face. "Not if you don't want to. But I'll tell you what's fun. When you sleep over with Mel and Harm, and you're tired of wearing jeans, they'll let you try on their dresses."

"What?!"

"Sure, haven't you ever done that before?"

"No, not with guys."

"Who said anything about guys?" I said.

"You did. You know, Mel and Harm?"

"Oh," I said, pretending to catch on. "I guess you got the wrong impression. Mel is what everyone calls Melody, and Harm is what everyone calls Harmony. Everybody knows the Johnson sisters."

Lacey shook her head. "You set me up, didn't you? I bet this isn't the first time you've done this routine." Then she laughed. "I should have known there was something funny when you started on the part about the dresses."

"You mean the sleeping over part in high school, that didn't bother you?"

"Well, I did think it was a little strange to sleep over with both guys."

"Oh, I'm not that wild," I said. "I like cowboys, but one at a time. It's safer that way. But I am serious about going riding. Hey, if you like it you can ride in the rodeo parade next month. Mel and Harm and I always ride together every year. I'd like to see the look on your cowboy's face when he sees you in the parade."

"Yeah, me too," Lacey said. "I did ask him to teach me about horses and cattle sometime, but this might be better. As long as I don't embarrass myself by falling off."

"Nah, you won't fall off, not if I'm your teacher. You know, you've got to start working on a wave if you're going to be in the parade. That's something you can practice anytime, even at work. Hey, we need to get moving if we're going riding. Can you go now?"

Lacey glanced at her watch and then at a folder in front of her on the desk.

"I guess I can take this home tonight," she said.

"Great!"

"Thanks, Donna, you're a real friend."

"That's right, and don't you forget it. You're lucky to know me. Isn't your life more exciting since you met me?"

Just then we heard a little knock and Victor was there in the doorway. Today the GQ guy had another one of those gorgeous suits on. I got this picture in my head of what his closet must look like back in San Francisco. One of those walk-in deals, no doubt, with a long row of Italian suits, and on one wall a small herd of fancy Italian shoes.

"Excuse me," he said. "Lacey, are we meeting after work?"

"Victor," Lacey said, "can we do that tomorrow? Donna's offered to take me riding this afternoon."

"Riding?" Victor said. "Horses?"

"Yep, on a real ranch. You want to come with us? That is, if it's okay with Donna."

Ha! Okay with me? Victor on a horse? In that suit? What was wrong with that picture? Just about everything. I wanted to say no, but then I got a picture of Victor falling off the horse on his well-dressed butt. That might be worth seeing.

"Sure," I said, "Mel and Harm will give you a horse."

"I don't know," Victor said. He looked as if he had just swallowed something that he had neglected to take out of his salad. "I have a lot of work to do."

"Oh, come on," Lacey said. "It'll be fun."

"I don't have anything to wear," Victor said.

"You can stop by your hotel room," Lacey said. "You must have brought some jeans with you?"

"Jeans? No, just suits and slacks. I thought I'd be working most of the time in Reno. Or taking you out."

"Heck," I said, "there's no law against riding a horse wearing a suit."

"No, you two go without me."

"I've got an idea," I said, "just ride in the car with us part of the way and I'll show you a really cool place. No horses involved."

"What's that?" Victor said. Lacey was looking at me all curious too.

"It's a surprise. Just trust me."

Victor looked as if he wouldn't trust me to give him the time of day, but just then Lacey jumped him.

"Come on, Victor," she said, "trust Donna. Don't you like surprises? For once in your life, do something spontaneous."

"I can be spontaneous," Victor said. He had his arms folded, feet planted squarely, ready to defend himself against any further accusations.

"Good," I said, "let's go then. You'll like your surprise. It's a place that all guys like." Lacey gave me a funny look, but she trusted me. That's where she was different from GQ boy.

"I'll have to stop at my apartment to change," Lacey said.

"Of course," I said. "Let's go, you two. The law firm will survive without you for a couple of hours."

Victor insisted on driving his Mercedes, so Lacey and I rode together in my truck and he followed us in his fancy car. We headed south on Virginia Street until we reached King's Hardware. We climbed out and there was Victor pulling into the parking stall next to us.

"What is this?" he said.

"Somebody I want you to meet," I said. "Trust me."

Inside the hardware store I spotted Shorty Rogers first. He was at the information counter. That was the job Shorty was born for, giving out information. If he didn't know the answer, which was not very often, he'd make something up, or start talking about something he did know. For a guy in his twenties he had accumulated a large amount of knowledge.

"Hey, Shorty," I said. "Have you seen Darryl?"

"Hi, Donna, how you doing? Yeah, he's was over in the power tools the last time I saw him. That's always the first place to look for Darryl anyway."

"Oh, I'm sorry, I want you to meet a couple of friends. This is Lacey Anderson. She lives in my building."

"Pleased to meet you," Shorty said, shaking Lacey's hand. He had always been polite, back to high school, where I met him and Darryl, and probably before that.

"And this is Victor Kleindich," I said.

"Pleased to meet you," Shorty said. He has a good handshake and I saw

Victor wince a bit.

"Let's go find Darryl," I said. "He's my boyfriend," I told Victor. "Darryl can answer all your hardware questions."

"I don't have any hardware questions at the moment," Victor said as we started down an aisle.

"All guys have hardware questions," I said. "Darryl will show you some cool power tools anyway. He can show you stuff you didn't know you needed and all of a sudden you can't live without it. You'll love this store."

"I'm sure," Victor said. He was looking around as we moved toward the back and the power tools. Maybe he was calculating which items would involve getting his hands dirty. The thing about guys, though, is they will never admit they don't like hardware. There's some kind of unwritten law. Just like they would rather die than shop for their girlfriend when she asks him to pick up a feminine hygiene product. That's something I'm sensitive about myself. I would never ask Darryl to do that, not in a million years, not even as a test of his love. If he did agree to do it, I know it would half kill him.

"Darryl, there you are," I said. Sure enough, he was hanging out by the chain saws. It was easy to spot him in that orange vest they all wear. There's something comforting about seeing Darryl at his daddy's hardware store. He looks so at home there. Like seeing Mel and Harm at the Lazy J, or Celia surrounded by pastries and gourmet coffee at Stella's. With guys, it's always good when they feel at home. I walked up and gave him a kiss on the cheek.

"Darryl King, this is my friend Lacey Anderson, the one I told you about."

"Ma'am," Darryl said, nodding.

"Glad to meet you," Lacey said.

"And this is Victor Kleindich," I said, "from Lacey's law firm."

"Vic," Darryl said, sticking out his hand. Victor shook it.

"It's Victor," I said, before Victor could correct him.

"Oh," Darryl said.

"Darryl," I said, "why don't you show Victor around the store. I bet he has a million questions."

"Be glad to."

"Lacey and I are going riding at Mel and Harm's. I'll call you later."

"OK, babe," Darryl said. I like the way he calls me "babe" sometimes. It's so cute.

So before Victor knew what had happened Lacey and I had disappeared and he was stuck with Darryl and a big store full of hardware. It would be good for him, and he would learn a lot if he kept his ears open, but I'm sure he would rather have been doing legal stuff, or maybe shopping at a fancy clothing store. I didn't much care as long as I could keep him away from Lacey.

Lacey and I stopped at our apartment building so she could change. I was already wearing boots and jeans, and my hat was in the truck. Soon we were headed out of town. The cowgirl life was calling to us, and kind of strong.

The Johnson sisters lived with their parents on the Lazy J Ranch, but there was nothing lazy about it. It was a full-on working Nevada ranch. Chance and Audrey Johnson had done things right on the Lazy J, and all their dedication and hard work had paid off in a profitable ranch business and a happy family. Audrey, Chance's favorite cowgirl and cook, had presented her husband with a remarkable pair of twin daughters. When they knew they were going to have twins, Chance had suggested that Audrey name the first-born and he would name the straggler. Audrey, well known locally for her love of music and her silver singing voice, named the first daughter Melody. Chance, never one to argue with his wife's good judgment, followed right along by naming the second daughter Harmony. The doctor was delighted to be bringing so much music into the world, and from the day of the twins' birth, these two outstanding daughters charmed everyone—from the nurses, to the relatives, to the friends, to perfect strangers.

With the Johnson sisters, as with any top singing group, it was difficult to tell where Melody left off and Harmony started. Like most identical twins, they were inseparable. Audrey Johnson dressed them alike, and even their parents took a while to distinguish between the two. Others were constantly guessing. Mel would often pose as Harm, and vice versa, on the telephone, in the classroom, and even later in high school, on dates.

Their best friend growing up was me, Donna Cooper. I was like a sister to the twins, and like a daughter to Audrey Johnson. Mel and Harm, who got their nicknames early from Chance Johnson, grew up as tomboys. They mostly hung around the ranch with their father, who treated them like a couple of sons. Not that Chance was disappointed to have daughters. Quite the opposite. He was the proudest parent in town, and he simply acted as if his two girls could do anything. And he let them do everything on the ranch. When the girls first brought me home to meet their mother, Audrey Johnson was delighted to have a girl around who had been raised as a girl. So Audrey had her daughter, and Chance had his twins who were as good as any sons could be.

Most people around Reno said that Mel and Harm were better at cowboying than most cowboys. No one actually referred to them as "cowgirls," they were just "two of the best hands around." Chance had taught them everything he knew about cowboying, which was plenty, and he had instilled in them an unswerving loyalty to the cowboy code. They were both straight shooters, hard working and never complaining. I had learned riding and cowboying from the twins, and had learned everything about being a rodeo queen from the mother, who had been Miss Rodeo Nevada in her time.

Mel and Harm never wanted to be rodeo queens; they were too busy working on the ranch. When they did start to rodeo, it was barrel racing that became their passion. Every chance they got, when they could take a break from ranch work, they would head off to a rodeo somewhere to race their quarter horses around some barrels, and more often than not they would bring back some prize money. Nobody could say which twin was better at rodeo, and judges and announcers were thankful they wore numbers.

So Lacey would be learning to ride from the best. When Lacey and I arrived at the Lazy J Ranch, Mel and Harm were waiting. From a distance Lacey spotted the twins, who were dressed in identical shirts and jeans. Lacey was grateful that they were wearing different color hats. I knew what was up with the hats, but kept it to myself.

"Howdy, you must be Lacey," one of the twins said as they walked up to my shining white pickup.

"Lacey, these are my two best friends," I said after we had climbed out and set our feet on the Lazy J. "That's Mel in the white hat and Harm in the black hat."

"There ain't no harm in a black hat," Harmony said, winking at me.

"Harm, that wasn't funny ten years ago, and it's still not funny," Melody complained.

"That's my older sister," Harmony said to Lacey. "Ever since Dad told her she was born first and he started calling me the straggler, I've had to put up with this abuse."

I had to laugh. "Listen to you two. You know you two love each other more than anything in the world. Don't pay any attention to their fussing, Lacey. Mel just likes to get in Harm's way," I said, emphasizing the last three words.

"Now you're doing it," Melody complained. "Enough with the puns. Let's get Lacey up on a horse and show her the ranch."

Lacey was a fast learner. She learned to saddle a horse, climb on it, and not fall off. She had to put up with a certain amount of teasing, such as being told to "stop looking for the turn signals on that animal," but she took this as a natural part of her initiation.

And what teachers she had. If she had told God that she wanted to learn to paint, and God had given her a choice of any artist, she would have had a hard time deciding between Michelangelo and Vincent Van Gogh. But having Mel and Harm teaching her to ride, it was as if God had said, "Lacey, you're one of my favorites, so you can learn from Michelangelo and Vincent."

I had learned riding from the twins, and they had learned from Chance Johnson, and Chance Johnson, well follow it all the way back and you'd probably find someone with a God-given talent for riding. And now Lacey was the next student, and one of the best ever to come to the Lazy J. I wondered what in her life had prepared her to be such a successful student. Was it law school? Was it the perseverance that her father had exhibited in building up his produce business and had passed on to his daughter? Or was it Lacey's desire to impress her cowboy friend, Cody? Learning from Cody would have been fun, but this was even better. He would never see any mistakes she might make today.

Mel and Harm gave Lacey a fine horse named Angel. Indeed, there were no devilish horses on the Lazy J. Lacey barely had to do more than think about going left, or right, and Angel would read her mind. It was like the responsiveness of a fine sports car, but with a warm-blooded animal beneath her and a spectacular view in every direction. She said she liked the views from Angel even better than the views from Cody's pickup. All the cattle and mountains and ranch scenery brought back the movie she had watched with Cody and Charley and me. She wanted to yell "Yee-hah!" and she did.

At the end of Lacey's first riding lesson, the twins and I lined up to give her a hug. We found it hard to believe that she had never ridden before. Mel and Harm excused themselves and went "to check on something," stopping first to wink at me. When they returned, the twins asked Lacey if she could settle a bet for them. They wanted to know which sister was taller. Lacey scratched the back of her neck and grinned, and stalled some more, and then finally asked them to stand side by side. They did, and then Lacey asked them to remove their hats.

The twins said they couldn't do that, because it was part of the bet.

Lacey studied the two, walked around to look at them from different angles, and then finally gave her decision. "I guess you're just a bit taller, Mel, with your white hat."

That's when I jumped in. "You mean Mel wins the bet?" I asked.

"That's it," Lacey said. "What's this bet all about anyway?"

"Well," I said, "whenever they meet someone new, these crazy girls bet each other which one is taller."

"What does the winner get?" Lacey asked.

"She gets a date with the boyfriend of the person who's doing the judging," I said.

"What!" Lacey almost yelled.

"It's just a friendly bet," I said nonchalantly.

"Not very friendly, if you ask me," Lacey said.

"What's wrong," I said, "don't want to share Cody?"

At this point one of the twins asked if Lacey's decision was final, that Mel was the winner, but I interrupted, saying it was time to stop the foolishness. "There's no way Mel's the winner, she's wearing the black hat."

"What?" Lacey said, still confused.

"Those two played a trick on you," I said. "They disappeared so they could switch hats. They do it every time. And don't let them get near your cowboy, much less go on a date with him."

About this time Mel and Harm were just about rolling on the ground laughing, having pulled off the hat trick one more time. They had done it so often they were polished performers, and no one had ever caught on. They apologized to Lacey if she had taken it as a mean trick, but she was a good sport, seeing it as part of her initiation. I think the real lesson was not about twins and hats, but about how Lacey had revealed her true feelings for her cowboy.

Inside the ranch house, as the four of us sat down to a hearty lunch, Mel asked Lacey if she wanted to ride in the Reno Rodeo parade with them. Lacey was so confident after her first cowgirl lesson that she didn't hesitate to accept this invitation. Mel told her that if she wanted she could ride Angel in the parade. Harm invited her to come back again for some more riding. I suggested that Lacey might be ready to practice her parade wave the next time. This led to a lengthy discussion of different waves. I offered to demonstrate my latest rodeo queen wave, which caused some groaning and hooting from the twins, but I did it anyway, and Lacey applauded. The twins tried to do my wave, but they got it all wrong, and I told them so.

In short, it was another happy time at Chance Johnson's Lazy J Ranch. If Chance and Audrey had been there, it would have been perfect, but they had gone to see some horses and hadn't returned by the time Lacey and I waved goodbye and headed back to town.

"I told you they were a kick," I said as I pointed my truck back towards the highway.

"Are they always like that?" Lacey asked.

"No, sometimes they're all business, working the ranch with their dad. But they like you. Are you sure you're not a cowgirl disguised as a San Francisco lawyer?"

Lacey smiled. "Do you think Cody will be surprised?"

"Don't tell him till the parade. Let him think he's a big, strong cowboy, and you're just a lady who's willing to bask in his glory."

"Is that the way you act around cowboys?" Lacey asked.

"Never you mind, girl." I wasn't about to give away all of my secrets. I pulled onto the highway and gunned the truck toward Reno. Once I turned to Lacey and smiled. She looked right at home in cowgirl clothes, riding in a truck. She might as well have been a million miles from San Francisco and big city life. And Victor.

12 Donna

"Charley, what's your dream…"

The next month went fast. I was busy with the rodeo queen competition and classes. My unofficial moonlighting job of love cop was going great. True, it was a part-time volunteer position. I never got a nickel for all the work I put in to make sure the right people were with the other right people, and that Mr. Wrong didn't mess things up.

Victor Kleindich, who could have tried to fit in better by becoming Vic, and riding with Lacey, and thereby having a chance at her, just stayed Victor, his own handsome but snooty self. His week in Reno passed without him making any new progress with Lacey Anderson. That was a busy week for me, always checking in with Lacey and keeping her occupied as much as possible, and imposing myself on her and Victor when the two of them went out to lunch or dinner. Lacey was still seeing Victor, however, and she still talked about making partner.

In the weeks after that, with Victor safely back in San Francisco, I watched Lacey and Cody spend more time together. Sometimes Lacey would call me with the latest report, but more often I'd call her, just to see how things were going, and to reassure her that maybe some of the things she had heard about cowboys, if she had heard some of those negative things, were not always true. I know that cowboys get a bad reputation, and if you listen to just a few of those songs, like Willie Nelson's advice to all the mamas not to let their babies grow up to be cowboys, you might want to run the other way when you see one, rather than chasing them. That's a fact.

But chasing cowboys, or at least chasing Cody West, was something that Lacey seemed quite willing to do. I enjoyed watching the way she chased him too. It was a good, honest kind of chasing. No silly games, no playing hard to get. No playing easy to get either. I'd see the two of them together and they'd be talking like old friends.

I've always thought that was important in a romantic relationship, to be friends first. Heck, Darryl King and I were friends before he ever asked me out. I'd go to his daddy's hardware store with my older brother, Rooster, and Darryl was always friendly and talkative. He'd help Rooster with whatever hardware needs he might have, but he'd be talking to me too in a friendly way. Sure, he checked me out more than once, you know the way guys do. I have one of those figures that guys can't seem to resist staring at. But Darryl always did it in a fast way and didn't have any rude comments to make either. When he finally did ask me out it was to dinner and a movie, and he behaved like a gentleman. It was one of those action movies, with Bruce Willis. He was nice about picking out the movie, too. He said that next time we could go see a chick flick. Darryl can be real considerate at times.

Anyway, I was talking about Lacey and Cody being friends and all, as well as a couple. That's one reason I thought they were good together. I wish I had made a bet with someone the first time I saw them together that those two would make it last. Maybe Charley Meyers would have taken that bet. I didn't know what his experience with women had been. It was something he never talked about, and I never thought to ask him. I guess I was too busy showing him my latest wave and asking him about cowgirl clothes at Parker's.

★

One day, about a week before the opening of the rodeo, I decided to make time for Charley. It was about noon when I walked into Parker's. There he was, leaning on the counter the way an old cowboy might lean on a corral fence. Not that Charley was old. You might think that forty-five is old, but if you stood him up next to a really old geezer Charley would look very young by contrast. Age is relative, that's what I always say.

"Charley, it's lunchtime," I said as I charged through the front door at Parker's.

"Donna, you sneaked up on me. Where have you been keeping yourself?"

"Busy with school and all that rodeo queen stuff," I said. "Did you miss me?"

"You bet," Charley said. "It's been kind of gloomy without you around. I was just about to hang black curtains in the front window."

"Oh, Charley. Say, why don't you take your lunch break? I brought some sandwiches and sodas."

"Hey, good idea. What's the big loaf of bread for? How many sandwiches are we going to eat?"

"Oh, the bread is for the ducks," I said. "Let's go eat down by the river. It's a beautiful June day."

"Sounds good," Charley said.

So before you know it we had walked the few short blocks to the park that borders the Truckee River. We found a place down by the river to sit and eat. Most of the ducks were down by Virginia Street, but the word must have gotten out that someone was throwing bread upstream, so we quickly became very popular with the duck population.

"So how's Cody?" I asked, after we were settled and started in on the peanut butter and banana sandwiches. Charley smiled on the first bite, pleasantly surprised, I think. I guess there are some people in this world who have lived all their lives without having a peanut butter and banana sandwich. Charley appeared to be one of those people.

"He's a good kid. I think he's going to make a decent cowboy."

"That's good to hear," I said. "I didn't tell Lacey the whole story about Cody's background. Just as I promised you."

"Do you think she'd still love him if she knew he was a cowboy wannabe from Iowa?"

"Probably," I said. "I just wouldn't want to take a chance that it might spoil things."

"Yep. Anyway, he's turning into a real cowboy, so it doesn't matter much anymore." Charley stopped to take another bite of peanut butter and banana, then he washed it down with some soda. "Rodeo's just a week away. You ready to become the next rodeo queen?"

"I've done everything I can do," I said. "It's up to the judges. Competition is fierce this year."

"It's fierce every year," Charley said.

"Life is fierce," I said. I just had to go him one better.

"How would you know? You're only eighteen."

"And I guess you're a hundred and eighteen and know everything."

Charley laughed. "Not quite," he said. He took another bite of his sandwich and threw some more bread to the ducks. Then he looked down for a while. When he looked up again I had the feeling that he had just taken a long mental journey somewhere.

"What you thinking about, Charley?"

"Nothing." He threw some more bread in the river. The ducks loved him.

"Come on, tell me," I said. I had to know.

"Well," he said slowly, "I was just thinking about dreams. You're pursuing yours pretty good. It's fun to watch."

"And? There's more than that on your mind."

"It's the dreams. I haven't thought about dreams for a long time. I just go along from one day to the next."

"What's your dream, Charley Meyers? What are you dreaming about these days?"

"I don't dream," he said. "Haven't for years."

"You never dream in your sleep? I find that hard to believe."

"No, it's the other kind, the waking dreams. I don't have them anymore. Nothing I really want or something I'm working for."

"How about your old dreams then? What was your dream when you weren't so old."

"So old? Thanks a lot."

"You're welcome," I said. It was fun teasing Charley. He never got upset. He was a like a favorite uncle to me. If I were a little kid again I'd probably be sitting on his lap and telling him what I wanted for Christmas. Or maybe that's Santa Claus I'm thinking about.

"Dreams," Charley said. "Old dreams." I kept quiet now because he seemed ready to talk about it. He took out another slice of bread and sailed it at one old duck that was off by itself and looking kind of forlorn.

"I guess I used to have dreams," he said. "I dreamed about becoming a rodeo champion. I was good enough to get a rodeo scholarship at Wyoming. Made a little money on the circuit after college. Not a lot though. I chased that dream a number of years, but it never got any closer. One morning I woke up and decided to do something else with my life."

"Ranch work?" I asked.

"Yep, I decided to settle down once and for all in Reno and be a regular cowboy instead of one those migrant buckle chasers. My buckles are all store bought anyway."

"And that's all? That's the only dream you ever had?"

"Nope, that was the rodeo dream. I guess I lived it for a while. Can't complain. There was one other dream I pursued for a while." He reached into the bag for the last slice of bread.

"So stop stalling," I said. "The ducks are stuffed anyway. Tell me your other old dream."

"That would be Angel."

"Who's Angel?" The only Angel I knew was the horse at the Lazy J.

"A girl I used to know. When I was a young ignorant cowboy."

"Ignorant?"

"Ignorant about women. When you're in your twenties you think you know everything, but I didn't know jack." He stopped, a little embarrassed.

"Jack shit?" I said. That was an expression I had heard a few times from Darryl, although I would never use it myself.

"Yeah, that's it, pardon my French. I didn't know beans about women. Angel and Mud were a couple of cowgirls I ran around with in those days."

"Mud?"

"Mud was Angel's best friend, like a sidekick. She was short and red-headed and quite a . . ." He stopped again.

"Pistol?" I offered.

"I was going to say 'pisser,'" Charley said.

"Oh, I get the picture. Mud was her real name?"

"Nickname. I never did know her real name. She may have told me once but I was too drunk to remember. Nobody ever called her anything but Mud, her mom included."

"Tell me more about Angel. You chased her for a long time?"

"Not long enough," Charley said. "Or fast enough. She was a beauty, and I think she loved me. She had that long straight dark hair almost down to her waist, and beautiful eyes and a sweet smile. She had a great laugh too."

"So she was your angel?"

"For a while."

"What happened, Charley? How did you lose your angel?"

"I think she got tired of waiting for me. I wasn't ready to marry anyone, although she would have been the one if I had decided. Funny thing is, I was just starting to think about how it would be, married to Angel, and then one day she was gone. Left town, out of my life."

"And you never saw her again?"

"I got a postcard from up in Washington State. She was staying with a cousin up there, helping on her cousin's ranch. It was just a short message, but she had a return address on it."

"So you wrote to her?"

Charley looked down. He picked up a handful of small rocks and started chucking them into the river. The ducks had moved off a ways, so don't worry about them getting hit.

"You did write to her," I said.

"Never did," Charley said. "I didn't know what to say."

"Didn't know what to say? You might have told her you loved her," I said. "I swear, you were telling the truth when you said you didn't know jack about women."

"I know now," Charley said. "I was just a kid back then."

"Well, it's too late," I said, "you lost your angel. Charley Meyers, that has to be the saddest story I've ever heard. And I've heard some sad stories."

"Now you know why I don't talk about her. I don't want to make everybody around me sad."

"So you never found another woman to take her place?"

"Who could? She was perfect for me."

"And you were a perfect idiot," I said.

"Can't argue with you there. Maybe I should just throw myself into the river."

"Oh, Charley, don't do that, you'll scare the ducks." That made him laugh. I could always make him laugh. I put my arm around him and gave him a little hug. "Cheer up, Charley, it can't get any worse."

"Thank you very much. Very encouraging."

"No," I said, "I'm serious. Think about it, it's got to get better. Just try to focus on a new dream."

"But I kind of like the old dream."

I patted Charley's shoulder. There was nothing left to say. He was going to focus on that old dream, and there was nothing I could do to stop him. I was frustrated. He was frustrated. At the moment only the ducks were content.

I stood up and pulled him up, before he could launch himself into a watery grave. Then I walked him back to Parker's. Maybe working would be good for him, help him out of his sad mood. I gave him a smile and a wave before I left the store, but my heart wasn't in it.

All the way home I kept thinking about Charley's old dream. His Angel had flown away, and he was left to ponder where he had gone wrong. The truth is that he wasn't the least confused about it. Maybe confusion would have been better for him. You see, Charley knew exactly where he had screwed up. But now it was too late.

I have to tell you that when I went home that afternoon I couldn't concentrate on the rodeo queen competition. Normally I'd be in front of the mirror, practicing my wave, or maybe checking out my wardrobe. I picked up one of my schoolbooks and stared at it for a while before I finally closed it and left it on the kitchen table.

I headed for my bedroom and just lay there a long time staring at the ceiling. That was a mistake. All I saw up there was a beautiful young cowgirl with long dark hair riding away from a young Charley Meyers. It was like a scene from an old Western movie, and I was seeing it for the first time. How many times had Charley seen that movie in the twenty years since Angel had left him? At least now I understood why he always seemed to have a lonesome side. He'd been carrying that weight around a long time. It was enough to make a person cry, and I did.

13 Charley

"Get along, little dogies..."

Rodeo week arrived in Reno, finally. It was like Christmas in lots of ways. You waited a whole year for it, prepared for it, and then there it was, right on time. It was a dependable event. It was the biggest thing in town in June. For some folks it was the biggest thing of the year. Take Donna Cooper, for example. All those years of dreaming about being rodeo queen, all that riding, all that smiling and waving. It made me tired just to watch that girl sometimes.

For me personally, Reno Rodeo week came as a blessing, a relief. I'd been feeling blue for the whole week before, ever since Donna had gotten me talking and thinking about the old days. Most of the time I was able to keep my memories of Angel stowed away in a special compartment of my mind. I was always aware of those memories, I knew they were there, but I didn't open the door and confront them any more than I had to. It was like the few photos I had of her, tucked away in the back of a dresser drawer at home. I can't remember the last time I pulled those photos out.

If I close my eyes right now, though, I can see them clearly. Angel with her dark eyes and long black hair. I always thought there was some Indian blood in that girl, especially with those cheekbones, but she said there wasn't. It wasn't just Angel in the pictures, of course. Mud was there in every one. She was the faithful sidekick who was always there. Well, not always. Sometimes Angel would manage to lose her so the two of us could be alone. Sometimes I bribed Mud to go off and buy something, the way you'd bribe a little sister if you were visiting your girlfriend in her home.

Visiting those memories, all that week before the rodeo started, I redis-covered the meaning of that powerful word "bittersweet." I'd start thinking about Angel and the good times we had and how much I loved her, although she seemed to love me more. That would be the sweet part. Then my thoughts would ride on down that trail of memories, a little farther than I wanted to go but I couldn't help it. At the end of the trail comes the bitter part. Angel rides out of my life. I don't ride after her. I miss her but I'm not smart enough to ride after her. I'm 25 at the time and what do I know about women? I thought that when a woman left you that was it, she's gone. I got the postcard from Washington State, but I never wrote to her. I never tracked her down. Now I have no idea where she is. I imagine she fell in love with someone else, someone who had the good sense to marry her. I see her with two or three kids, sending them off to school, maybe out riding with a friend. I can't see the face of her husband, and I don't want to. I imagine Angel in her forties, still beautiful, still smart and funny.

Then I have to stop. I have to turn my horse around and head back down that trail. Back to Reno. Back to the life I've made for myself. Funny thing is I'm the same person I was twenty years ago. Still doing pretty much the same things, a little ranching, a little retailing right now. I hang out with Bob Morgan and some of his hands. Every couple of weeks I drive down to Carson and visit Cheryl at the Starlight Ranch. She relieves my frustration and regrets for a while.

★

Oh yeah, rodeo week. On the Tuesday before the Saturday of the parade and first performance, I brought in my tape of *City Slickers*. We had one of those little combination TV and VCRs in the store. In the past we would play Western movies, mostly John Wayne classics, which entertained the customers and put them in the right mood to buy hats and boots. It also relieved some of our boredom. Lately we'd stopped doing that, I don't know why.

This was all part of Cody's cowboy education. I'd taught him to ride and even rope a little. He'd had the *Red River* orientation lesson, so he appreciated the history of the cowboy and the great trail drives of the past. Now it was time for something he could relate to in the present. *City Slickers* was all about becoming a real cowboy. True, Cody was a lot more eager than the Billy Crystal character in the movie, the one who only goes along for the ride because his friends want to. On the other hand, Cody had not been tested. He had not done anything heroic, the way Billy Crystal does at the end of that movie. He had not brought in the herd. He had not jumped into the river and risked his life to save a calf. For Cody, the expression "cowboy up" still only meant climbing into his pickup or into a saddle and not falling off either one. There was more to it, of course, and I hoped that watching *City Slickers* would help complete his education. Most ranch work is just hard and long, the way that most days on the trail drives were just hard and long and dusty. Sometimes, however, you have to be ready to do something heroic, and that's the lesson I was trying to teach Cody.

He was a good student. I think the lesson stuck. We watched it over the course of three days, and by Friday he was ready to move on to the next lesson. That would come the following week in the businessmen's steer decorating competition at the rodeo. First there was the matter of a modern day trail drive, the one that brought the rodeo animals from a ranch in northern California to Reno.

Donna Cooper bounced into Parker's that Friday afternoon, as she had warned me she would. She and Lacey had come to escort Cody and me to Virginia Street to watch some of the trail drive cowboys bring a small herd of steers right down the main street of Reno, under the arch and toward the rodeo arena. I heard the door open and turned to see who it was. There was Lacey, and for a moment I thought I was seeing double.

"Charley, hi!" Donna said. "This is my new friend Mandie. She's the Tucson rodeo queen." Mandie was a couple inches shorter than Donna, with lots of blonde curly hair spilling out beneath her white cowgirl hat. She had a smile as bright as Donna's and a personality to match.

"Glad to meet you, Charley," Mandie said as she gave me a firm handshake.

"My pleasure," I said. "You two look like sisters." That made them laugh.

"I guess we do," Donna said.

"Where's Cody?" Lacey asked.

Cody came walking up, right on cue, from the back of the store. He stood next to Lacey and gave her hand a squeeze. They made a cute couple. Now it was Cody's turn to be introduced to the visiting rodeo queen.

"Mandie, this is Cody West," Donna said.

"Now there's a good cowboy name," Mandie said as she shook Cody's hand. "I'm Mandie. Mandie Rawl."

"Rhymes with y'all," Donna said. I had the feeling that Donna had invented that one, and would be using it again. "Mandie's the Tucson rodeo queen, Cody."

"Great," Cody said. "Now there's a good Western town."

"Lots of cactus and horses," Mandie said. "And a big university."

"That's why she's so smart," Donna said, then she looked at her watch. "Hey, let's go, or we're going to miss the cowboys." With that we scooted on out of the store, locking the front door and putting the closed sign up. It was a tradition to close Parker's during the downtown trail drive.

We found a good vantage point under the Reno arch and waited for the cowboys to arrive. The cattle drive had become an annual event in town. For five days cowboys had been herding 300 head of cattle to be used in the rodeo, moving them from Doyle, California, to the Livestock Events Center in Reno. Some were real cowboys and the rest were city slickers who had paid over a thousand dollars to experience a trail drive. At the end of the drive, some of the herd would be driven down Virginia Street, past the casinos and under the famous arch.

While we waited, I told about the time a few years back when one of the critters had broken loose and walked right into a casino, starting a human stampede. It had scattered the customers and banged into one of the slot machines, which caused a bunch of coins to fly out. A couple of the cowboys had charged right in after it and roped it in the middle of the casino floor before it hit any more jackpots. The following year they drove just the smaller cattle down Virginia Street. "Just the ones that were too young to gamble," I said.

"That's a wild story," Mandie said.

"Do you expect us to believe that?" Lacey asked.

"Well, some of it's true," I said. "You believe the parts you want to believe."

"Here they come!" Donna said. People who had lined up on both sides of Virginia Street tried to get a better view.

"Bet you can't tell which are the real cowboys and which are the city slickers," I said.

"You're right," Lacey said. "They all look dusty and tired."

"They've been working hard this week. It's been five long days for those drovers, but they're here. They made it. The new fellows have earned the right to be called cowboys. It's like baseball, when you have a rookie in the World Series. He's been through six long months of competition, including a pennant race, so you can't really call him a rookie. Same with city slickers."

"Hey, that one's kind of cute," Donna said.

"Are you talking about a critter or a cowboy?" I asked.

"I was talking to Lacey, so just hush up," Donna told me.

"You're right," Lacey said. "I think he's my type." She stopped just then because Cody was giving her a serious look.

The cattle drive moved on past the arch, past the Eldorado and the Silver Legacy, and finally down a side street, where the cattle would be loaded onto trucks and driven the last couple of miles to the rodeo site. The crowd scattered, some back to the casinos, some looking for dinner, and some of us making dinner plans.

Donna insisted that we all go out together, including Mandie, so we ended up at the Coyote Bar & Grill. We were in luck, not just because the food was good—it always is at the Coyote—but also because there was live music that evening. Teri Autrey, who had just started performing at the Coyote, was doing a solo act, strumming some chords and singing Western songs. She could play guitar all right, but it was her voice that made her special. I had heard her once before in town. It was exciting discovering someone new like that, someone who clearly had a future. She sang mostly familiar tunes, some old and some recent, but she put her own stamp on them. There was something heartfelt in her singing that made everyone at the Coyote stop talking and listen. When Teri sang, the waitresses walked more carefully and everyone tried to chew more quietly.

When Teri finished her set, we talked and ate, chewing freely now. Donna and Mandie entertained us with their waves. Mandie demonstrated the traditional Tucson rodeo queen wave, which was not a wave at all but more of a salute. She told us about a rodeo queen friend of hers from a small town in northern Arizona who said that the girls there did one of those low waves, with the hand about hip high. Mandie said that when her friend demonstrated the low wave, it looked like she was waving at the ground. Donna asked what was the point of waving at the ground and Mandie said, "Exactly, there's no point in that!" Lacey and Cody and I just sat back and listened to those two as we enjoyed the ribs and baked potatoes. Between Teri Autrey's music, and the rodeo queen conversation of Donna Cooper and Mandie Rawl, we were thoroughly entertained.

That evening reminded me a lot of a time twenty years ago, when I used to hang out at the Coyote with Angel and Mud and my cowboy friends Sam and Cookie. Back then it was just the Coyote Bar, and it was just beer and music and friends and no ribs, but it was what we wanted. I closed my eyes for a moment and saw the old gang sitting around a table, maybe this same table, on a Friday night in Reno, Nevada, and when I opened my eyes again it was a different gang. I closed the door on those memories and returned to the present. That's where you have to live your life anyway, if you stop and think about it.

Later that night, lying in bed, as I thought about the excitement of the next day, especially for Donna and her rodeo queen dream, my thoughts turned to the yee-hah scene in *Red River*. It's early morning on the Red River D, just before the start of the great cattle drive, as all the cowboys and cattle wait for the trail boss's word to begin the drive. All is silence and anticipation before John Wayne gives the command and the cowboys yell "yee-hah!" to get the cattle moving. That's the kind of night it was for me, lying awake and waiting for the word to ride. But now it was time for the cowboys to sleep. I imagined a campfire flickering until it gradually went out and only the moon and the stars remained to light our dreams.

14 Donna

"Once in the saddle I used to go dashing…"

So there I was, not a little girl dreaming rodeo queen dreams, but all grown up and sitting on a big horse alongside the other contestants in downtown Reno on a bright Saturday morning in June, waiting for the parade to begin. By the end of the day, a little after 7 p.m. actually, I would know whether the next Miss Reno Rodeo was me or one of the other girls. I kept telling myself it's awfully hard to win on the first try, but deep in my heart I wanted to win the first time around. But I kept telling myself the other thing. Every day. But I kept on wanting to win. In my heart.

In the meantime my horse was all saddled and decorated. Heck, *I* was decorated. I was featuring a lot of blue and silver again, the university colors, which I figured would carry some weight with the Reno judges, although I loved those colors together anyway. My horse and I made a good combination, our colors all coordinated, both well groomed and feeling strong and ready to ride. We had some waiting to do, however. While we waited, the rodeo queen coordinator was giving us some tips, mainly warning us not to show up at the rodeo performance with dirty horses. The horses had to be clean, that was her point. She made it several times. I think she was intending the warning for just one of the girls, but she disguised it by warning all of us. Parents do that, teachers too.

She also reminded us to smile during the parade. I didn't need to be reminded of that. Then she reminded us to wave. I guess you know by now that there was no way anybody was going to stop me from waving. If my horse stopped right in the middle of Virginia Street and wouldn't budge, and if I had to walk the rest of the way, or ride in a convertible, I would still be waving. And smiling. Those were my strong suits, as Charley Meyers well knew. I'd been practicing at Parker's for months.

There were seven other contestants that year. I guess if you compared this year's crop to other years, you'd have to say it was a typical group of girls. We all had long hair and knew about grooming. We knew how to handle a horse. We could talk on our feet, some better than others of course. Five of us were blondes. Ha, big surprise! Two were brunettes. Then there was Dayna Green.

Dayna was different in so many ways that I hardly know where to start. I guess you'd have to start at the top, with the hair. It was naturally red, like the brightest carrot in the bunch at the supermarket. She had these intense green eyes and freckles. Dayna was pretty, and she knew it. She was tall, the tallest of our group. She walked among us on those long legs like some kind of big bird. Not the Big Bird of Sesame Street, but some kind of unusual bird that looked down its beak at the other birds. She seemed to have an attitude that God had given her the longest legs and the best looks, so naturally it was in the divine cards for her to become the next Miss Reno Rodeo.

Please don't think I'm being catty, or jealous of her. All the other girls felt the same way about Dayna Green. The rest of us got along great. We all liked each other, honest we did, and we'd be happy if any of the rest of us won. Dayna, however, just never fit in. She never tried to fit in. I think we were beneath her. Did I mention that she was articulate? When she spoke in front of the judges, or any time, she spoke very carefully, making sure she hit all the consonants along the way. I always got the feeling that she was the first grade teacher and we were her little uneducated students, and she was showing us the correct way to pronounce all those words.

If they gave out an award for the contestant with the most superior attitude, Dayna would win it in a landslide. She was intending to win the whole thing, of course, and she acted as if it was only a matter of time before the title was hers. Just for luck, however, she had added four leaf clovers, in sequins, to all of her outfits. I could see them even now, when the morning sun reflected off the sequins on her Western shirt. If the unthinkable happened and she did win the competition, would we have to hug her and pretend we were happy? I prayed that sorry moment would never arrive. I think we all prayed for that.

I was studying those four leaf clover sequins when I heard a familiar voice behind me.

"Hi there, honey!" I turned and there was my mom. And right behind her my dad. Carol and Hank, as everybody else called them. Since my dad had landed a better job in Las Vegas a few months earlier, and Rooster and I stayed behind in Reno because of school and jobs, and the rodeo queen contest, I didn't get to see as much of them as I would like.

"Great, you made it!" I said. I leaned down to give my mom a kiss. Then my dad stepped up.

"How's my little girl?"

"Doing great, Dad," I said. I leaned down to give him a kiss too.

"How was the flight from Vegas?" I asked.

"Very smooth," he said, "and on time. Your mom was so worried we wouldn't get here in time."

"Was Rooster in time to pick you up at the airport?"

"Yep," my dad said, "he's parking the truck now. Look at you," he said. "You look just like—"

"A rodeo queen," my mom interrupted.

"No, I was going to say a princess."

"Rodeo queen," my mom repeated.

"I guess she can be both," my dad said.

"Well, read my sash, Mom. It does say 'Rodeo Queen *Contestant*,' doesn't it? Anyway, I'm so tickled you came," I said. Then I introduced them to the rest of the contestants, all but Dayna, who was off by herself, posing in the saddle, although I didn't see any cameras around. It was almost time for the parade to begin. I asked my mom and dad to walk down to the next block and say hi to Mandie, the Tucson rodeo queen. I had told Mandie they would be here and she was looking forward to meeting them.

Soon after that we started riding slowly toward Virginia Street to join the parade. People were all over the sidewalks, waving at us, and we were waving back and smiling. I'd ridden in the parade before, but never as a rodeo queen contestant. I tried to wave at everyone who was waving at me, as well as some of those who weren't waving. Lots of people responded by waving back. It's a simple thing, but it's an important Western custom.

My mom was waving and my dad was taking pictures when I rode by them. I gave them one of my fast waves, with lots of wrist action, and of course a big smile.

Darryl King had planted himself right beneath the arch and called out when I rode up. I blew him a kiss and he caught it. When I looked back a moment later he was gone. He had to work at his father's store that day, so I guess he was racing back to sell hardware.

At one point I spotted Cody and Charley on the sidewalk and gave them a big wave. Then I pointed in back of me. They said "What?" and I said, "Somebody you know is coming along later." Then they were out of sight. I'm sorry I wasn't there when Lacey rode up with Mel and Harm and a few of the other local barrel racers. I heard later that Cody was so surprised he just stared. It was only after Lacey waved at him and shouted his name that Cody waved back, but he was still speechless. He could only think of her as a lawyer, and seeing her as a cowgirl must have really opened his eyes.

I knew that years later I would remember this moment. I was so close to making my dream come true. Every step my horse took was moving me closer. I also took pride in the job I had done in promoting the romance of my new friends Lacey and Cody. I tried not to think of Charley's loneliness, although he seemed happy enough standing along the parade route with Cody and waving to everyone.

When we reached the bridge over the Truckee River, I spotted Rooster. He had missed me at the beginning of the parade and must have run ahead so he could catch me at the bridge. I gave Rooster a big wave. He waved back, and called to me, but I was surprised to see a camera in his hand. Rooster's not one to take a lot of pictures, and he's always on the move himself, but I guess he wanted to capture this moment. I stopped my horse and struck a pose, with my hand out in a wave, and Rooster snapped the picture. Then he called out "thank you" to me and gave me another wave. As I caught up with the others I turned and threw him a little wave over my shoulder. I guess growing up I always had to have the last word, and here I was having the last wave.

Then before I was ready for it to be over, the parade came to an end. I returned my horse to its trailer. There was more to be done before the rodeo that evening. I was meeting my mom and dad, and Rooster, for lunch. I waved goodbye to the other girls.

I even waved at Dayna Green and she gave me a little wave back. In that moment I felt sorry for her, for the first time. Now I regret those things I said about her earlier, even if they were all true. I just don't want to carry them around with me. I don't want them to darken my smile or put a hitch in my wave. Not today, that's for sure. Come to think of it, I wish Dayna a happy life.

I said a little prayer for her, that God would teach her some humility. Then I prayed that God would see to it that anyone but Dayna would be named rodeo queen. Then I stopped praying before I asked God to let me be rodeo queen. I don't think that's a proper thing to pray for. I'm sure God's got a lot more important business to take care of anyway. So I said a little prayer for Charley instead, that God would do something about his loneliness. That prayer felt better. I thought it was a prayer I would trot out again in the days ahead, just to make sure God knew I was serious.

15 Charley

"The wildest, richest rodeo in the West..."

Saturday night at the Reno Rodeo. Opening night. Or "First Performance," as it is billed in the world of rodeo. This is the part I'd been looking forward to writing down. I couldn't wait to see Donna Cooper be named rodeo queen and ride around the arena with that big smile and special wave of hers, and then, a few days later, Cody and me win the steer decorating competition, and everybody live happily ever after like in the books and movies. But this was real life, so a number of things were bound to go wrong. I guess the trick is how you handle it when things do get screwed up. In that way it's a test, which is a good way of describing rodeo, a test of man and beast, and you just might find out what you're made of.

I've been going to rodeos all my life, and for a number of years I was one of the cowboys in the arena, sitting on top of a bucking saddle bronc for eight seconds, and sometimes quicker when I'd be flying off the bronc and eating dirt. You don't lie there and feel sorry for yourself, of course. You jump up and run off, or limp off, because it's somebody else's turn to take the test.

As part of Cody's cowboy education, I had been telling him everything I knew about rodeo, with tales of past champions, remembered adventures, and misadventures, in the arena. "Kid," I had told him one day in Parker's, "you don't know how lucky you are. Competing in your first rodeo, and it's a mighty special one. It may not be the wildest rodeo in the West, although it's right up there. And it may not be the richest. Cowboys can make bigger money at the National Finals in Vegas. But I'll tell you one thing, the Reno Rodeo is the best rodeo in the West, and I'll fight anyone who says it ain't. You know, if God had a day off and decided to take in a rodeo, this is where he'd be, right there near the bucking chutes. Not indoors at the Astrodome or Vegas, and not at some small town rodeo that doesn't attract the best cowboys or the best broncs and bulls. No sir, he'd be right here. The Reno Rodeo is just like this town, not too big and not too small."

Cody had continued the thought. "And after the rodeo was over, God could check out all the stars in his sky." Cody and his stars. Now and then you'd get a glimpse of the poet in his soul, and I think that's one reason Lacey Anderson was so attracted to the kid.

At the moment, however, the stars were not out yet, and before all the cowboys took over, the rodeo queens would have their moment in the sun. The sun was going to disappear soon over the Sierra Nevadas, but for now it was lighting the bright red stagecoach that carried the rodeo queen contestants into the arena for the naming of the new Miss Reno Rodeo. One of those girls was my good friend Donna Cooper, which was why I was sitting in the stands with a large group of her friends and family. I'd been lucky enough to get Parker's box of seats, right down on the fence and facing the bucking chutes, so the riders would be coming right toward us. To our right were the roping chutes, so the ropers and steer wrestlers would be racing from our right to the center of the arena, and again we'd have a great view of the action.

I guess I should tell you who all was there. I know I'm going to have a devil of a time keeping all these people straight here, but I'll do my best. Cody and Lacey, the Reno newcomers, were sitting next to me. They looked good in their Western clothes and boots and hats. I'd never seen Cody wear anything but cowboy clothes, but Lacey was a beautiful cowgirl on this day. At other times I'd see her and she'd be a beautiful lawyer. If I were ever on a jury and she was there making her opening statement, or closing argument, I'd probably be thinking "whatever you say, little darlin', I'm voting for your side." It wasn't just the looks, either. She was smart, and I'm sure she'd outsmart the other side in the courtroom.

Lacey had surprised me by showing up with two men. Besides Cody, she had Victor Kleindich in tow, the San Francisco lawyer. Seems that Victor had driven to Reno earlier that day because he had some legal business to tend to at Lacey's firm on Monday and thought he'd surprise her and spend the weekend with her. I'm sure he hadn't counted on being dragged to a rodeo because he was dressed for some kind of yuppie weekend, what with the pressed khaki slacks and polished loafers, pink button-down shirt, and sweater tied around his neck. If I forget to call him Victor, and start talking about GQ, you'll know who I'm referring to. I guess you'd have to say that he was handsome, but a little too handsome and too much aware of it.

So we had Lacey and Cody and Victor and myself. Then there were the Reno people: Celia Moon from Stella's, that singer Teri Autrey, and Donna's older brother, Rooster. Mel and Harm Johnson were probably somewhere down around the arena at the moment, waiting to cheer on Donna. Darryl King, Donna's boyfriend, was in our group, which meant that Shorty Rogers was there too. Darryl was wearing jeans with work boots, a blue work shirt, and a John Deere cap. He had left his hardware store vest behind on this occasion. If Donna had been chasing cowboys before she met Darryl, she had found herself a different sort of guy.

Shorty was dressed Western, however, with cowboy boots and a big old sidekick hat that looked one size too large for his head. He would have blocked everybody's view, except that sitting down he was more like a little kid, and he slouched, so the hat was no problem. Shorty had a can of Copenhagen in the back pocket of his Wranglers, although I've never seen him chew, and neither has anybody else. Cody asked him what his tee shirt said, so Shorty stood up and showed us all. What it said was "Cowgirl's Motto: Party till he's cute!" and "Cowboy's Motto: Party till she's pretty!" Shorty told Cody he had a tee shirt at home that said "Cowboy foreplay: 'Get in the truck!'" and another one that said "You've been a bad cowgirl, go to my room!"

Seems that Shorty could never pass up a humorous tee shirt. My favorite tee shirt, however, was one that Mel and Harm Johnson had given me. It had a photo of a barrel racer and words of scripture, "Run with perseverance, the course is marked out for us ... Hebrews 12:1." You have to agree with the perseverance part, although sometimes it seems that the course is not clearly marked out. I guess that shouldn't stop you from running though. Donna always tells me to have a little faith, that it goes a long way, so I try to remember that.

Let's see now, who else was there at the rodeo that day? Oh yeah, Donna's parents, Hank and Carol, had flown up from Las Vegas, and they were the most excited of anyone. Hank had the video camera going, and Carol was doing the commentary for anyone who cared to listen. You had to watch out for her hands and arms flying about when she talked, which I guess is where Donna picked up that habit.

When the stagecoach came to a stop in the arena, and the rodeo queen contestants stepped out, Carol Cooper spotted Donna first and started waving like crazy. Lacey waved and cheered, then we all started waving, except for Hank, who was busy making the video. Even Victor the GQ boy gave a little wave. His wave lacked the enthusiasm that Donna deserved, but it did match his weak handshake.

The contestants lined up, facing the stands, and were introduced. Donna's cheering section was the loudest, of course. The judges had already reached their decision, of course, but we all cheered and hollered as if the winner would be the young lady with the loudest fans. The outgoing rodeo queen, a blonde named Cindy, rode around the arena waving goodbye, and we all waved back at her. In rodeo there's no end to the waving. She circled the arena twice, the second time at a gallop. It was a beautiful sight to see, and a very emotional moment I'm sure for her, and for a lot of other folks as well.

Then they started to give out the various awards to the queen contestants. I noticed that Donna's mom was squeezing her hands together in a kind of prayer. You can't blame her, but she had this intense life-or-death look on her face, as if they were going to name one big winner and the rest of the girls would be lined up and shot. I have to admit that I was rooting hard for Donna too, as were the rest of us. Except Victor, who had this bored look kind of frozen on his face. He was obviously one of those people who think that such contests are a silly waste of time. I pity the fool, because he was missing the whole point of selecting a good spokesperson for the rodeo, but I find it's best just to ignore fools, so I did.

There were lots of awards to go around: congeniality, spirit, photogenic, speech, horsemanship, personality, and appearance, as well as first and second runner-up. The redhead, Dayna Green, won for horsemanship, and the other blonde contestants were scooping up the other awards, and we kept waiting for Donna's name to be called. Finally they got around to the personality award and you just knew they had to give that one to Donna Cooper. If you looked up "personality" in the dictionary, well you know. Sure enough, Donna won that award, and we all whooped it up. She waved that unique wave of hers and they gave her a western purse and silver pin, which she got to hold, along with the roses they gave out when they introduced the contestants.

Then the time came to announce second runner-up. Carol Cooper's hands were squeezing each other harder. Lacey kept saying "Donna, Donna, Donna" under her breath, and then Celia and Teri picked up the chant. I guess we were all thinking Donna Cooper, Miss Reno Rodeo, but the chant started a bit early and, sure enough, Donna's name was called out for second runner-up. That's like good news and bad news all wrapped together. We cheered, but not as wildly as we would have a couple minutes later if she'd won the whole thing. Being in the top three on your first try, of course, is an achievement. Donna, as you'd expect, was gracious and charming as ever. She now had more stuff to hold. She'd just won a silver bracelet, a gift certificate, and a $200 scholarship.

One immediate consequence of Donna winning second runner-up was that Carol Cooper could finally unlock her hands and begin to relax. I glanced over and there was a lot of pride and love in her eyes, as well as a tear. I had a little dust in my eye at the moment and had to blink and rub it for a second. It can get dusty in the arena, you know.

We all applauded for the first runner-up, then finally for the new rodeo queen when she was named (one of the blondes, surprise surprise). The outgoing queen gave roses to the winner, and put the shiny rodeo queen banner on her. Then came the part I always like. She bent down to remove her Miss Reno Rodeo chaps and then put the chaps on the new rodeo queen. I don't know why, but that's a special moment. If they did that for the Miss America pageant it would be a lot better pageant. I guess they do put a crown on the new Miss America's head, but it's not the same as the deal with the chaps. Then again, Miss America's not wearing jeans, so the chaps would look ridiculous. Never mind, I'm sorry I brought it up. I do like those chaps, however.

Next the new rodeo queen climbed into the saddle and circled the arena waving. We hadn't had a good chance to wave for several minutes, so we were grateful. She didn't have Donna's wave, although she did look good in the saddle. The new Miss Reno Rodeo gave us all that quick wave that's all wrist. I looked over and noticed that Lacey had a very nice wave going. You could tell she'd been hanging around Donna Cooper.

Then the queen program was over and it was time to rodeo. The rodeo began with the Grand Entry, featuring the flag girls, entering the arena with their horses at full gallop and carrying the flags of the rodeo sponsors. When the last flag girl arrived carrying the American flag, we all stood and removed our hats for the National Anthem. With his hat off, I noticed that Shorty was a whole lot shorter.

The first event on the program was the wild horse race. This is one of the three original rodeo events, along with steer roping and bronc riding. "They've been doing this for a hundred years," I told Lacey. "They work in teams of three cowboys. Six teams and six unbroken horses. The first team to corral a wild horse, put a saddle on it, then a man in the saddle, and race it around a barrel at the finish line wins."

"Sounds simple," Lacey said. "Three strong cowboys to each horse. The odds seem to favor the cowboys." This made me laugh.

"You just watch and see who the odds favor," I said. "The total purse is over $17,000 this year, so you're going to see some determined fellows out here."

Just then the gates flew open and the wild horse race began. The event took less than two minutes, but there was more action in that time than the roaring crowd could take in. Confusion reigned in the arena as the horses ran and bucked and the eighteen cowboys found themselves in every kind of awkward position and situation: from diving past flying hooves, to hanging on to a moving rope along the ground, to trying to stay on a saddle that was not firmly attached to a wild bucking horse. As with all events at the rodeo, the animals were competing as well. The wilder the horses, the better. The more they ran and bucked, the bigger the challenge for the cowboys and the better the entertainment for the rodeo fans.

I caught Cody's eye. "Don't even start," he said. "You're not talking me into competing in this event."

A team from Oregon was the first across the line and won the applause and cheers of the crowd. The winning cowboy in the saddle had hung on as his horse ran right at our section and then turned away just before reaching the wall. Lacey leaned back as the horse drew nearer, and if she had been looking at Victor she might have noticed his hands tightening on his chair, but I just laughed through it all.

Next up was the calf roping. "Watch the quarter horses," I told Lacey, "how they work as a team with the cowboys, matching the speed of the calf, stopping at just the right time, and then backing up to keep the rope taut as the cowboy runs to tie the calf. Your good quarter horses have a lot of cow in them." We all cheered for Bob Morgan's nephew, Landon, the one named for a popular star of the old *Bonanza* show on television. Landon performed well, finishing with the third best time of the eight calf ropers in the opening night go-round. A cowboy from Duncan, Oklahoma, won the go-round with a time of 9.1 seconds.

There were some familiar names in the bareback bronc riding, including the reigning world champion and a former champion. We whooped it up for all the bareback riders as they broke out of the bucking chutes and tried to stay on for the required eight seconds. "Hey, Cody," I said, "imagine riding one of these animals without a saddle or stirrups or a rein, just a leather pad with a leather handhold. And you have to spur him the whole time, and the higher and wilder the better."

"Yeah," Cody said, "that would be a waltz."

"How would it feel to be bucked off," I said, "to go flying through the air and not know how you're going to land or if you're going to be kicked by the bronc on the way down?"

"Cody," Lacey said, "you seem a little pale. Are you all right?"

"Sure," Cody answered, "why wouldn't I be?"

Cody and I had a friendly competition going to see who could guess the judges' score for each rider and bronc. Most of the scores were in the 70s and a couple of times we predicted the exact score before it was announced. Cody may have been an Iowa farm boy in his former life, but he had seen his share of rodeos and knew something about the scoring. When Cody's score was off by a point or two, he blamed the judges for missing something that the horse or rider did. Lacey joined in this judging game, and discovered that she was getting better at it with each rider.

"I think I'd rather be a judge than a bronc rider," Cody said at one point. He had a point. The two judges in the arena were close to the action but never once went flying through the air. They stay rooted to the ground for the full eight seconds and beyond.

"Hey, is there room for one more?" a voice in back of us asked. We turned and there was Donna Cooper. She collected a round of hugs and congratulations and then squeezed in with us. The women had to take a look at her new silver bracelet. Darryl ended up holding the rest of the loot for her. Donna handed the roses to Darryl and he gave them to Shorty, who would smell them from time to time when he thought nobody was watching.

A cowboy from Fort Worth, Texas, won the bareback competition, but his win had barely been announced when Donna's eyes suddenly lit up. "Here they come!" she announced, pointing to the arena entrance. Donna, who had been studying the program after the last bareback rider had limped away, knew what was coming. Cody, who had been feeling the limping cowboy's pain, wondered why she was so excited. The arena announcer soon cleared up this small mystery. It was time for the visiting rodeo queens to ride in, some of whom we had seen earlier that day in the parade.

Miss Rodeo Oregon, a cowgirl named Meg Shorter, came riding in first, wearing lavender jeans and a lavender shirt. We all decided to sit back, ignore the announcer, and listen to Donna's play-by-play description of what we were seeing.

I knew we were in the presence of greatness. Cody told me later that listening to Donna on the subject of rodeo queens was like listening to famous voices from his early childhood in Iowa. He remembered Harry Carey doing the play-by-play on ballgames for the Cubs, and he could still hear the deep resonant voice of newscaster Walter Cronkite telling him how it was in the big world beyond the cornfields. He said he suddenly remembered the sound of his mother's voice. He was no more than five and his mother had taken him to a John Wayne movie, and as they sat in the darkened theater she spoke softly to him about the cowboys up on the big screen and real cowboys out west. This was one of his earliest memories, and one of his strongest. And it was Donna who had brought it all back to him, just by talking about the visiting rodeo queens.

"Hey, it's Mandie!" Donna said. She began waving like crazy. The Tucson Rodeo Queen rode right in front of us and gave us all a big wave and a howdy. Even Victor leaned forward for a better view.

"Wow, she looks great," Darryl said. He hadn't said two words since the rodeo began, and now he saw Donna staring at him. "But not as great as you, Donna," he said quickly. A fast recovery for the hardware guy. Shorty seemed to be staring after the Tucson queen, but it was hard to see him for all the roses.

After the rodeo queens had ridden out of the arena, the saddle bronc riders took over. I gave Lacey a quick lesson in what to watch for, and how this event differed from the bareback riding. The saddle bronc riders, when they weren't being bucked off, rode in a more straight-up position, with one hand on the rein and the other flying high above the head.

The crowd buzzed when the announcer introduced the all-around champion cowboy, a young fellow with a baby face from one of those countless small Texas towns. Like most great athletes, the Texan exhibited a grace and economy of motion that, as Lacey put it, "made it look easy."

"You've got it right," I said. "Did you ever see film of DiMaggio running down a fly ball in Yankee Stadium? Different sport, same idea. Last year I saw this Texas kid get bucked off by a bronc, but even then he performed kind of gracefully. I didn't see a whole lot of dirt on him after he bounced up from the ground."

The Texan received an 81 on this night, which was good enough to win the go-round. Lacey and Donna were rooting for a handsome veteran saddle bronc rider from Hawaii named Keahi Port, the one who had waved right at the two of them at the end of his ride. They were disappointed when the judges gave him a score of 79. "That's all right," Donna said, not loud enough for Darryl to hear, "he can score with me anytime."

"This is my favorite event coming up," Cody said, "steer wrestling."

"Most people would say bull riding or bareback," I said.

"No," Cody said, "for me it's always been steer wrestling. It's so basic, man against animal. Why rope the critter, or try to ride him, when you can just jump off your horse and grab those horns and pull it down, show it who's the boss?"

"I like the big muscles on those steer wrestlers," Donna chimed in. "Those are the biggest, strongest cowboys, the ones who can grab you and throw you on the ground."

"You *are* talking about steer wrestling, aren't you?" Cody asked.

"Why, of course." Donna laughed. "You think I'd want one of those big old cowboys to grab me and throw me on the ground?" Cody and the rest of us decided not to answer that question.

The steer wrestling began, and this time Cody took over the commentary, telling Lacey about the basics as well as some finer points to watch for. The best steer wrestlers were so quick and efficient that they could complete the event in just a few seconds. Success demanded a combination of strength and timing and coordination. You needed to be aggressive but not break the barrier on the way out. You needed a good hazer to ride on the steer's "off side" and keep it going straight. You had to time your slide from the saddle and onto the steer. And you needed a good pair of boots to put on the brakes so you could wrestle the critter to its side. The steers weighed anywhere from 450 to 750 pounds. Steer wrestlers were built like linebackers, whereas bull riders could be smaller.

Of the ten cowboys entered in this opening round, three missed the steers and had no time. The others were within three seconds of each other. Half of the steer wrestlers, not surprisingly, were from Oklahoma, and had names like Kurt and Ote and Mike. A cowboy from Checotah, Oklahoma, was first out and set a time of 7.1 seconds for the others to shoot at. Nobody could match it on this night. By the time the winner was announced, Lacey was a big fan of steer wrestling.

"Time for some fast women," I said.

Donna laughed and turned to Lacey. "Don't get agitated, he means women's barrel racing. Mel and Harm are racing tonight."

"They go third and fourth," Lacey said, "I already checked."

The first barrel racer entered the arena just then. A cowgirl from Cut Bark, Montana, guided her quarter horse through the clover leaf pattern around the three barrels that were painted like cans of Coors beer, then raced back to the finish line for a time of 18.85 seconds. Hundredths of a second separated the competitors in this event, and meant the difference between no prize money and a chunk of the total purse, which this year was over $55,000.

"If she knocks over a barrel, she's penalized five seconds," Donna said. "That's like an hour in barrel racing. And if she doesn't head into a turn just right, or shifts her weight at the wrong time, she's going to lose enough time to keep her out of first place."

"Do they ever have wrecks?" Lacey asked.

"Rarely," Donna said. "It's not as dangerous as riding a bronc or a bull, of course, but I have seen a couple riders go flying off their horse before, even once in the National Finals. It happens when they're going around a barrel, usually the last one, and trying to make up hundredths of seconds."

The barrel racers on this night were from towns like Canby, Oregon; Salinas, California; Montalba, Texas; and Guthrie, Oklahoma. Lacey Anderson, the attorney from San Francisco, imagined herself as a barrel racer.

"Say, Donna," Lacey said, "do you think I could try some barrel racing at the Lazy J sometime?"

"Sure, why not?" Donna said.

"If I'm ever good enough to enter a rodeo," Lacey said, "I'll have to tell folks I'm from some small California town like Chowchilla."

"You're halfway there with a hometown like Chowchilla," Donna said. "You could also say you were a Reno cowgirl and not be lying. That way you'd have the local rodeo fans all cheering you on. You'd get your name in the paper too."

"I can see it now," Lacey said, following an imaginary headline in front of her with her hand, "'Local Barrel Racer Knocks Down All Three Barrels.'"

"Not you," Donna said, "you'd be good. You'd have Mel and Harm teaching you. Then when they gave you your gold buckle you could give everyone that special wave of yours. I can see it now. By day a mild mannered Reno attorney, but by night a champion barrel racer kicking all the other cowgirls' butts!"

The winning barrel racer on this first go-round was a cowgirl from Lampasas, a small town deep in the heart of Texas. It had been a big night for cowboys and cowgirls from Oklahoma and Texas, but a pair of brothers named Dylan and Nathaniel, from Big Piney, Wyoming, were about to put on a team roping clinic. When the flag dropped on their run, rodeo fans stood and cheered and pointed at the scoreboard, which flashed a time of 4.5 seconds.

"Ain't nobody gonna touch that time tonight, no way, no how," I said to Lacey. "You saw that start, very aggressive without either roper breaking the barrier. Before you could say 'get 'em, cowboy,' the header had roped the steer's horns and turned the animal into the best position for the heeler to throw his loop around the hind feet. The timing was perfect because it had to be. You probably didn't notice that after their catches both men had to wrap, or 'dally,' their ropes around the saddle horns. That why they call them dally ropers, and they have to be careful not to lose a finger. When the steer was roped the two horses had to turn to face each other, with the ropes taut and the steer right in the middle, pretty as a picture. Then the judge can drop his flag for the official time. All this in just four and a half seconds. Watch the replay on the screen."

It was still too fast to see everything, but Lacey studied the other team ropers and began to appreciate the various elements and the teamwork in team roping. I remembered a conversation I'd had with Cody weeks earlier. I'd compared Donna and Lacey to a couple of team ropers who could catch you and stretch you out before you knew what had happened.

When the team roping ended, the stagecoach entered the arena, pulled by six horses at breakneck speed. It was the same one that had brought the rodeo queen contestants into the arena earlier. This coach, an annual attraction in Reno and at many other rodeos, was owned by a cattle rancher in Montana who wanted to share a part of the Old West with rodeo fans throughout the country. The coach had been hand built by a cabinetmaker in Texas, and its wheels were the work of Amish woodworkers in Iowa.

"Reminds me of that old classic John Wayne movie," Cody said. "Did you ever see *Stagecoach*?" he asked.

"You think the Apaches are coming over the ridge tonight?" I asked.

"Of course," Donna said, "with the cavalry right behind."

"I like the part where the Duke and the lady are flirting," Lacey said. "She was run out of town by the proper ladies, but she had a heart of gold."

"I guess you've all seen it then," Cody said. "Let's rent it and watch it together one night."

"Are you going to do your John Wayne impression again?" Lacey asked.

"If you insist," Cody said, smiling.

This was met by a chorus of "We don't!" and long groans from Donna and me. Lacey patted Cody on the shoulder and told him it was a great idea, the *Stagecoach* idea anyway, and he could even do his John Wayne if he also provided the Lone Star.

The words "Lone Star" made me look around for the beer man, who, with perfect timing, was just making his way toward us. We had to settle for Coors in plastic cups with a picture of a saddle bronc rider on them, but the beer was cold and delicious, even on a cool June evening. As the stagecoach raced out of the arena I asked Donna the question I'd been dying to ask.

"Donna, how did someone beat you out for the spirit award?"

"Oh, that's one of the consolation prizes," Donna answered. "I call it the spiritual award, because it usually goes to a girl who tries real hard but doesn't have a prayer."

16 Charley

"Impressing the ladies…"

Some strange things began happening the following Monday, the day before Cody and I were scheduled to compete in the steer decorating. These unusual events coincided with the monthly arrival of the full moon. If I had bothered to study the calendar at Parker's, an old fashioned one with the phases of the moon clearly indicated for the month of June, I might have seen this coming. When it came to the effects of a full moon, Nevada was not that different from Iowa or any other part of the country. As has been well documented—and observed keenly by those whose jobs involve having to deal with some of the craziness that accompanies a full moon—animal behavior, in particular that of the two-legged animals that walk upright and pretend to have reached a highly evolved state, changes at that time of the month.

But I had not checked the calendar, being too busy thinking about having to decorate a steer with Cody at the rodeo on Tuesday evening. The time was growing short. Soon it would be the moment of truth, time to cowboy up. So the full moon sneaked up on us, and on many others.

In downtown Reno, for example, it sneaked up on an old cowpoke who had found a faded ten-dollar bill stuck inside the coin pocket of his Wranglers, just as he was walking past the Eldorado. He moseyed inside and decided to change the ten-dollar bill into three shots at a Megabucks slot machine. Six dollars disappeared quickly into the machine. The next three dollars, however, made some friends. Lots of friends, actually. The symbols on the reels lined up like angels waiting to escort the old cowboy to jackpot heaven. He looked again at the numbers above the machine and counted all the numbers after the first number, which was a nine, and started to shake. Nine million dollars and change. A lot of change, actually. He had won just under ten million. He was oblivious to the commotion around him, as word spread throughout the casino. He could think only of his old dream—to buy a little ranch of his own, some cattle and horses, a new pickup, and then just be his own cowboy. Like the faded ten-dollar bill, he had stuck that dream away and forgotten about it. Now he pulled it out and looked it over, decided it was still what he wanted, and knew it was more than a dream now.

Down Carson City way, the full moon sneaked up on the Starlight Ranch. Nobody hit any jackpots at the Starlight on Monday evening, or expected to, since there were no slots to play there. But someone did find true love, which is a kind of jackpot after all. A young cowboy—one that Cheryl had never seen before—rode his horse up to the ranch, exhibited good manners by tying his horse outside rather than trying to ride it inside, and politely asked Cheryl to introduce him to the nicest lady at the Moonlight. Two hours later the young cowboy left the ranch accompanied by Annie from Wisconsin, who climbed onto the horse, put her arms tightly around her cowboy, and never looked back as the two of them rode off to a new life together. It was apparent from the bright smile on Annie's face that the cowboy had not told her stories of cemeteries.

Back in Reno, the full moon was shining on the Stella by Starlight Bakery and Gourmet Coffee Emporium. Celia Moon, the owner—who had named her shop in honor of her mother's favorite song—was rushing to close up and spilled the coffee beans. Rushing even more, Celia spilled some more beans, as well as a handful of cinnamon sticks, until she had several different kinds of coffee beans and the cinnamon sticks in a big pile on her work table. Just then Teri Autrey walked in and said she needed a hot mug of coffee and someone to talk to. Celia grabbed a handful of beans and a couple of the cinnamon sticks from the big pile, threw them in the grinder, brewed a fresh pot for Teri and herself, and the rest is history. Thus was born Celia's Special Blend. Its fame would spread so fast that Celia's business would double within a month.

A number of other notable things happened that night, some of which would find their way into the newspaper the next morning. It seems there was a ruckus out at The Lucky Cowboy that attracted the attention of the police and fire departments. Then there was the UFO sighting, this time closer to Reno than anyone could remember and witnessed by a local minister and his wife, as well as a dozen other sober citizens. At the rodeo arena, a bull named Bad Attitude threw its rider and then broke through a gate near the roping chutes and ran wild in back of the stands. Cowboys were scattering all over the place and rodeo fans were climbing to the top of the stands to look down on the excitement, and by the time the cowboys had gotten the bull penned another bull had broken loose and the fun started all over again.

Other events, like the happy ending at the Starlight Ranch, were not reported, but lots of folks knew about them. In the animal kingdom, it seemed as if every dog in town was howling at the moon. Half the cowboys in town, which was more cowboys than normal with the rodeo in town, joined in with their own howling, even if it was only Monday night.

The lucky old cowpoke at the Eldorado, once he was able to speak, told his story to a television reporter, and the next day everyone in town was digging through the pockets of their old jeans, searching for lucky money they had forgotten about. Some actually found money in this way, including one fellow who found a hundred dollar bill he thought he had lost the night before at The Lucky Cowboy. Others were surprised when they fished out old neglected dreams from their memories. But all were recharged with hope.

Cody awoke that Tuesday morning with the realization that the big day had arrived. He had his pickup, he had been learning to cowboy at Bob

Morgan's ranch, and now he was about to be a rodeo cowboy for one day, even if it was just the steer decorating event. With so many teams competing, it would be great to win, especially in front of Lacey. Cody and I had even practiced with one of Bob's steers, and I thought we were as ready as we would ever be. I told Cody I had a lot of confidence in him. I'd even asked Donna to stop by the day before to talk to us about focusing. She was only too happy to share her thoughts on a subject so dear to her heart.

Even so, Cody told me later that as he sat in the coffee shop at the Eldorado, eating a big breakfast and reading all the strange news in the morning paper, his imagination began to run blooper film clips of all the things that could go wrong. All these pictures ended with me holding nothing but a ribbon and Cody lying in the arena all dirty and beaten up and our steer running freely away. Cody finished his breakfast quickly and headed for work, trying to leave the blooper clips behind him.

I spent a good part of the day boosting Cody's confidence one more time. By the time we drove to the arena Cody was ready to take on two steers.

The rodeo began as the sun was beginning to set. In the middle of this the fourth performance of the Reno Rodeo, the full moon rose and shone like God's spotlight on the arena.

One highlight of the evening was Chance Johnson's twin daughters in the barrel racing. The program listed Melody as the second racer and Harmony as the last of the eight racers. Mel had the advantage of going early, riding "on top" of the ground before the course was dug out by the others. Harm, on the other hand, had drawn the least desired position and would have to overcome that handicap. Harm had followed Mel into this world, and now she would have to follow her around the barrels.

The first rider tipped over a barrel and had five seconds added to her time. Now it was Mel's turn. The arena announcer could have saved his breath when he told everyone to cheer on the Reno's twin cowgirls, because people were cheering and whistling already. In the stands, Donna and Lacey leaned to their left, toward the arena entrance, where Melody Johnson came roaring into the arena on her favorite quarter horse. Mel made a neat, tight turn around the first barrel, then headed across the arena and circled the second barrel. Her horse flew toward the third and final barrel, circled it without a slip, then raced back toward the finish line. The crowd roared as the official time was announced: 17.81 seconds.

"Yes, Mel!" Donna yelled. "Put that time up there and let 'em shoot at it. Let's see what the others have."

The others didn't have enough, not the Texas cowgirl, or the ones from California, or the one from Oregon. Mel's time held up going into the final run. If Mel was going to lose this go-round, and the first place check that went with it, it would have to be Harm to keep her from the prize.

"At least we know it's going to stay in the family," Lacey said. "Who do you want to win, Donna?"

"That's hard to say," Donna answered. "How can you cheer for one of them over the other? I just hope they finish first and second. But if I had to choose I guess I'd have to cheer for Harm. She's always had to run twice as fast to catch up with Mel, from the day they were born. Nothing's come easy for her."

Just then Harmony Johnson raced into the arena, crossing the line and heading for the first barrel. She matched Mel's first turn, then headed for the second barrel, which she circled even more closely than the first. Her horse gave her everything it had as they went after the third barrel. Looking for an edge, and running on "the bottom" of the arena after the other racers had torn it up, Harm knew she had to take chances. She headed into the final turn as close to the barrel as she could get without crashing into it.

In the middle of the turn, Harm's horse bumped the barrel and it started to tip over. With disaster imminent, with Mel about to beat her again, Harm did something remarkable. She couldn't afford to stop or slow her horse to save the barrel, so she had to take another chance. With her right hand still on the reins, and urging her horse on, Harm reached down quickly with her left hand and punched the front of the barrel before it could fall. The barrel rocked back the other way after her punch, but she was racing to the finish line, with her eyes ahead on the prize, and could only pray that the barrel wouldn't fall behind her. When she didn't hear a moan from the crowd, she knew that the barrel was still standing. She raced across the line and waited for her time.

"The official time for Harmony Johnson is 17.75 seconds," came the announcement. "She is your winner by six one-hundredths of a second." The crowd roared its approval. Mel ran up to Harm and threw her arms around her.

"I don't believe what I just saw," Donna said. "Did you see what she did to that barrel?"

"It looked like she hit it so it wouldn't fall," Lacey said.

"Oh yeah. She punched that sucker because it was the fastest way to save the barrel. That's taking a big risk. I've seen her do that once or twice at the ranch, but never in competition."

"Well, you got your wish," Lacey said. "The girls finished one-two."

"They sure did. And Harm got the Reno win she's been after for so long. But it's the same old story. Nothing comes easy for her. She has to work hard for everything she gets."

When the time finally arrived for the Businessmen's Steer Decorating, Lacey and Donna both leaned forward to try to catch an early glimpse of Cody and me. Our names were in the program, representing Parker's, so Lacey knew that this was not some joke we were playing on her.

"There they are!" Donna shouted, spotting them first.

"Come on, Cody, you can do it!" Lacey called out.

And then it started. Steers were running and twisting every which way around the arena, each steer with one cowboy fighting hard to hang onto the rope and another cowboy trying to perform the delicate job of tying a ribbon to the steer's tail. The evening would have been perfect if Cody had held his steer in check while I tied the ribbon quickly and neatly and the judges had awarded us first place. But life is usually far from perfect, a fact that Lacey must have known, a fact that helped her earn her living as a lawyer.

For weeks afterwards, Cody and his friends would sit and discuss the events that transpired that Tuesday evening in the arena, each one recalling from their own viewpoint the particular details that had stuck in their minds. Donna remembered me dancing back and forth with the ribbon in response to the steer's wild movements. Donna said she had never seen such a dance before and decided that it deserved a name of its own, which she promised to work on.

Lacey remembered Cody stretched out on the ground, hanging onto the rope with both hands, a picture of determination and courage as the steer led us on a deluxe tour of the arena. She remembered cheering us on as loudly as if we had won the event.

As for myself, someone who had truly believed that we could win, I remembered the surprise I felt when I realized that all we were doing was providing a large part of the entertainment and laughter. But laughter is a good thing, as long as nobody gets hurt.

Then there was Cody, the cowboy from Iowa who just wanted to ride a horse that didn't spook easily, and to rope the odd calf without roping himself. I had talked him into entering the steer decorating, and I had convinced him that we could win. Cody told me he remembered it all, every second that he held onto that rope and simply refused to surrender, every bit of dirt that met him during our deluxe tour, every aching muscle that reminded him for days afterward, every hand that shook his hand afterward for the gutsy way he had hung on, and every emotion he had felt when Lacey ran up to him afterward and threw her arms around him. "I'm proud of you, cowboy," she had said. Cody said he had the strangest feeling that he had won something, that her response could not have been more rewarding if we had in fact won the event.

As Cody walked away from the rodeo that night, his aching right arm around the lady lawyer, he looked up and noticed the full moon for the first time.

"Nice moon," he said.

"Kind of romantic," Lacey said. "Somebody here got a little dirty and bruised tonight. Why don't you come home with me, cowboy, and let me take care of you."

It was not a question, and all Cody had to do was keep walking, hold on tight, and not let go.

17 Donna

"Do not hasten to bid me adieu…"

A couple of weeks later, after the full moon had been replaced by the new moon, after the Fourth of July had been properly celebrated—including, among other patriotic highlights, my new cowgirl fireworks shirt—and after the rodeo cowboys had left Reno for other towns and other rodeos, Cody West and Lacey Anderson found themselves on the road to Virginia City again. Lacey told me about it later, and I wrote it all down, so I don't think I've left anything out.

There's always a letdown when rodeo week is over. When I was a little girl I felt that way about Christmas. I guess I still do. The magic and the excitement are over for another year. My dad says that when I was four I asked him why Christmas couldn't last forever.

That's how I feel about rodeo week in Reno. I know that the rodeo cowboys have to move down the road, that all the volunteers have to get back to their regular lives. When I was a little kid, and I'd be all sad after Christmas was over, my dad would tell me, "All good things must end." He always said it twice, maybe trying to convince himself that it was true. I refuse to believe that saying, and I do my best to make good things last, but sometimes I suspect that my dad was right.

Does love have to end? I believe that true love never ends. Call me a romantic fool, but that's what I believe. On the other hand, when you think you're on that road to true love there's a world of speed bumps slowing you down, and detour signs, and muddy roads. My dad used to pull out his guitar and sing some old country songs. One of those songs was about detours and muddy roads ahead, and one line went "should have read that detour sign." Looking back at how Cody and Lacey had met at Parker's that day, and how everything had fallen into place for them, what with Charley and me helping them along, I should have realized it was too easy. So pardon me for a second while I put on a pair of old boots. There's a muddy road ahead, you know. And some tears and heartache too.

On this day, two weeks after the rodeo had left town, it was another Saturday morning, and Lacey had suggested to Cody that they return to see more of the old mining town of Virginia City. Lacey had been unusually quiet on the drive out of Reno. She slipped a CD into the stereo and they rode along to the sounds of Cody's pickup and cowboy songs. As "Red River Valley" began, Lacey hummed along softly with the familiar old tune and looked out the window at the passing sage.

> From this valley they say you are goin',
> I will miss your bright eyes and sweet smile,
> They say you are taking the sunshine
> That has brightened our pathway a while.

Lacey put a hand over her eyes and turned her head farther away from Cody. The truck was filled with the sweet, sad music of a harmonica, steel guitar, and a plaintive voice.

> Come and sit by my side if you love me,
> Do not hasten to bid me adieu,
> But remember the Red River Valley

And the cowboy who loves you so true.

I've been thinking a long time, my darling,
Of those sweet words you never would say,
Now, alas, all my fond hopes have vanished,
They say you are going away.

Cody looked over to see Lacey with her face in her hands. "What's the matter?" he asked.

"Can you pull over to the side up there?"

Cody pulled the truck off the road and parked at a scenic lookout. Lacey got out and walked about thirty feet across a clearing and leaned against a Ponderosa pine. Cody followed and caught up with her under the tree.

"Are you feeling bad?" he asked.

Lacey looked up and shook her head. "No. I mean yes. I guess I am feeling bad. I got a call yesterday from my law firm in San Francisco. It was Victor."

"Victor?"

"Yep. They have a big trial coming up and..." She paused to catch her breath before continuing. "And they asked me to go back and help with the trial preparation."

"Can't they find someone else?" Cody asked.

"I guess not," Lacey said. "It's a client I've worked with a lot over the past two years, and he wants me there. I told them I wanted to stay in Reno, but they said it's only for a few months. The trial should be over by the end of September."

"You'll get to see your parents," Cody said, trying to cheer her up.

"I know, but I just feel that Reno's my home now, and I have good friends here, and I love to ride, and of course there's you."

"Hey, I'll be here when you come back," Cody said. "And they do have telephones in San Francisco. Maybe we can get together for a weekend."

"Telephones are frustrating. I want to be here, not talking to you on the phone. And they'll have me working seven days a week until the trial's over. It's just hell. Sometimes I wish I had another job, working on the Lazy J maybe."

Cody looked down the mountain towards Reno. "All I know is that if you believe Reno is your home, well then it is, and anything else is just temporary. And if we want to be together we will be, and anything else is just temporary."

Lacey put her arms around him and leaned her head on his shoulder. "I know, I know," she said. "I guess I'm more of a worrier than you are. I think of all the things that can happen when we're apart."

"If the cable car's brakes fail, just jump off," Cody said.

"Stop joking. Anything can happen."

"You think you might see an old boyfriend when you're back there?" Cody asked. "You and Victor will be thrown together a lot. Maybe that's why he's calling you back."

"I don't know," Lacey said. "Maybe you're right. Victor's been phoning me twice a day, talking about the case as if it's going to be a great adventure for me and telling me how lucky I am. I sure don't feel lucky. But don't worry about Victor. You're the only cowboy I want. Besides, I'll be too busy working to see anyone."

"You're telling me not to worry? I'm not a worrier. Ever since that steer dragged me halfway across Reno and everyone shook my hand, I've stopped worrying."

"That's right," Lacey said. "You're one lucky cowboy."

Cody laughed. "You bet. So you'd better stick with me."

"Oh, Cody, I want to, but I have to go back to San Francisco for a few months. What am I going to do?"

"You have to go, I guess. When do you leave?"

Lacey paused. "They want me there on Monday. I was planning to pack tomorrow and drive back early Monday morning."

"That soon? Damn. You know, I don't want you to think that I don't mind. I'll miss you a lot. What will I do with myself? We've been spending so much time together."

"You can do things with Charley and Donna," Lacey said. "They've been great friends. Donna will make sure you stay out of trouble while I'm gone. It's Charley I'm not so sure about."

"Oh, Charley's like a big brother," Cody said. "He won't let me get into any serious trouble. It's Donna I'm not so sure about."

They stopped talking and looked at Reno in the distance for a while, then turned and walked back to the truck. Cody pointed his pickup toward Virginia City and Lacey smiled at him and then looked up the road to try to see what lay ahead for the two of them around the next curve. She didn't have the heart to play the sad cowboy songs again, so they rode the rest of the way with only the faint echoes of "Red River Valley" in their heads.

Lacey's abrupt news ticked in their heads like a noisy old alarm clock throughout the weekend. Early Monday morning the alarm finally went off. Much too soon for both of them. Lacey had her bags packed and in the trunk of her car just as the warm July sun was rising. Cody talked her into stopping for breakfast with him before she drove across the mountains. Lacey followed his truck until they pulled into a cafe on the way out of town.

The food was hot and tasty, their waitress was friendly, and it was the start of a fine July day in Reno. But Lacey picked at her food and finished less than half her breakfast. Cody had a good appetite, although he was having a difficult time trying to cheer up the lawyer lady.

"Want some more coffee?" he asked.

"Not me," Lacey answered. "I just want to go back to sleep. Do you remember my parents' phone number?"

Cody laughed. "I should," he said. "You only put it in my pickup and on my refrigerator and on the back of my hand."

Lacey smiled for the first time that morning. "Oh, that's just ink. It'll wash off."

"I thought for a while there you were going to have it tattooed on my chest."

"Actually that was Donna's suggestion, the tattoo, but I thought if my parents had their number changed it might be painful for you."

Cody laughed. "That girl is dangerous."

"She can be." It was good to talk about something else on this morning.

When the check came, Cody grabbed it first. Out in front of the cafe, standing next to Lacey's car, Cody gave Lacey his best smile. Lacey gave him her best kiss in return and climbed in behind the wheel. She started the car toward the road but slowed to a stop and jumped out. Cody stood and watched her give him her best rodeo queen wave, the one from the parade. He waved back and heard her call out to him. "Take care of yourself, cowboy," she told him.

"You, too, missy," he said, in his own voice instead of John Wayne's this time. Then she got back into her car and drove off toward San Francisco. Cody stood and watched the car get smaller and smaller until he couldn't see it at all, then he walked to his pickup and headed for Parker's.

18 Charley

"I will miss your bright eyes and sweet smile…"

The days and weeks following Lacey's departure from Reno were nothing to write home about. I was the one who suffered the most from Cody's unhappiness. Watching Cody mope around the store, I missed the spirited young cowboy I had known before. Not that Cody whined or expressed his misery openly, but it was clear that a major change had occurred in the fortunes of the lucky cowboy. He was like a horse that was off its feed. Something was missing. Or, to put it more accurately, someone was missing.

I had suggested to Cody that he take a ride down to the Starlight Ranch one night for some female companionship, but Cody showed no interest. That was when I knew I had a serious case of melancholy on my hands.

Now I believed I could become accustomed to Cody's quiet sadness, eventually, but I could never become accustomed to "that song." Cody's quiet mood gradually became kind of bearable and even comfortable, in a way, but the repetition of "that song" became increasingly impossible to stand. One afternoon at Parker's, when business was slow and Cody was listening to his favorite CD, I decided to complain.

"Say kid," he began, "how long are you going to keep playing 'Red River Valley'?"

Cody looked surprised. "I only play it now and then. Why, does it bother you?" Cody was a tough one to be upset with. He had that innocent little kid quality that women liked and men didn't know how to handle.

"Well, no," I said. "I mean, hell yes. If you're not playing that CD you're humming or whistling the tune. I'm starting to hear it in my head when I'm driving down the road. And I've heard the words so many times they just sound like nonsense now."

"Oh, I'm sorry," Cody said meekly. "If it bothers you I'll stop playing it."

I was in trouble. This reminded me of trying to stay upset with a big puppy. "Wait a minute there," I told Cody. "You don't have to stop it altogether. Let's just set a limit on it, before I go crazy, although I think you're more likely to go crazy before I do."

"Whatever you say," Cody replied.

But it was too late. The tune and the words were so planted in my head that I could no longer tell whether I was actually hearing the song or just imagining it. There was only one solution. The next morning I stopped Cody just as he was about to play that song again.

"Stop right there. You know, kid, there's nothing worse than a lovesick cowboy, unless it's a cowgirl scorned. But right now I don't see any cowgirls around, so let's you and me have a good talk."

Cody put the CD down on the counter and folded his arms. "Okay, Charley, what's eating you?" he asked.

I took a big breath and then shook my head. "It's not what's eating me, it's what's eating you," I said. "We both know what it is and dammit there's only one cure for it."

"What's that?" Cody asked. He had not been able to think straight for the past couple of weeks. Lacey had been right. The telephone was a frustrating kind of deal. It tried to trick you into thinking somebody was right there, when they weren't.

"Only one cure," I repeated. "You've got to go to San Francisco and see her."

"She's working seven days a week," Cody said.

"To hell with seven days a week," I said, raising my voice. "You're driving yourself crazy seven days a week, and you're driving me crazy five days a week. Just go see her."

Cody had never seen me so forceful. He seemed to be considering my argument, searching for a good reason not to go but failing to find one.

"Okay, tomorrow's Saturday, I'll drive to San Francisco then," Cody said, reaching for the CD.

I spotted the "Red River Valley" CD moving closer and closer to the stereo. I knew I had to act fast. "Not tomorrow, go today," I said quickly.

"Today? I have to work today."

"No, you don't. It's slow, and I don't mind covering for you."

"Are you sure you don't mind?" Cody's mood was brightening rapidly.

"Oh, I'm sure. You go ahead and don't worry about me. I'll have a nice, quiet day here." Right after I said that, I hoped that I had not been too obvious.

"Well, all right then," Cody said, his mind made up, "I'll go. Thanks, Charley, you're a true friend. What would I do without you?"

"God only knows. Just leave that CD here with me, where I can keep an eye on it. I'll take good care of it for you."

"Promise you will?" Cody asked.

I had to promise, although I was torn between loyalty to a friend and a strong desire not to hear "Red River Valley" again for the next few years. I felt sorely tempted to accidentally misplace the CD while Cody was away in San Francisco, but then I realized that he could just buy another copy. I finally decided it was a good sign that Cody was ready to ride off and leave the CD, and his sadness, behind.

I shooed the Iowa kid out of the store. He hadn't been gone five minutes when guess who walks in. It was Donna Cooper, searching for Cody.

"Too late," I said, "you just missed him."

"Rats," Donna said. "I need to talk to him. He needs to go to San Francisco and see Lacey before something happens."

"Oh? What could happen?"

"Well, that GQ boy might get his hooks into her."

"Victor?" I asked.

"That guy. He's not my type, but maybe he will seduce our Lacey. I bet those two are spending a lot of time together working on that case." Donna leaned closer. "You know what they say about propinquity."

"Pro what?"

"Propinquity," she said. "Look it up sometime. That's when two people are together for long periods of time. They acquire an attraction for each other."

"And that's what you're afraid is going to happen with Lacey and that Victor fellow?"

"It could happen. And where does that leave Cody? Out in the cold, that's where."

"Well, you can stop worrying. Cody's on his way to San Francisco right now. I chased him out of here. If I had to listen to 'Red River Valley' one more time I was going to do something violent to that CD."

"Oh," Donna said. "So you sent him off to see Lacey?"

"Yep," I said. "Proud of me?"

"Charley Meyers, you know what? I'm very proud of you. Here I thought I was the love cop in charge of everything and it was all up to me. That takes a load off my mind."

"Donna, want to deputize me? I think you need a good deputy to help you."

"You've helped already. I think I'll call Lacey and let her know that Cody's on the way."

"Don't do that," I said. "He wants to surprise her."

"Oh. Well, okay." Donna scrunched up her forehead, trying to focus on this news. "I guess that's good. I'll just call Lacey tonight and see how it's going."

"For cripes sake, Donna, give them some time alone without the love cop checking up on them."

"Okay, but..." She had those forehead wrinkles again. You could tell when she was doing her hardest thinking.

"But what?" I said.

"But I want to hear all about it at some time, and—"

"Hey," I interrupted her. "I'm the one writing the book about all this."

"Yeah," Donna said. "And I'm the one in charge of directing the romantic traffic. If this all comes crashing down, where does that leave your book?"

"*Chasing Cowgirls*? It'll have to end with a crash then, that's all."

"Charley, don't you know anything?" Donna was talking louder, the way she did whenever I said the wrong thing. "Your book needs a happy ending. It's a romance."

"Who said it was a romance? It's just a story. Romances don't always end happy anyway."

"You mean like you and…" Donna stopped. She had stumbled into a room that I wanted locked up good and tight.

"Me and Angel?" I said.

"Sorry," Donna said. She patted my shoulder.

"That's all right. Anyway, Cody's off to see Lacey. Everything's going to be all right."

"I hope so," Donna said. "For their sake. And for the sake of your book. You'd better start praying that Victor doesn't screw everything up. I don't trust that guy."

"Okay, I'll put Cody and Lacey in my prayers tonight."

"You pray every night?" Donna looked astounded.

"Always have," I said. "Ever since I was a little boy. My mama always told me that life is too hard to handle on your own. That's where the praying comes in."

"Charley Meyers, you're an interesting human being." Donna smiled and headed for the front door. She always had someplace to go. Before she disappeared, though, she turned and gave me a little wave.

"There's hope for you after all," she said. Then she was gone. She had managed to have the last word, again. I pulled out my composition book from under the counter and jotted down a few notes. I wished I knew how the story was going to end. The suspense was making us all a little crazy.

19 Donna

"Cody and the cable cars..."

Pardon me if I take over the story from Charley Meyers here. This is a critical part, and I don't trust him with it. He'd probably leave out something very important. It wouldn't be his fault, but the simple fact is that he is a man, and what do they know about romance? So here's what I pieced together from talking to Cody and Lacey. I confess I did make up some of the details, but you won't know which ones, so it doesn't matter. Oh, I need to warn you that there is some delicious food involved, so you might want to have some of your favorite snacks handy for the following chapters.

An hour after leaving Parker's, or being pushed out by Charley, Cody was on the road to San Francisco. Moving more quickly than he had in weeks, he had dashed home, thrown a few things together for the weekend, and jumped into his old Dodge pickup. To say that his spirits had improved would be an understatement, like saying that the spirits of the old cowpoke who had hit the full moon jackpot at the Eldorado had improved.

Cody didn't seem to miss his "Red River Valley" CD at all. He spent the first part of the trip listening to Willie Nelson sing "My Heroes Have Always Been Cowboys" and "Always On My Mind" and "Blue Eyes Crying in the Rain." When Willie began singing about how he couldn't wait to get "On the Road Again," Cody's spirits were soaring.

He decided to surprise Lacey at her office in downtown San Francisco. She had been springing all of the surprises up to now—learning to ride without telling him and leaving suddenly to work on that dang trial in San Francisco. So he owed her one.

As his pickup climbed the Sierras and crossed the border into California, Cody realized that he was going places this day where he had never been. In his life he had seen a great deal of the Midwest and the East, but the West Coast was a large gap in his geographical education. Not that he shared the prejudices of his Aunt Alice and Uncle Max, who had raised him after his parents died. Aunt Alice always believed firmly—more firmly because she had never been West—that everything west of Iowa, or maybe Nebraska, was still pretty much as it had been during the time of General Custer, and that anyone who left God's heartland to risk their neck in that forsaken wilderness did not have the good sense they were born with.

When Aunt Alice had heard that her nephew was going out to Nevada, she had tried to dissuade him before it was too late. Nevada is where they set off those atomic bombs, she had told him, and when they aren't doing that they're gambling their homes away and going straight to hell. Aunt Alice had seen the *Godfather* movies, as well as some news film from the 1950s, and for her that was Nevada. When she discovered that he was going anyway, she tried to minimize the dangers he would encounter. "Alan Cody West," she had said, "if you have to go out there, stay away from the casinos and from wild women. And go straight to Reno. Don't be taking any side trips to the Little Big Horn or the Badlands." Aunt Alice was not sure exactly where the Little Big Horn or the Badlands were, but she knew that George Armstrong Custer had come to a bad end at the former, and that outlaws were hanging around the latter, which is why they called it the Badlands in the first place. Cody had assured his aunt that he would go straight to Reno and avoid wild women, although he did not mention casinos in his promise. Aunt Alice satisfied herself that she had done her best and that the boy's guardian angel would have to take over from there.

Uncle Max was more adventurous than this. He was the uncle who had made it as far as Denver as a young man before turning back. Uncle Max might have tried again, but then he met Alice and settled down for good in Iowa. Secretly he kept waiting for a time when he would buy a new car, one that could make it safely all the way to California, but that time never came. Cody often thought that the family name should have been changed from West to Midwest, but instead he had taken it upon himself to live up to the name.

As Cody's old pickup flew down the Sierras and toward Sacramento, he changed CDs. Michael Martin Murphey began singing a wildly romantic song about a horse named "Wildfire" and the lady who loved him. Cody remembered how good Lacey had looked riding in the rodeo parade back in Reno. Funny, he thought, how his memories of Lacey were all back in Nevada, but Lacey herself was ahead and waiting for him in San Francisco.

The past always seemed more real than the future, which was usually cloudy. Willie Nelson had sung about cowboys and their slow moving dreams. Cody's dreams had been racing along at a pretty good clip, from the April day four months earlier when he had stepped down from the train with new boots and a new name. Lacey had been an unexpected addition to his cowboy dreams, and their teaming up had occurred with all the speed of a barrel racer blazing toward the finish line.

Cody checked the speedometer and discovered that the pickup was roaring toward San Francisco at over 75 miles an hour. He eased it back to 65 and cars began to pass him. What was waiting for them down the road, Cody wondered. The old traffic cop greeting was "Where's the fire?" or "Do you know how fast you were going?" Cody remembered rehearsing answers to these questions with friends back in Iowa. "Gee, officer, I think something's wrong with the speedometer" was a favorite. Cody preferred an honest answer. "No, officer, I've had so many things on my mind, and the rest of the cars were going at that speed anyway, and I just...well, you know." Sometimes it worked and sometimes it didn't, but the police, who had heard all the alibis, seemed to appreciate an honest answer and sometimes gave you a break.

As he drove through farm country, Cody compared it to Iowa. Iowa had corn and cattle and pigs, and lots of memories. He couldn't tell what was growing in California. He knew that southern California grew oranges and movie stars, and he had heard that northern California grew interesting things like almonds and walnuts and artichokes and grapes. Around Sacramento he saw fields being irrigated, but didn't recognize the crops. Was it soybeans and alfalfa? He remembered that Lacey's father had a produce business. If he got to meet him would they end up talking for hours about vegetables?

Cody glanced at his jeans and Western shirt. Would Lacey's parents approve of her seeing a cowboy? Cowboys had a general reputation that would put a mother on guard to protect her daughter. Cody made a mental note to be especially polite if he met Lacey's folks, not to act too colorful like Charley, to compliment the mother on her cooking and engage the father in talking about his business and hobbies. Cody thought he would probably feel like a high school kid meeting his date's parents, sitting on a strange sofa and getting the third degree. What the hell, she was worth it. As long as she didn't have a date tonight with Victor or some old boyfriend, Cody thought everything would be all right.

Five hours after he had left Reno, Cody finally saw the hills of San Francisco. On the Bay Bridge he saw the impressive skyline across the bay and wondered which tower Lacey was working in at this moment. He had picked up a map of the city and had an address, and he figured that he could stop and ask someone if he got lost. He found Lacey's building without much trouble, pulled into a parking garage, and recovered from the shock of the parking rates by the time he got out of the elevator and walked into the law offices of Peterman, Biggen & Kleindich.

Now it was Lacey's turn to be shocked. The receptionist, thinking that they didn't get many cowboys walking in, greeted Cody with a "howdy" and asked him if he was there to see someone. Cody asked the receptionist to tell Miss Anderson that if she had a moment there was someone who would like to see her. The receptionist went along with this and picked up the phone to relay the message. Lacey came walking out of her office with an armful of files, took one look at her visitor, and dropped the files on the floor. Cody helped her pick up the files and they went back into her office. By now several secretaries had noticed the cowboy and were exchanging glances and looking to the receptionist for a clue. Lacey closed her door behind them, and they did not come out for a good ten minutes.

When they did return to the main office area, Lacey, who was trying to keep from smiling too broadly, introduced Cody to everyone as "my friend from Reno." The workers greeted Cody with "howdy" and "welcome, cowboy," and Cody just grinned and nodded to everyone. Lacey walked Cody out to the reception area and found a corner where she could give him one more hug.

"Why don't you go have a bite to eat?" she suggested. "You must be hungry after that long drive. I'll be done about 5:30 or 6:00. That will give you time to ride a cable car if you want. Take the Hyde Street car, the one that goes down to Fisherman's Wharf. You can catch it by walking a couple of blocks west to Powell Street. The view's spectacular. Just don't get bucked off."

"Okay," Cody agreed, "I'll meet you back here and take you out to dinner."

"I have a better idea," Lacey said. "Come home with me and meet my folks. Mom's the best cook in the city anyway. You can relax and take off your boots if you want. You'll be more comfortable than in a restaurant. Cody, Cody, Cody. I can't believe you're here."

"This is better than talking on the phone, don't you think?"

Lacey smiled. "No comparison," she said.

Cody left and Lacey walked back towards her office. The receptionist and secretaries greeted her with applause and comments like "Yes, Lacey!" and "Does he have a brother?" Lacey just smiled and kept on walking. Victor Kleindich stepped out of his office and almost bumped into her. Victor had been on the phone and missed Cody's visit.

"Lacey, can you step into my office?" Victor said. "I want to go over a few things with you. And we need to plan the weekend."

Lacey sighed, then managed a professional smile before disappearing into her mentor's office. She had other plans for the weekend, and they didn't involve Victor and work. It was time to use her negotiating skills. Maybe she could bargain for Saturday off and work on Sunday. She hated it when something came between her and Cody. Was it the work, was it Victor, or was it both?

Down on Powell Street, Cody spotted a cable car and decided he'd ride it to Fisherman's Wharf and grab a sandwich there. He jumped on the side of the car, which was loaded with tourists, paid a few bucks, and hung on with one hand as it moved slowly towards Chinatown. Cody knew he wasn't in Iowa any more, or Reno. The sights and sounds and smells of the city occupied his senses.

Lacey's warm welcome had filled him with renewed hope and energy. As the cable car turned from Jackson Street onto Hyde, and Cody had become comfortable with its vibrations and rhythms, he did something natural and impulsive. With his free hand he took off his cowboy hat, waved it in the air, and gave a rousing "yeeee-hah!" If there had been any critters in the neighborhood they probably would have been persuaded to start moving down the trail.

The cable car grip man and conductor laughed, rang the bells some more, and joined in with their own "yee-hahs!" The tourists, already in a festive mood, were amused and inspired by this happy cowboy. In a matter of seconds the whole car was a chorus of cowboy yells, as each of its passengers tried out their vocal cords on their own version of "yee-hah!" A couple of pedestrians on Hyde Street stopped to watch and listen. As local residents, they were accustomed to the daily sight of the cable cars on their streets, but this one was different, sort of a Red River cable car. In fact, more than one witness that day recalled the John Wayne movie, even if they had not seen it in years.

As it moved down the hill toward Fisherman's Wharf, the Powell-Hyde car became a moving party. Strangers introduced themselves to each other. The grip man and conductor worked some cowboy lingo into their patter; for weeks and months afterward they would be saying things like "Head 'em up, move 'em out" and "Get along, little dogies" and "Whoa there, don't start a stampede." And, of course, the passengers wanted to meet Cody and ask him where he was from. When Cody told them his name—Cody West—and said he was from Reno, they thought that was just about perfect. They began to tell their own Reno stories, or Las Vegas stories.

This party continued after the cable car had reached its destination at Beach and Hyde streets. A group of the friendlier tourists were stopping for a late lunch and offered to buy Cody a beer and sandwich. At lunch someone asked Cody what kind of cowboy he was. Cody was surprised that he could tell the truth now and it would sound pretty good. He told his new acquaintances that he cowboyed some on a ranch outside Reno, and that he also helped out in a big western wear store in downtown Reno. Someone asked him if he ever entered a rodeo. Cody stated that he had rodeoed back in June in Reno but he had to confess that it was only the steer decorating. When everyone heard what was involved in steer decorating, however, and what Cody had been through trying to decorate the steer, they were duly impressed and ordered another beer for the Reno cowboy.

It was at some point during this second beer that Cody started doing his John Wayne impression. The next day, when he told Lacey about this part of the afternoon, Cody would not be able to say whether he had finally perfected the voice, and walk, of the Duke, or whether everyone was just having such a good time that they decided the impression was perfect. At any rate, Cody did about ten minutes of John Wayne, including scenes from *Red River*. At the end of the ten minutes, Cody had to visit the restroom, but when he returned he walked up to the table with that distinctive John Wayne walk. Everyone at the table applauded and whistled, until Cody gave them a signal to hush.

"Just hang on there a minute, pilgrim," he said.

"What is it, Duke?" one man in his group asked.

"Well, fellows...and ladies," he said, removing his hat, "I hate to break up this little party, but the sun's startin' to go down, and you know what that means."

"No, what does it mean?" Cody's audience asked, right on cue.

"Well, it means there's a certain young lady who's waitin' for me back at the ranch. If I don't get back there soon she's gonna be a regular hellcat."

Cody's new friends laughed and whooped it up.

"So let's ride," Cody said. Someone insisted on picking up the check and they walked back to the cable car turnaround. Everyone wanted to know more about Cody's "hellcat." When they found out she was a San Francisco lawyer, they had to know how Cody had met her. When Cody started talking about

Reno he happened to mention Donna Cooper's name, and as they waited for the cable car, the group received a brief glimpse into the world of rodeo queens. Cody even showed them some different waves, including Lacey's wave, and everyone practiced waving for a while.

When the cable car arrived, Cody and his new friends jumped on for the trip downtown. Climbing Hyde Street, the group made some new acquaintances, as they worked on their "yee-hahs!" and encouraged others to join in. Because the group included a couple of Western music fans with strong voices, the return trip featured a little singing. "Mamas, don't let your babies grow up to be cowboys," they began, and stuck with that one song because it was easy to sing and the chorus was familiar to everyone. By the time the cable car turned onto Washington Street, just about everyone was singing this song of advice to mothers.

No one could have guessed that only a few minutes later the high spirits and innocent fun of the souls on the cable car would meet with impending tragedy. No one saw the little Chinese girl wander away on a crowded sidewalk and walk out to the edge of Powell Street. The two-year-old was intent on locating her mother and did not see the delivery truck moving up Powell. In the opposite direction she saw a cable car coming slowly down the street and heard the people on it singing about "mamas."

"Cable car," she said, and remembered riding a cable car with her mother. Maybe her mother was on the cable car. She walked into the street and started to call out "Mama" to the people on the cable car. Her mother, back on the sidewalk, heard this small voice and ran towards the street. She would never arrive in time. The little girl had her back to the truck now and was walking toward the cable car. The truck, the little girl, and the cable car were on a course to arrive at the same part of the street in three or four seconds.

The driver of the truck saw the cable car up ahead, and noticed a cowboy standing on the outside, but he never saw the little girl walking into the street. Cody, singing away and looking down the street, saw the little girl first. Then he saw the oncoming truck. If he had paused to shout or tell someone what he saw, it would have been too late. Instead he jumped off the cable car and dove headfirst for the little girl. He caught her with one arm and rolled with her toward the side of the street. As he rolled he saw, and felt, the truck go right by them, and felt one tire brush his boots.

Cody rolled to a stop against the curb. The little girl was still startled, but she was all right. All around them people were reacting to what had just happened. The truck driver had slammed on the brakes when he saw the cowboy flying in front of him. The cable car grip man, not sure what had just happened, had brought the car to a halt. The mother was the first on the scene, followed by the truck driver and Cody's friends on the cable car. The sidewalk was buzzing with the talk of dozens of bystanders.

The little girl jumped up and hugged her mother, then pointed back at Cody. "Cowboy," she said to her mother.

Satisfied that her daughter was unhurt, the mother turned her attention to the man who had just saved the little girl's life. "Are you all right?" the mother asked Cody.

"Yes, ma'am. She seems okay, too. I guess we were lucky."

"How can I ever thank you?" the mother asked. "You were so brave."

"That's all right," Cody answered. "I guess I was in the right place at the right time."

They were joined now by Cody's new friends and admirers from the cable car, and, surprisingly, by a news crew from a local television station. It turned out that the crew was filming a feature that afternoon about a visiting exhibit at the Jade West jewelry store on that block. When they heard the brakes and noise out in the street, the cameraman and reporter had run out of the store to see what was happening. They quickly forgot about the jewelry story—that could wait. How often does a cowboy leap from a moving cable car in downtown San Francisco to save the life of a little girl from the onrushing wheels of a truck?

The reporter interviewed Cody and a couple of the passengers before they climbed back on the cable car to continue their trip. She interviewed the truck driver, the mother, and even the little girl. She also interviewed the owner of the jewelry store, to explain how they were on the spot so quickly. The reporter could have stayed longer—everyone had something to say about the event—but she had to rush to try to get the story on the early news.

Before Cody was able to leave the scene, he had to do the interview, give the mother his Reno address so she could write to him, accept the praises of his friends on the cable car as well as some of the bystanders, and accept a kiss and hug from the little girl. Cody refused to give a San Francisco address to the news reporter because he didn't want Lacey or her folks being bothered. At last he was back on the cable car and managed to complete his remarkable cable car ride in a less eventful way. When he stepped down and waved goodbye to the grip man, the conductor, and all of his new friends, Cody felt that pain again and realized that he had twisted an ankle during his impulsive leap into the street.

He limped back to Lacey's building. Checking his watch, he saw that he was not late and that Lacey would not have to know what had happened. It had been her idea that he ride the cable car, but he didn't feel like bragging about his heroics. It wasn't as if he had planned it or intended to risk his neck to save a life. It had just happened, and now it was over. He was glad that he had been riding on the outside, and on the truck's side of the cable car.

Cody knew that he would remember that little girl for the rest of his life. It was kind of funny to realize that the one detail that stuck in his mind was what the kid said after it was over. She had pointed to him and said "cowboy." It had been a long time since Cody had asked himself if he was a cowboy yet. Then he realized that jumping off the cable car was like being a steer wrestler, only he had a little kid to wrestle to the ground instead of a big old steer. And how many times had he seen rodeo cowboys limp across the arena after their event?

When he walked into Lacey's office, she noticed his limp right away. "What happened to you?" she asked.

Cody chuckled. "Oh, I guess I jumped off the cable car before it stopped," he said.

"You ought to be more careful, cowboy," she said.

"Yes, ma'am. It's different from a horse, you know. It goes kind of slow but it doesn't have a saddle."

"Take off your boot, and let me have a look at it," Lacey said.

Lacey wouldn't leave until Cody took off the boot and let her massage his ankle. It wasn't swollen, so she let him put the boot back on.

"It doesn't really hurt," Cody assured her.

"You cowboys are all the same," Lacey said, grinning. "You don't show pain. If it did hurt you'd hide it."

"I swear, it doesn't hurt," Cody said.

"Well, don't walk on it any more than you have to." They walked out to the elevator together. "Can you drive?" Lacey asked.

Cody sighed. "Of course I can drive. You act as if I broke my leg or something. It was just a little cable car ride. What do you think happened?"

"Oh, I don't know," Lacey answered, "you probably met a bunch of tourists and they asked you questions about cowboys and they bought you a couple of beers at Fisherman's Wharf and that's why you fell off the cable car."

"You're good," Cody said.

"I thought it was something like that," Lacey said, proud of her guess. "If you can drive, then follow me back to my mom and dad's house for dinner. You can soak the ankle in hot water later."

"Are you going to be my nurse?" Cody asked, smiling.

"Don't get any ideas," Lacey said. "I told my mother you're coming, so she's making a big salad and cooking steaks for you. She thinks that cowboys eat steak or chili all the time."

"Steaks for me?" Cody asked.

"She said you could eat a couple of steaks by yourself. I don't know what she thinks cowboys do that they have appetites twice as big as the rest of us."

"Well, I did work up an appetite today, falling off the cable car and all."

"Anyway, you only have to eat one steak if you want," Lacey told him. "But you'd better eat a lot of salad. My dad is so proud of his produce that he'd never forgive you if you didn't like his vegetables."

As they walked to the parking garage, Lacey noticed the condition of Cody's hat. "What happened to your black hat, cowboy?"

Cody took off the hat and inspected the damage. "It must have gotten banged up when I fell off the cable car," Cody said.

"Let me see what I can do with it," Lacey said. She worked on it until it no longer looked as if Cody had been wearing it in a saloon brawl. "You want to make a good first impression with my parents."

"Are they suspicious of cowboys seeing their daughter?" Cody asked.

"I never went out with a cowboy before," Lacey said. "They want to like you. I told them you're a gentleman and treat me very well. Just be sure to eat a lot and take an interest in the vegetables."

"And use my napkin instead of my sleeve?" Cody asked.

Lacey laughed. "Just get in your truck and follow me home, if you know what's good for you."

Cody knew. On the way out of the office he turned back and caught a glimpse of Victor, who looked like a model who had decided to become a lawyer. Victor was standing and studying at a file, which he held open in his right hand while he smoothed the hair along his left temple with the other hand. Cody thought it was a very feminine gesture, or something a peacock might do if it were human.

Back in the garage Cody climbed into his old Dodge pickup, trying not to put much weight on his right ankle. He waited for Lacey to drive up in her car. When she rolled down her window and said, "Head 'em up," Cody called back, "Move 'em out," and off they went. Time to meet the folks.

20 Donna

"Meeting the parents…"

Lacey was glad her parents lived in the city. After a long day at work, it was so much easier going home to their house in the Sunset neighborhood rather than having to fight the traffic across the bridges or down the peninsula. On the way home she checked her mirror frequently to make sure Cody was behind her. The blue pickup, with the cowboy behind the wheel, was easy to spot. She wondered how her parents would react to Cody. He was about as different from her former boyfriends as he could be.

After she pulled up in front of her parents' comfortable, middle class Sunset home, Lacey walked up to Cody's truck and was there to help him out. He assured her once again that he was all right, and then he limped up to the Andersons' front door. Lacey unlocked the door and was greeted by her mother's voice.

"Lacey, is that you? Come quick! Cody's on TV!"

"What?" Lacey said, as she dragged Cody with her into the family room in the back of the house.

"Hurry!" Mrs. Anderson called again. "He's about to be interviewed by Lisa Nakasone."

Cody knew at once that his secret was out. As he entered the family room, he saw Lacey's parents on the edge of their chairs. They gave Lacey and Cody a quick wave and pointed at the television screen. There was the reporter with her exclusive coverage of the heroic cowboy who had jumped from a moving cable car and rescued a little girl from being crushed by a truck on Powell Street that afternoon, only a little more than an hour earlier.

Lacey was the most surprised. As she sat on the sofa with Cody, she stared at the screen, trying to hear every word of the report. Then she stared at Cody, who was trying to avoid her look. Finally, she stared at his ankle and his damaged cowboy hat. She was about to ask him why he hadn't told her about this, but she wanted to hear his interview.

On the screen, as the reporter quizzed him and held a microphone in front of him, Cody looked kind of embarrassed about the whole thing. He kept saying how lucky it was that the cable car came along just at that moment, and how he was riding along one second and the next thing he knew he was flying through the air and then rolling on the street. He said he was happy the little girl wasn't hurt, that he had tried not to hurt her as they scrambled out of the way. He gave the reporter his name, said he was from Reno and had just driven in today to visit a friend. Yes, this was his first cable car ride ever. No, he didn't think it would be his last one.

There were more interviews to watch. Lacey was amused by Cody's friends on the cable car, who were interviewed as a group. They related how Cody had been riding on the outside of the car and yelling "yee-hah," and how they had all become cowboys on this ride, and how they had been singing a Western song when they saw Cody suddenly fly off the cable car. They thought at first he had fallen off, and it was only after the cable car stopped and they got off that they realized what had happened. They told about how they had lunch with Cody and told the reporter she should see his John Wayne impression, but when they looked around he was busy talking to the little girl and her mother.

When the report ended, the news team in the television studio kept talking about what a remarkable story it was, how they had heard different cable car stories but never one as good as this. Lacey's dad turned off the television, stood up, and walked toward Cody. "Let me shake your hand, young man," he told Cody. "I'm Lacey's father. Everybody calls me Sonny."

Cody stood up and shook Sonny's hand. Mrs. Anderson, tall and attractive like her daughter, was right behind. She kissed Cody on the cheek. "Cody, I'm so glad to meet you. Please call me Ellen. Lacey has told us so much about you. She didn't tell us what a hero you were."

"I didn't know," Lacey spoke up. "He doesn't tell me everything. I saw him limping this afternoon, and he told me he fell off the cable car."

"Well, that's sort of what happened," Cody said.

"I bet you worked up a big appetite today, Cody," Ellen said. "Why don't you sit down and rest and I'll finish preparing the dinner. How many steaks can you eat?"

"One will be fine," Cody said.

"That means two," Ellen said. "Lacey, why don't you help me in the kitchen? We'll let the men sit here and talk about whatever it is they talk about when women aren't around."

"Sure, Mom," Lacey said. "I think we ought to let Cody take his boots off first. He twisted his ankle jumping off that cable car and I'm afraid it's going to swell up. He can soak it later."

Cody protested, but to no avail. Lacey insisted on helping him take his boots off, and Ellen had to inspect the famous ankle before pronouncing it a minor sprain. The women went into the kitchen to finish the dinner, leaving Cody and Sonny to get better acquainted.

Cody sat on the sofa, less uncomfortable than he had imagined, now that the fame of his cable car heroics had preceded him. Sonny wanted to hear more about the afternoon's events, especially how close he had come to being hit by the truck ("very close," Cody had said) and whether he had felt any fear while jumping in front of the truck ("didn't have time for that"). Cody thought the conversation would never get around to the subject of vegetables and other produce, and eventually it did, but only because he himself was a bit uncomfortable talking about his heroic deed. Cody tried to change the subject.

"Lacey tells me you have a big produce business," Cody said.

"There are bigger ones," Sonny said, "but Anderson's is large enough. We started out small, of course, but now we have over thirty employees. I could give you a tour of some of the fine restaurants that buy from us, but the vegetables you'll be eating tonight are the same, maybe fresher."

"Lacey said her mom's the best cook in town," Cody said.

"That's the truth," Sonny said. "You ought to taste her seafood dishes. Do you like seafood?"

"Sure," Cody said, "but tell me more about the vegetables."

Sonny was soon off and running with his favorite subject. Cody had asked out of politeness as much as anything, but the lesson he received about vegetables surprised him. He had never known there was so much to learn about produce—all the varieties, all the things to watch for. It was endless. Cody had grown up in Iowa appreciating fresh corn and tomatoes and such. He remembered his aunt saying how corn should be picked and shucked and slipped into the pot quickly, and to ignore the telephone if it rang while you were rushing the corn to the boiling water. He knew not to overcook the corn, or any other vegetables.

His education in vegetables had been like a grade school education, however, and now he was experiencing higher education. His teacher was a master, a man whose life was fresh fruit and vegetables. "Do you like artichokes, Cody?" Sonny was asking.

"Artichokes are great," Cody said. He had eaten a few of the strange things over the years.

"How do you like them prepared?" Sonny asked, and waited for an answer.

Cody struggled for an answer to this. He knew about stuffed artichokes, but not enough to discuss them. "I usually just boil or steam the artichoke and eat it with some melted butter or mayonnaise," Cody said.

Sonny studied this answer. "Steaming's better."

"I agree," Cody said.

"How about stuffed artichokes?" Sonny asked. He could have gone on about artichokes for an hour. It was Ellen who usually interrupted him at these times and changed the subject.

"I've had some good stuffed artichokes," Cody said, trying to hold his own in this uneven conversation. "I remember mushrooms and breadcrumbs."

"You haven't had Ellen's stuffed artichokes," Sonny said. Cody had to admit that he had never had the pleasure of encountering Ellen's stuffed artichokes, but that he looked forward to it.

"Good," Sonny said, louder than before. "You're having stuffed artichokes tonight." Sonny sat there in his favorite chair, a smile of contentment on his face. Business was good, Lacey had found a fellow that any father would be proud of, he was married to the best cook in San Francisco, and Ellen was making her stuffed artichokes. Life was good.

Sonny was about to launch into the nutritional value of fresh fruit and vegetables when Ellen walked in from the kitchen to ask Cody if he would like something to drink. Sonny suggested a steam beer and asked Ellen to bring two, one for himself and one for "our cowboy." When she returned with the steam beer, Ellen also brought a large plate of appetizers, filled with different cheeses, crackers, thinly sliced apples and bell peppers, carrot sticks, and Greek olives. "That looks fantastic," Cody told her. His lunch at Fisherman's Wharf had been a light one, and so much had happened in the hours since then. The food was garden fresh and delicious, and the steam beer was cold and wonderful.

"Fiber," Sonny remarked.

"Excuse me?" Cody responded.

"Fiber. The body needs fiber. That's where fresh fruit and vegetables are so vital. People these days are in such a hurry. They get filled up with all this fast food and convenience food and think they've eaten. Then they get sick and wonder why. Not enough fiber. Why do you think they call it junk food? This plate of food here will give you plenty of fiber."

"Yes, sir," Cody said, "and it all tastes great."

"Sonny."

"Excuse me?" Cody said.

"Call me Sonny."

"Oh, sorry, Sonny," Cody corrected himself. Calling Mr. Anderson "Sonny" took some adjustment, probably because Cody was used to having himself called "Sonny" by older people, especially some of his aunts and uncles back in Iowa.

Just then Lacey walked in see how Cody was doing, if he needed any help. She took one look at Cody attacking the appetizers and smiled. "Fiber," she told him, then turned around and went back to the kitchen.

"Hear that?" Sonny asked. "That girl's an Anderson, all right."

"I guess she knows a lot about produce, too," Cody said.

"When she was growing up she used to ride in with me on Saturdays and hang around the business," Sonny said. Cody could almost see the memories parading before Sonny's eyes, and he tried to imagine what Lacey looked like as a young girl. He made a mental note to ask Ellen if he could see some old photos.

"She was a real tomboy, that one," Sonny said, remembering those old days. "Her mom named her Lacey because it's a nice feminine name. Even if you shorten it, you've got 'Lace.' But Lacey was all tomboy, always wanting to go fishing or play ball. She would have pitched right in at Anderson's and driven a delivery truck if I had let her. Ellen used to ask me if I regretted that we never had a son. I would just smile and tell her I never missed a thing, and that was the truth. I used to take her to the Giant games. You should hear her yell at the umpires."

Cody was enjoying this conversation, learning more about artichokes and Lacey. Ellen walked in again to announce that dinner was ready. Cody and Sonny picked up their glasses of steam beer and joined the women in the dining room.

"Cody, you sit here across from Lacey," Ellen said, "so you two can look at each other all you want."

"Candles?" Sonny said to Ellen.

"Why, of course," Ellen said, "in honor of our cowboy hero."

Lacey offered to pour the wine, and then Sonny stood up to offer a toast.

"Here's to the best cook in San Francisco, and to the best daughter a father ever had, even if she works all the time and we don't see enough of her. And to Cody West, who risked his life today to save a little girl, and who has put the sparkle back in Lacey's eyes. Salud!"

They all said "Salud," touched glasses, and tasted the good California chardonnay. Cody saw Lacey looking at him and guessed that he needed to make a toast as well. Cody raised his glass and began his little speech. "Lacey never told me she was a tomboy and used to yell at umpires, or that she had such terrific parents, or that she lived in such a friendly city, where you can ride a crazy cable car and make lots of friends and have all kinds of adventures."

As they were sipping the wine again, the telephone rang. Ellen excused herself and went to answer it in the kitchen. She returned immediately to tell Lacey it was her office calling. Lacey was in the kitchen for a few minutes before she returned to the dining room.

"You'll never guess," she said.

"You have to go in?" Cody asked.

"No way," Lacey said. "That was Adrienne, the receptionist. She saw you on the news and phoned the station and the newspapers to tell them she knew who you were. The papers want to interview you and get your photograph with the little girl and her mother. Adrienne decided to phone me and let us decide if we wanted to talk to the papers. She gave me the reporters' phone numbers. It's up to you, Cody."

As they started in on the stuffed artichokes, Cody pondered his fifteen minutes of fame. It had its interesting points, but he did not want to spend his whole stay in San Francisco talking to reporters. "Maybe I'll call them after dinner and answer their questions," he finally said.

"Cody, I can take a day off from work tomorrow," Lacey said. "I'd like to show you the city. Maybe we could go up to the wine country and visit a few wineries. Unless you're tired of driving."

"No, that sounds like fun," Cody said.

"Mom's made up the guest room for you, so you can rest your ankle tonight and we can have breakfast here and then drive up north. If you're lucky you can ride inside and you won't have to jump in front of any trucks."

Cody chuckled. "I'm always lucky."

"I'm afraid I'll have to work on Sunday," Lacey said.

"Well, we have all day tomorrow," Cody said. "I have to be back at work on Monday."

Sonny spoke up just then. "Say, Cody, I have a couple of tickets to the Giants game with the Dodgers on Sunday afternoon. Ellen's going shopping with a friend. You want to go to the game with me? You could drive back to

Reno after the game."

"Maybe he doesn't like baseball, Sonny," Ellen said.

"Oh no, I love baseball," Cody said. "Thanks, Sonny, I'd like to go. Have you ever been to Wrigley Field or Fenway?" The conversation turned to baseball stadiums they had visited, and games and players they had seen.

"You should have been here when Mays and McCovey and Marichal were playing for the Giants," Sonny said. "Now that was baseball. The hottest games were with the Dodgers, when L.A. had Koufax and Drysdale. I saw Marichal hook up one night with Drysdale—what a game. The Giants won and I was hoarse the next day at work."

As the two men reviewed the baseball highlights of the last thirty years, Ellen and Lacey smiled at each other and talked about Ellen's latest shopping trip and Lacey's work. The stuffed artichokes were a big hit, as were the T-bone steaks and rice pilaf that followed. Ellen brought out a large wooden bowl containing the best tossed green salad that Cody had ever tasted. The salad featured a variety of fresh gourmet vegetables from Anderson's Produce, along with several different kinds of nuts, as well as artichoke hearts, sourdough breadcrumbs, and Parmesan cheese. The salad dressing, which Ellen identified as "the house dressing," was a sensational creamy blend of secret ingredients. Lacey said she knew the recipe but wasn't allowed to tell anyone.

Ellen beamed as Cody complimented her cooking. "If you two are going to be back from the wine country in time for dinner tomorrow," she said, "I can cook you up some chili."

"Mom, do you think that cowboys only eat steak and chili?" she asked.

"I make a mean shrimp creole, too," Ellen said.

"I love shrimp creole," Cody told her, remembering what Sonny had said about Ellen's seafood dishes.

Lacey watched all of this interaction between Cody and her parents—from the toasts, to the baseball talk, to the talk about her mother's cooking—and let out a big sigh.

"Are you tired, Lacey?" her mother asked.

"No," Lacey replied, "it's just been such a big day. Lots of surprises. Not only did Cody appear out of the blue, he became the local hero of the day. And he has one more surprise coming."

"What's that?" Cody asked.

"Mom's New York cheesecake," Lacey answered.

"New York cheesecake, in San Francisco?"

"Of course, it's Mom's specialty."

Ellen brought out the cheesecake and gave Cody a wedge that was twice the size of anyone else's. Then she sat and watched him eat every bite while Lacey disappeared into the kitchen and returned with steaming coffee. The cheesecake was so good that Cody was speechless. All he could do was grin and hum. After every bite he would savor the taste and hum a little more. Cody laughed at himself and all his humming, but just kept going till every crumb on his plate had disappeared.

"You'd better call the newspapers, Cody," Lacey said, handing him the names and phone numbers that Adrienne had relayed. "Your public is waiting."

"I guess so." Cody excused himself and went to use the phone in the living room. When his calls were completed, Lacey and her parents were in the family room awaiting his news.

"Did you answer all their questions?" Lacey asked.

"I tried. They were nice. They want to get their pictures, but I told them I'd be out of town tomorrow and that they'd have to wait till Sunday."

"Anything else?" Lacey asked.

"Well, then there's the mayor's office."

"The mayor?" Sonny asked.

"It seems the mayor caught the interview tonight on TV and the reporter says the mayor wants to meet me and give me some kind of award."

"And when is this happening?" Ellen asked.

"Whenever it's convenient for me, they said. I don't want to disrupt your weekend."

"Don't worry about that," Sonny said. "I have a friend in the mayor's office. If he wants to give you an award he'll have to do it at the ball game. You're going to be with Lacey all day tomorrow, and we're not going to let the mayor cancel our baseball plans. I'll call my friend tomorrow and let him know. The mayor will probably go for it—it's worth a few thousand votes, I'd say, even if the fans enjoy booing the mayor when he's introduced. I've never been at a game where the politicians were introduced and some fans didn't boo. I guess they're just warming up before the umpires come out."

Cody liked Sonny Anderson. Because he was an only child, and because his father had died when he was three, Cody tended to look for substitute siblings and parents. Charley Meyers was the older brother he had never had, and maybe Sonny was the father he had never known. And perhaps Donna Cooper was a wild younger sister that he had found in Reno. Then there was Lacey. Cody now knew where she got her good looks, her high spirits, and her love of life. Sonny and Ellen were happy with their lives and generous to others, and they had welcomed this cowboy into their home like a long absent son.

After they watched the cable car story again on the late news, and Cody soaked his right ankle in a pan of hot water, and Lacey escorted Cody to the guest room, Cody felt suddenly tired. Was this really the same day that had started like a regular Friday workday at Parker's? If Charley hadn't grown tired of having a lovesick cowboy around in Reno, would the little girl on Powell Street still be alive right now? If Cody had not stayed for a second beer with the group of tourists at Fisherman's Wharf, would he have been on a different cable car?

"What are you thinking, cowboy?" Lacey asked

"I was just thinking about all the coincidences today. You know, all the things that had to happen so that I could be on that particular cable car at the moment the kid walked into the street. Kind of eerie, if you stop to think about it. And it all started with my moping around and missing you."

"That's a nice thing to say," Lacey said, and she moved closer to kiss him. "You have a good rest. If you need anything I'll be down the hall. We'll have the whole day together tomorrow. Just like a Saturday in Reno."

"Good night, missy," Cody said as Lacey left. Before he fell asleep, Cody thought again about how Charley had been so insistent that he go to San Francisco today, and not wait until Saturday. Charley, as usual, had been right. Saturday would have been too late.

21 Donna

"Where's the Lone Star..."

"Wake up, cowboy. Breakfast is almost ready." Cody had been riding a cable car in his dreams, and in this dream he had looked out on the sidewalk and seen Victor Kleindich walking arm in arm with Lacey. He was just about to leap off and confront Victor when Lacey's voice made the cable car fade and he opened his eyes to see her sitting on the side of the bed, her green eyes gazing at him.

"Bacon in the pan, coffee in the pot," she said, trying to entice him to wake up and join her for breakfast.

"Good morning," he said.

"Have breakfast with me and I'll show you the wine country today," she said.

"Sounds like a good deal," Cody said. "How much will I owe you?"

"The breakfast is on the house," Lacey answered. "The tour is free as long as you drive. I want to ride in your pickup again."

"Is it me you missed, or the truck?"

"Both, I guess," Lacey said, and she reached down and mussed his hair. "How's the ankle?" Lacey felt Cody's ankle through the sheet. "It doesn't seem swollen."

"I think it's all right," Cody said. "Just feels a little sore."

"Good. Come on into the kitchen when you're ready. Dad's already gone to work. Mom's making you bacon and pancakes with real maple syrup."

"Lacey," Cody said, "does Victor know I'm in town? Do you think he'll be upset?"

"Why would he be upset?"

"I don't know," Cody said, "maybe because I'm pulling you away from the work."

"Or away from him?"

"I didn't say that."

"No," Lacey said, "but maybe you were thinking it. Now who's worrying?"

"I just dreamed about Victor, that's all."

"Hey, you're supposed to be dreaming about me."

"You were there too," Cody said. "Never mind. It's not important." He smiled at Lacey and she kissed him on the cheek, and that was the end of the Victor talk.

When Cody stepped out of the shower he heard the phone ring and Lacey telling her mother she would grab it. Cody put on a clean pair of jeans and a shirt that he had brought with him, then walked down the hall toward the kitchen.

"You'll never guess who that was," Lacey said when she saw him.

"Good morning, Cody," Ellen said as she flipped another pancake.

"Good morning, Mrs. Anderson. So, Lacey, who was calling?"

"Would you believe the White House? Would you believe they heard about your heroics and want you to fly to Washington next week? Would you believe they have a special medal they give to cowboys who jump off cable cars to save little kids?"

"No, I wouldn't believe it," Cody said.

"Stop teasing him and let him eat his breakfast," Ellen said.

"Oh, Mom, don't spoil my fun," Lacey said. "Actually it was Dad. He talked to his friend in the mayor's office, and they're setting up your award deal for the ballpark tomorrow. They want you and Dad to sit down in the front row box seats with the mayor."

"Do I get to throw out the first pitch?" Cody asked. "That would be better than going to the White House."

"How did you guess?" Lacey asked. "You'd better warm up with Dad tomorrow before you go to the game. You can use my old glove."

"Great!" Cody said.

"You two have a seat," said Ellen, as she brought the pancakes and bacon to the breakfast nook. "I hope you like blueberry pancakes, Cody. The blueberries are big and fresh."

"Yes, ma'am," Cody said. As he sat down he noticed the morning paper next to his plate.

"Anything interesting in the paper?" Lacey asked.

There it was, right on the front page, below the fold. Cody recognized the little girl and the mother in the photograph first, then began to read the article.

Cody chuckled. "It calls me the 'mysterious cowboy.'"

"Well, you are," Lacey said.

Cody read some more. "Somebody said I jumped over 15 feet to save the kid. That'll probably get longer every time they tell the story."

"It didn't say anything about your ankle," Lacey said.

"I didn't tell them. If they knew I twisted my ankle they'd probably turn it into a broken leg."

Cody went back to the article. "What? How did they find out I was doing my John Wayne impression at Fisherman's Wharf?"

"I thought you must have told the reporter last night on the phone," Lacey said.

"No way," Cody said. "It had to be one of the tourists on the cable car. They must have called the paper. Those guys."

"Either your John Wayne has gotten a lot better, or they remembered it because it was the worst they'd ever seen," Lacey said. "Did you do the walk, too, or just the voice?"

"Both," Cody said. "You should have seen it. I think it was the best one

I've ever done. I don't know why, but I think it was because I was feeling so good and because they were a great audience."

"Tell me, Cody, did they offer to buy you lunch before you did your John Wayne impression, or after?"

"Never mind," Cody said quickly. "Let's eat."

Ellen poured the coffee, then whispered something in Cody's ear.

"Come on, Mom, no secrets," Lacey complained.

"Please?" Ellen begged Cody. "As a favor to me? Just pretend I'm one of the tourists and we're at Fisherman's Wharf."

"Oh no, Mom, you didn't ask him to do John Wayne, did you? You don't know what you've started."

But it was too late. Lacey was forced to eat breakfast with John Wayne instead of Cody. Ellen Anderson was delighted, but Lacey just looked up at the ceiling and shook her head. During the second cup of coffee, Ellen pretended she was the television reporter and began to interview Cody.

"Tell me, cowboy," she began, "why did you jump off that cable car?"

"Well," Cody answered in his deep John Wayne voice, "a man's gotta do what he thinks is right."

Lacey tried not to encourage him, but she could not help laughing at Cody.

"Someone said you broke your leg," Ellen continued the interview.

"Shucks, ma'am, a little thing like that's not gonna stop me. I've gotta ride out and round up a few strays before this day's over. Just pass me another one of those flapjacks, if you will, and I'll be on my way."

"Cody, stop it," Lacey said. "Give me a break." She had put her hands over her ears, but Cody had just leaned closer and talked louder.

"How about another cup of cowboy coffee?" Ellen asked.

"Thanks, ma'am. It's mighty nice of you to feed me like this. I haven't had a good home cooked meal since..."

"Since last night," Lacey interrupted.

"Come to think of it, you're right," Cody said. "That was some good eatin', all right. Looked like a side of beef and half a garden of vegetables. Gives a fellow the strength to round up the dogies and take 'em to Missouri."

"Not today, cowboy," Lacey said. "Today you're taking me to the wine country. All you have to round up is me, and I'll make it easy for you to catch me."

After thanking Ellen for the delicious breakfast, and returning to his own voice and walk, limping only slightly, Cody escorted Lacey to his blue Dodge pickup. They waved goodbye and Cody pointed the truck toward Golden Gate Park. Lacey tried to point out various features as they drove through the large city park, but the park and the city were wrapped in a cold morning fog. Cody said he expected to see Mr. Hyde jump out from behind a tree, but Lacey said that was London. Finally she gave up and directed Cody toward the Golden Gate Bridge. Lacey said they could return this way later in the day, after the fog had burned off, so that Cody could actually see the bridge and the city.

Cody drove up through Marin County, headed east above San Pablo Bay, then turned north again toward Sonoma and the Valley of the Moon. In the town of Sonoma they stopped and walked around the central plaza. Cody was happy to be out of the fog and feel the warm August sun.

"Are we going to be shopping this morning?" Cody asked, following Lacey into a small crafts shop.

"Not really," Lacey said. "If we were on a shopping trip, I don't think you could keep up with me."

"Are you one of those marathon shoppers?"

"You bet," Lacey said, smiling. "You might keep me in sight for a while, but eventually you'd hit the wall. No, I was just thinking we should check out our first winery. Sebastiani is right here in town. Are you ready?"

"Are we too early?" Cody asked.

"No, they're probably waiting for us right now."

At the Sebastiani winery, Cody and Lacey took the tour with a small group of visitors. This was Cody's first trip to a winery, and he listened carefully as the tour guide explained the wine making process. At the end of the tour, when they moved toward the tasting room, Lacey whispered some instructions to Cody.

"When they ask you which wines you want to taste, just don't say, 'Where's the Lone Star?'"

Cody was surprised, but he only adjusted his black cowboy hat and said "Yes, ma'am." How had she known what he was planning to ask?

As they sampled the first wine, a chenin blanc, Cody licked his lips. "This is outstanding," he said to Lacey.

"I don't know why, but wine always tastes better at the winery, after you've taken the tour," she said.

"Breweries are like that, too," Cody said. "I visited a Coors brewery once, on a hot summer day. I still remember how that beer tasted."

They sampled two more wines before leaving. "Hey, this is fun," Cody said. "Where to now?"

"Let's go up to Glen Ellen," Lacey said. "I want to show you Jack London's home. He's the one who named this the Valley of the Moon."

"I used to read his books when I was a boy," Cody said. "*The Call of the Wild. White Fang.*"

"In his time he was the most famous writer in the world," Lacey said. "I guess he was more famous even than you."

"Did he jump off cable cars, too?" Cody asked.

"I don't know, but he was an oyster raider, a gold prospector, and a war correspondent, among other things."

"Cowboy?"

Lacey laughed. "Probably, in his spare time. I don't think he ever tried his hand at steer decorating, though."

Cody's pickup wound its way through the hills west of Glen Ellen until it reached the Jack London State Historic Park. They wandered through the museum in the House of Happy Walls, which had been built by London's wife after his death in 1916. Cody stopped to read about each exhibit.

"He was only forty when he died," Cody said.

"But he led a very full life," Lacey said. "They say he invented himself, like the Great Gatsby."

"Scott Fitzgerald," Cody said.

"Very good, cowboy," Lacey said.

"Everyone's read that," Cody said. "Or seen the movie. Do you think a person can really invent himself?"

"Sure," Lacey said. "You're born in a certain place, to certain parents, and a certain set of circumstances, and at some point you decide who you're going to be. You usually have to travel around and taste different ways of living. Before you know it you're this new person. Gatsby grew up in the Midwest and planned his whole life. He had a dream and followed it wherever it led him, for better or worse."

"I guess you're right," Cody said. "I always remember the daily outline that Gatsby wrote as a boy. He had every hour planned for self-improvement. I think the seeds are planted early in life."

"Sometimes," Lacey said. "When I was a little girl I always wanted to follow my father into the produce business. Somewhere along the way I developed other interests."

Lacey pointed to one of the photographs. "That Jack London was a handsome devil. He looks a little bit like Charley Meyers in this one, don't you think?"

Cody stared at the photograph. "I guess so. Don't tell Charley."

Cody and Lacey walked out of the museum and along a trail. About a mile later they reached the stone ruins of Wolf House.

"This place is so sad," Lacey said. "I always come back here and I always feel the same emotions when I'm here."

"So this was his dream house?"

"It burned before Jack and Charmian could move into it. I always try to imagine how that felt. Did you ever build a dream and have it taken from you suddenly?"

Cody stared at the rock walls and thought back over his life. "I guess not. My father died suddenly, and my mother died when I was six. I guess that's the closest. I love my Aunt Alice and Uncle Max, and they treated me well, but they're not my parents." Cody looked around at the ruins. "You can build another house, but it's not the same."

Lacey took Cody's hand and they walked to Jack London's grave, then retraced their steps down the trail to the museum. Once inside the pickup, Lacey leaned over and kissed Cody on the cheek.

"What was that for?" Cody asked.

"Just felt like it," Lacey said. "Thanks for bringing me here."

"No, thank you," Cody said. "When I woke up this morning I didn't know we'd be visiting Jack London. I thought we were just visiting wineries."

"Well, you introduced me to the cemetery in Virginia City, so I thought I should return the favor. I don't know why, but places like this are very romantic."

"He led a romantic life," Cody said.

"You won't see any tumbleweeds rolling through here, though," Lacey said. "It's not dry enough."

"But there are spirits around, especially down at the ruins."

"You felt that, too?" Lacey asked. Cody nodded and drove back along the same winding road.

Lacey took out the CDs from the glove compartment and was looking through them. "Where's the CD with the old cowboy songs?" she asked.

"Did you want to hear 'Red River Valley'?" Cody asked.

"No, 'Streets of Laredo,'" Lacey said.

"Dying cowboy songs?" Cody asked.

"I can't find the CD," Lacey said.

"That's because Charley has it."

"Oh darn," Lacey said. "Is Charley listening to dying cowboy songs now?"

"No," Cody said, "it's a long story."

"That's all right, we have a way to go before the next winery. Tell me the long story."

"He's taking care of the CD for me," Cody said.

"He's what?"

"Taking care of it for me. That's what he said anyway." Cody paused, reflecting on Charley's behavior. "I think he was tired of listening to that song, that's all."

"'Streets of Laredo'?" Lacey asked.

"No, the other one. 'Red River Valley.'"

Lacey smiled. "I see now. How often were you playing it?"

"Not that often, really," Cody said.

"Too often for Charley, I imagine. Is that why he threw you out of the store and sent you to San Francisco?"

"I suppose. Do you think the CD is safe with Charley?"

"Oh sure," Lacey answered. "If he loses it, I'll buy you another copy."

Lacey put in the Willie Nelson CD, and they sang along with the Western ballads.

"You should have been on the cable car yesterday," Cody said between songs. "Someone started singing 'Mama, Don't Let Your Babies Grow Up to Be Cowboys,' and before you knew it everyone was singing it."

"My favorite is 'My Heroes Have Always Been Cowboys,'" Lacey said. "Even before you saved that little girl's life." Cody kept driving and singing.

One winery and one picnic lunch later, they were cruising through the Napa Valley and Cody had become more talkative than usual. Lacey had never pushed him to tell her everything about his life. She knew that he had grown up in Iowa, that his parents had died when he was a small boy, that he had been raised by his aunt and uncle, that he had gone to a small Midwestern college, that he had never been married, that he had moved to Reno and taken up the cowboy life. She did not know how recently he had moved to Reno.

What she did know, and all that really mattered to her, was that she loved him for who he was now. If Cody had a mysterious past, that was all right. Lacey thought that if they had been living some kind of 19th century, Wild West life, then Cody might have killed a man back in Abilene and was on the run from the law. What role would she have played back then? Did they have women lawyers in Reno then? She doubted it. She couldn't see herself as a dancehall girl. Donna yes, but not Lacey. A schoolteacher? There weren't too many careers open to women then.

If she had hooked up with Cody, would they have had a ranch near Reno? Would they have been outlaws together, hiding out at the Lazy J with Mel and Harm? Or would they have been up at Virginia City, seeking their fortune? If that were true, then they would have been buried alongside each other in the old cemetery up there. They might be a couple of tumbleweeds drifting along together, just like that old song. Lacey shivered.

"Are you cold?" Cody asked.

"I'm fine," Lacey said. "Tell me more about Iowa."

Cody told her about his mother taking him to Western movies, about how his full name was Alan Cody West, but that he liked his middle name better and decided to use that. Lacey commented that "Alan" was a good name, but that she liked "Cody" much better. Lacey asked if he had been named for Buffalo Bill Cody. Cody said only his parents knew the answer to that one, and they had never told him, and now he would never know. He said that Buffalo Bill was a showman, an entirely different kind of person from himself. Lacey said that there was no nickname for "Cody," unless it was "Cowboy."

Just about then they arrived at the Charles Krug winery, where the tour guide was very friendly, and very amusing, and in the tasting room he brought out some of the best wines for tasting. They asked Cody and Lacey, the two people on the tour dressed as cowboy and cowgirl, where they were from. Cody answered "Reno," and Lacey added, "by way of Iowa and San Francisco." The tour guide apologized that they didn't have any Lone Star, and Cody laughed and said that was all right. Lacey told the tour guide she'd have to find him a Lone Star before the day was over, "or else he'll get kind of ornery." It was that kind of tasting session.

When they left Charles Krug, Lacey, who had been more restrained than Cody in the tasting rooms that day, offered to drive. "I'll let you drive on one condition," Cody said.

"What's that, cowboy? Do I have to promise not to wreck your beautiful truck?"

"No, I trust your driving. You have to promise to do your Donna Cooper impression."

"My what? I don't do a Donna Cooper impression."

"Well, now you do," Cody said. "You be Donna and I'll be Charley."

"This should be good. Give me the keys."

"Yes, ma'am," Cody said and gave Lacey his best Charley Meyers salute.

Lacey drove back onto the highway and they headed down the road for the Christian Brothers winery. Cody kept staring at her. "You can start anytime," he said.

"I don't have the big hair to do Donna," Lacey protested.

"You don't need the big hair, just think like a rodeo queen and you'll be fine."

Lacey took a deep breath. She looked over at Cody, tilted her head a bit, and then flashed her biggest smile.

"That's it!" Cody shouted. "Excuse me, ma'am," he continued in a deeper, gravelly voice, "are you running for Miss Reno Rodeo?"

Cody started laughing and couldn't continue. Lacey found she had to stare straight ahead at the road, because each time her eyes met Cody's she started cracking up.

As they pulled into the Christian Brothers parking lot, Lacey told Cody that this would have to be their last tasting session today. "Are you going to just throw me in the back of the pickup after this one?" Cody asked.

"I may have to. Once you're in the back there I'll probably have to tie you down."

"That sounds interesting," Cody said. "What did you have in mind?"

"Hush up," Lacey said. "You behave. This is Christian Brothers, so don't be a devil."

After the tour, after the tasting session, Cody led Lacey into the gift shop. He noticed the lady behind the counter smiling at them.

"Nice shop you have here, ma'am," Cody said. "My name's Cody West."

"Howdy, cowboy. My name's Sylvia. Can I show you something?"

"Well, Sylvia," Cody said, "I need to find something special for my favorite cowgirl here."

"That's not necessary, Cody," Lacey said. "Don't mind him, Sylvia, he's just feeling unusually happy this afternoon."

"Something special," Cody repeated. Lacey knew it would do no good to argue.

"Take a look at these special wine glasses," Sylvia said, pointing out the best glasses in the shop.

"I like these," Cody said. "They're mighty pretty. And mighty tall."

"Elegant, aren't they?" Sylvia said, holding them up to the light. "A couple of these would give you years of enjoyment. You should see the way a good wine looks in these."

"Probably taste better in them, too," Cody said.

"You should be a salesman," Lacey told him.

"Do you like these?" Cody asked her.

"They're beautiful, but they're probably too expensive," Lacey said. But it was too late. Cody was already taking out his wallet.

"We'll take eight of them," Cody said.

"Wait a minute, two's enough," Lacey said.

"Eight," Cody said.

"Two," Lacey repeated.

"How about four?" Sylvia asked.

"Four's good," Lacey said. "We can use them tonight with my folks."

Sylvia carefully wrapped up four of the tall wine glasses.

"Thank you, cowboy," Lacey said. "You're so nice to me."

"Y'all have a good day," Sylvia called after them as they left the gift shop.

"You, too, Sylvia," Cody said. "Thanks for showing us the good stuff."

Back outside, at the pickup, Cody waited for Lacey to throw him in the back and tie him down. When she simply climbed behind the wheel instead, he was a little disappointed. "I thought you were going to tie me down," Cody said, exaggerating his disappointment.

"Later, cowboy, if you're lucky," Lacey said, and winked. Cody settled in for the ride back to San Francisco. It was late afternoon now and the sun was beginning to light the valley in a softer way.

Cody gazed out the window at the light and shadows of the passing vineyards. "All those grapes," he said. "I didn't miss my Lone Star at all."

22 Donna

"My heroes have always been cowboys…"

That Sunday evening, the day after their trip to Wolf House and the wineries, Cody was back on the road to Reno and Lacey was back at her parents' home in San Francisco after spending the entire day downtown at her office reading depositions and catching up on her trial preparation. Lacey sat at a small desk in her bedroom. The weekend had been unusually eventful, and she had been meaning to write to me anyway, so she decided to write the letter now. She took out her good stationery and began.

> *Dear Donna,*
>
> *I'm sorry I haven't written before. This crazy trial has taken up almost all of my time the past few weeks. Cody drove over Friday, so I took a whole day away from the office yesterday. I really needed the break. I'll be glad when the trial's over and I can get back to Reno. I miss you and Charley, and Mel and Harm, and everyone there.*

I hope that everything's going well with you. You've been such a good friend, especially when I was new in Reno and needed a friend. Thanks for helping me with the cowgirl lessons. I can't wait to get back to the Lazy J and do some riding with you and the twins.

You're probably wondering how this weekend went. Just believe me, everything that I'm about to tell you is true, even if it sounds incredible. Cody surprised me at work on Friday afternoon. Then he went off to ride the cable cars while I finished up at the office. When he came back he was limping and told me he'd jumped off the cable car before it stopped. Bucked off. I didn't think much of it until we got back to my mom and dad's home and Cody was on the news. It seems he jumped off the cable car to save a little girl who had wandered out into the street and was about to be hit by a truck. They had a TV news crew there and they interviewed Cody and the mother and the passengers. The newspapers called, and the mayor's office. Cody was a big hero. My mom and dad were so impressed, I thought they were going to adopt him.

Yesterday Cody and I drove up to the wine country and had a great time. I showed him Jack London's house in Glen Ellen. It was just as romantic as the Virginia City cemetery! I lost count of how many wineries we visited, but every one had a tasting room. Cody enjoyed the wine, a little too much. I offered to drive after a while and he just rode along looking at all those grapes and talking like Charley. His Charley Meyers is better than his John Wayne. What a kick! We stopped at the gift shop at Christian Brothers and he insisted on buying me four beautiful tall wine glasses. I think the gift shop lady was quite amused by her cowboy customer.

We drove back and had another nice dinner with my folks. My mom went all out feeding Cody. That cowboy can eat. I took him for a drive around the city last night to see the lights, and we ended up parking on a dark street near Coit Tower. I swear,

Donna, it was just like being a teenager again.

This morning we all went to an early church service at Grace Cathedral, then I went on to work. I heard that my dad and Cody took a couple of gloves and a baseball to Golden Gate Park and were warming up Cody's arm for the Giants game. I don't know if my mom was calling balls and strikes at the park, but I can imagine. Cody had to warm up because the Giants invited him to throw out the first pitch this afternoon, before the game with the Dodgers.

Cody and my dad sat down in the front with the mayor and with the little girl and her mother. They gave Cody a Giants cap, but he decided to wear his cowboy hat instead. The weather was warm and there was a big crowd there. I had the game on at the office, on my little portable, and some of us were watching it when we could. When they introduced Cody and the little girl, and told how he had saved her life by jumping in front of a truck, the crowd stood and roared. Cody took off his cowboy hat and waved it around.

They asked him to walk out to the mound to throw the first pitch, and he took the little girl's hand and had her walk out there with him. He let her throw the first pitch—it went about fifteen feet—then he picked up the ball and showed her how it's done. I guess he put some heat on it, and everybody laughed and cheered some more when the Giants catcher pretended to fall backwards from the impact.

Cody waved his hat some more, then he took the girl's hand and they walked off the mound and back to the box seats. I think at that moment the crowd would have elected him mayor, if they could. The mayor seemed a bit uneasy anyway.

I went back to reading depositions, and the rest of the story I heard from my dad over dinner this evening. He said that they had trouble watching the game because people kept coming down and asking for autographs. The people who came down generally ignored the mayor, they just wanted to shake Cody's hand and ask him for his autograph. The mayor was a good sport about it; he even asked Cody to autograph his program. I heard that by the end of the game the little girl was calling Cody "my cowboy." And all this time I thought he was my cowboy!

Dad said that Cody even brought the Giants good luck. They rallied in the bottom of the ninth to beat the Dodgers. There was a foul ball in that inning that came down in the first row, and the Dodger catcher was about to grab it, but Cody reached up and caught it first. I think the crowd would have voted for Cody for President at that point. His catch saved the inning, because on the next pitch the Giant batter hit one off the wall in centerfield and everybody went home happy. Except the Dodgers, that is.

I don't know why, but when my dad told me about Cody's catch in the ninth I wasn't at all surprised. I guess I've come to expect that sort of thing from Cody. He's one lucky cowboy.

Hi again. I just had to run and catch the phone. That was Cody, calling from Reno. He had a quiet trip back, he said. No cable cars, no wineries, no baseballs. I miss him already, but I'll be back in Reno in a few weeks when the trial's over. He's running up his telephone bill right now, because my mom insisted on talking to him, and my dad's waiting his turn. I guess they might adopt him after all. All through dinner this evening all they could talk about was Cody this, and Cody that, what a great guy he was, and how lucky I was to have met him, and on and on. I guess it's better than if they didn't like him, then we'd have a problem.

Well, it's getting late. If you have time write me a letter and let me know how everything's going. Say hello to Charley for me, and Mel and Harm. Take care of yourself. See you soon.

Love,
Lacey

★

A week later, I was at home in Reno, rereading Lacey's letter. I picked up a pen, grabbed my stationery, and wrote my reply.

"*Dear Lacey,*

Thanks for your letter. I know how busy you are. That was the most entertaining letter I've read in a long time. By the time it arrived I had already read about Cody's heroics. The Associated Press must have picked up the story from the San Francisco papers, and it was in the Reno paper on Monday morning. Charley spotted it first and called me. We decided that there could be only one Cody West jumping off cable cars in San Francisco. Charley remembered that Cody's favorite rodeo event is the steer wrestling, and he figured that studying the steer wrestlers probably helped him when the time came for him to jump off that cable car.

We are very proud of him, of course. Charley had the story framed—both the one from the Reno paper and the Sunday story from the San Francisco paper, along with a news photo of Cody throwing the first pitch at the game—and hung it all up on the wall near the front counter at Parker's. Everyone who walks in has to stop and read the story. Charley stands there, very serious, while the customer reads it, then tells them that's his good friend Cody, who works "right here at Parker's." I've been going over there this week just to hang around and watch it all. If you were here we'd have lots of good free entertainment at the store. Cody's been hiding out at Bob Morgan's this week. He'd rather haul hay around than face all the attention in town. After the noise dies down I guess he'll come back to Parker's.

I was out riding with Mel and Harm this morning, and they asked about you. I told them you could take care of yourself, but that running around with Cody seemed like a handful.

Sounds as if you had a good time visiting all those wineries. The next time you have to take the keys and drive him back to the city, just throw him in the back of the truck and tie him down. I find that works with Darryl.

Charley said something about misplacing one of Cody's CDs, the one with the old cowboy songs on it. He said he told Cody not to worry about it, that he'd probably find it as soon as you returned to Reno. What's that all about?

I bought a new Western shirt last week. It's kind of a tribute to the state of Texas—it's got this big Lone Star flag on the back and lots of Texas stuff on the front, like longhorns and horned toads, but tasteful. You'll have to see it next month when you come back. Mel and Harm want to get ones just like it. Maybe we can find one for you too. If we wear them in the rodeo parade next year folks will think we're some kind of riding team from Texas, in town to perform in the rodeo.

Your parents sound like a lot of fun. You should invite them to come visit Reno after you return. We could show them the sights, maybe get them up on horses. Charley can fix 'em up with some Western clothes if they don't have any. I bet they'd enjoy dancing at The Lucky Cowboy.

Well, Lacey, I'll close now. Hang in there. I'm sure you'll win your case and be back in Reno before you know it. Watch out for that Victor. I know you have to work with him but don't let him get any ideas.

Love,
Donna

P.S. Don't worry about Cody. I never saw anyone so crazy in love before. What's your secret?!"

23 Donna

"A discouraging word..."

In the first week of September, just before the trial was scheduled to open, Lacey uncovered some evidence in the case that made her a star in her law firm. With the evidence, Victor Kleindich was able to conduct some major negotiating with the defendants' attorney. He put some of his big cards on the table and hinted that he was still holding others. Victor told the other side that they could settle now and avoid the costs, and risks, of going to trial, or they could wait and see the other cards in court. Lacey sat in on the meeting. She stared at the other attorney with cold green eyes and a look of firm determination.

In the end, the other side blinked. Victor and Lacey won a big settlement for their client. Lacey received the praise of her colleagues at the firm and a look of gratitude from her client that she would never forget. Victor took her out to dinner that night to celebrate and praised her generously for her work on the case. He was the kind of guy you wouldn't want to be around for a second if he lost a case, but as a winner he was more tolerable. After dinner

Victor drove Lacey home and stole a kiss in the car when she wasn't looking. She tried not to encourage him, but you can guess what romantic fantasies were playing in the guy's head.

The victory restored Lacey's commitment to her career. And it brought her a special bonus—she could return to Reno several weeks earlier than anyone had expected.

Lacey sailed out of the office the day after the settlement and drove home to pack for the trip back to Reno. It was still mid-morning and she wanted to get to Reno before Cody left Parker's for the day. She owed him a good surprise. Lacey packed in a rush, kissed her mom goodbye, and was soon on the Bay Bridge and on the way to Nevada.

As she raced up the interstate toward Sacramento, Lacey thought about the past few weeks in San Francisco. What had it been all about? When she had found out in July that she was going to be leaving Reno for two or three months, she saw it as bad news, tempered only by the fact that she could spend some time with her family. When Cody dropped in on her suddenly that Friday afternoon in August, however, he brought his usual good luck with him.

Because Lacey was working in San Francisco, her parents were able to meet Cody, and under the most favorable circumstances imaginable. If Sonny and Ellen had been the type of parents who would devise a test for their daughter's suitors, which they were not, surely Cody would have passed the test the moment he launched himself from the cable car to save the little girl on Powell Street. Lacey realized too that the separation had been a more conventional test, that it had only strengthened their attraction to each other. And finally, she had won a big settlement for her client, which gave her the satisfaction and excitement that she had been missing in her career.

Lacey reached for her new Willie Nelson CD, which she had bought after Cody had returned to Reno in August. It was the same songs that they had listened to during the trip to the wine country. Lacey pushed the button till she found the one song she was wanted to hear just now. It told the story of someone who grew up dreaming of being a cowboy, but it told her story as well. Lacey sang along with the refrain, "My heroes have always been cowboys." In the middle of the song she reached over and pushed the repeat button. This was a song she could hear over and over and not get tired of. It was a sweet, sad ballad, but the music only made her smile.

By the time Lacey reached Reno it was late afternoon. She drove straight downtown, found a place to park, and walked quickly to Parker's. She wanted to see the look on Cody's face when he saw her walk in the door. She opened the door slowly and peeked inside. There was Charley at the front counter, but she couldn't see Cody. She walked up to the counter and said, "Howdy, Charley."

Charley, a little startled but recognizing the voice, turned and said, "Howdy yourself. What are you doing here? Are you here for the weekend?"

"No," Lacey said, "we got the case settled before it could go to trial. I packed this morning and drove over to surprise everyone. Where's Cody?"

Charley paused. "You just missed him. He was here earlier."

"Is he working out at Bob Morgan's?" Lacey asked.

"Well, no," Charley said. "He had to leave town kind of suddenly. He got a call from his aunt in Iowa yesterday. It seems there was some family trouble back there. Cody said his Uncle Max had open heart surgery and that he needed to go back and see him, and see if his aunt needed his help. They're the ones who raised him, you know."

"He told me," Lacey said. She felt as if all the air had gone out of her. She leaned both hands on the counter and looked blankly at Charley.

"I'm sorry," Charley said. "Cody said he'd call you tonight when you were home and tell you all about it. He asked me to tell you not to worry, that he'd try to come back as soon as he could. We thought you'd be in San Francisco at least another month."

Lacey saw Cody's newspaper clippings hanging in a large frame on the wall near the counter. She walked over and stared at the picture of Cody on the pitcher's mound at the ballpark, wearing his black cowboy hat and watching the little girl throw the baseball. She didn't want to cry, but she did. She felt Charley's hand patting her on the shoulder.

"Don't worry, he'll be back," Charley said. "He's so crazy about you that nothing's going to stop him from returning to Reno."

Lacey turned and buried her face in Charley chest. She couldn't stop crying. Charley reached for the phone and punched in a number. My number.

"Hi, Donna. It's Charley. Can you come over to the store? Lacey's here. She settled her case and drove in to surprise Cody. I told her about the business in Iowa. You can probably hear her crying." Charley handed Lacey a box of tissues. "We'll wait here," he said into the phone.

"Oh, Charley," Lacey said, "I'm being such a baby."

"No, you're not," Charley said. "I miss him too, the big galoot."

Fifteen minutes later I walked into Parker's. Charley had been smart to enlist my help. If someone needs major comforting, I'm the person to call. I learned a lot growing up just watching my mom. I don't mean to brag, but I do have a way of sharing your unhappiness and taking most of the burden on myself. I began by putting my arms around Lacey, assuring her that Cody would be back soon, and telling her not to worry about him. After all, I told her, he's the luckiest cowboy around. When Lacey's tears kept flowing, I began crying too, but not in the same way. My crying, as anyone who knows me might have predicted, was more towards the flamboyant side of the scale. I cried more tears and larger tears. My sobbing was about twice as loud as Lacey's. Lacey finally stopped crying and starting watching me cry. Then she put her arms around me and began comforting me, telling me all the things I had just told her. I could see that Charley was impressed. Leave it to me to handle any crisis.

"Say, I almost forgot," Charley said, after all the crying had subsided, "Cody left this note for you, in case you got back to Reno before he did. He handed a sealed envelope to Lacey, who stared at it a long time before finally opening it. She read the short note and then started crying again, so I had to come to the rescue once more.

"Not more bad news, I hope," Charley said.

Lacey reached for another tissue and wiped her eyes. "Oh, Charley, he says he loves me. He really knows how to make me cry."

"The rat," I said.

"Sounds like good news to me. He just got right to the point," Charley said.

"Can't you see, Charley," I said, "that's why she's crying."

Charley scratched his head. I think he decided right then to leave the comforting business to me. I suggested that Lacey and I go somewhere

where we could sit and talk. Lacey thanked Charley for all the tissues she had destroyed, then kissed him on the cheek and walked out with me. Calm returned to Parker's, and the only remaining evidence of the emotional scene that had just occurred was a wastebasket filled with tissues.

Lacey and I walked up Virginia Street, crossed the railroad tracks, and entered the Eldorado. We walked past the blackjack tables and roulette wheels and all the slot machines and video poker machines, and took the escalator to the second floor, where we found a dark, quiet booth in the international restaurant. When the cocktail waitress asked us what we wanted, I ordered a Coke for myself and a Fighting Cowgirl for Lacey.

"Excuse me?" the cocktail waitress said.

"You never heard of a Fighting Cowgirl?" I asked.

"No, but if you tell me what's in it I'm sure we can make you one." I carefully told her the forbidding list of ingredients.

"No rattlesnake venom?" the waitress asked.

"Not today, thank you," I said. "That's only used in the scorned cowgirl, and we're not having any of that drink today."

After the cocktail waitress left, Lacey said, "Is that a real drink, or are you just making it up.

"Of course it's a real drink," I lied. At the moment I was interested in a greater truth. "Wait till you taste it and then tell me if it's real or not."

"Why do they call it a Fighting Cowgirl?" Lacey asked.

"Glad you asked." I had started this Fighting Cowgirl business, so I guess I had to finish it. "There are two theories about that. One theory says that after a cowgirl has one of them she's ready to fight anyone. The second theory says that if you have a real fighting cowgirl on your hands you should give her one of these drinks because that's the only way to calm her down."

"I don't feel like fighting anyone," Lacey said.

"That's right. I subscribe to the first theory myself. After you've had one of these you'll be ready to fight anyone. It'll make you stronger. You're at a low point right now, and you need some strong medicine. The best medicine would be if Cody waltzed in here right now and sat down next to you. But that's not going to happen. Not just now. In the meantime we have to make you strong. You have to be one tough cowgirl between now and the day he returns."

"Donna, you're amazing," Lacey said.

"I know." I smiled at her. "There's just one thing I need to warn you about. After you drink your Fighting Cowgirl, you may feel the urge to order another one, but don't give into that urge. One of these drinks will make you stronger, but a second one will make you very weak."

"Sounds like the voice of experience," Lacey said.

"Yep, very weak. Sick as a dog, actually." Sometimes I surprise even myself. I hadn't lied this much in ages. Lacey laughed. Laughter is good medicine too.

The cocktail waitress returned with two tall glasses, one with my Coke and the other with a mixture the color of sagebrush. I took the red straws out of Lacey's glass.

"You won't be needing these," I said. I raised my glass and touched it against Lacey's, then we both took a good drink.

When the steam had stopped escaping from her ears, Lacey blinked, took a deep breath, and smiled. "So that's why they call it a Fighting Cowgirl," she said.

"You bet. It's hard to describe. You just have to experience it."

Lacey looked at her glass before taking another drink. "Is this a double?" she asked.

"No, ain't no doubles," I said, shaking my head. "There's just Fighting Cowgirls. By the time you get all of the ingredients in it this is the regular size."

"I don't think it needs the rattlesnake venom, do you?" Lacey said.

"Nope. It's just about perfect the way it is."

The cocktail waitress stopped by to see if the drinks were all right—they were—and to ask if we wanted to order some food. Lacey said she hadn't had any lunch, and I asked for two menus. I suggested a deluxe cheeseburger for Lacey, saying that she needed some beef to help make her stronger, then ordered a basket of tortilla chips and salsa for the two of us.

"That's going to make you thirstier," Lacey warned me

"Don't worry about me," I said. "You're the one that needs to eat the cheeseburger before your tongue gets numb and you can't taste it. They make great flame-broiled burgers here."

"Say, Donna, why didn't you tell me about the Fighting Cowgirl before now?"

"Never needed to until today." I reached over and gave Lacey a hug.

"Thanks," she said.

"Don't thank me, just keep working on your drink. Anyway, cowgirls have to stick together. Didn't you know that?"

Lacey smiled and nodded, but a few tears began making their way down her cheeks, as if they had missed the wake-up call earlier at Parker's and decided that they should head on down the trail and hope nobody noticed they were late.

24 Donna

"Adios to the dark side..."

As much as I tried to reassure Lacey that everything would turn out all right, that Cody would come back and put her heart back together, there was a little voice in my head that kept raising doubts. If I had a friend like that, someone who always saw the dark side of things and expected the worst, I don't think they'd be my friend for long. But when it's a voice in your own head that's spotlighting the dark side, how do you adios that?

Months earlier I had taken on the job of love cop, directing the romantic traffic for my friends. For a while there I thought I was doing great. Cody and Lacey were turning into cowboy and cowgirl sweethearts. Sure, Victor Kleindich was a threat. He was like some big old horsefly that keeps pestering everybody, except better looking and better dressed, if you like that type. Victor had considerable power over Lacey's career, and he did try to make his move, but she was not encouraging him.

There were other men interested in Lacey, especially with Cody back in Iowa. She said that one really nice young lawyer at her firm kept inviting her out to lunch. She'd had lunch with him a couple of times, but they were just friends, for now. Lacey's heart still belonged to Cody, but there was half a continent between them now. I know because I took out my road atlas one evening and checked it out. Darryl was over that night and asked me if I was planning a trip. I told him I was just seeing how far away Iowa was. I stretched out my hand on the map with my thumb on Reno. The tip of my little finger just barely reached the western border of Iowa.

Somewhere beyond my pinky Cody was back living his Midwestern life, maybe sitting on a porch swing with an old sweetheart, or a new one. The dark voice in my head was jabbering away so much I didn't hear a word Darryl was saying. Something about the last 49ers game. I nodded my head and he just plowed ahead with his story. I tell you, guys love football something fierce.

Anyway, I was beginning to wonder if I should retire from playing Cupid and trying so hard to make all my friends happy. Then, the morning after I looked up Iowa in the atlas, something happened to change my mind. Call it luck. Call it serendipity. Or give me some credit for having smart friends. That morning I was over at Lacey's office and Charley's name came up.

"How is Charley?" Lacey said. "I haven't seen him in a long time."

"He's the same. I think he misses Cody."

"We all do," Lacey said. "Me most of all. Charley's such a nice guy. I wonder why he's never been married."

"He almost did once," I said. "Or at least he should have. The girl he loved left town years ago and he never got around to proposing to her."

"Who was that?"

"A cowgirl. Her name was Angel. Charley told me about her once. He's still crazy about her, after twenty years. It's very romantic, but very sad too."

"Where did she go?"

"Up to Washington State," I said. "She sent him a postcard and then he lost track of her."

"Do you know her last name?" Lacey grabbed a pen and began taking notes.

"McHugh. Angel McHugh. Her best friend was a girl named Mud."

"Colorful name," Lacey said. "That'll help."

"Help what?"

"Help us find her." Lacey smiled.

"What?"

"We're going to track her down," Lacey said. "I know several private detectives, and they're good. If she's still alive we'll find her."

"Wow," I said. It was my turn to be in the presence of genius. I guess I wasn't going to be the only love cop in Reno after all. Here was Lacey, missing Cody like crazy, and she comes up with an idea of helping Charley. I was reminded again how truly blessed I am in my friends.

"You can applaud if you want," Lacey said. I did more than that. I clapped and cheered and jumped up out of my chair.

"How soon can we start?" I said.

"No time like the present," Lacey said. She flipped through her little phone directory and found a number.

"What else do we know about this Angel?" Lacey asked.

"She's tall and thin, with long dark hair. She looks like that movie star Madeleine Stowe."

"That'll help," Lacey said.

"Let's not tell Charley what we're doing," I said, "unless we have to. I'd like to surprise him."

"Donna, you know that Angel might be married by now, with a bunch of kids."

"She's not," I said.

"How do you know?"

"She can't be," I said. "She just can't be. Or if she is married she's unhappy and needs to leave the guy. And she would for Charley Meyers."

Lacey laughed. "You have it all figured out, don't you?"

"I like to win," I said.

"I noticed." Lacey punched in a number and started talking to one of her detective friends. She gave him all the information and told him it was urgent. Then she reminded the detective that he owed her a favor. I guess that would save us some money.

"The wheels are in motion," Lacey said, after she hung up the phone.

"Great," I said. I walked over to her and gave her a big hug. "Call me when you have any news."

"Don't worry," Lacey said. "I will."

"Thank you," I said.

"Don't thank me."

"Thank you anyway," I said. I gave her a little wave and turned and walked out, kind of fast. I didn't want her to see that I was crying. Happy tears. On the way home I said a few prayers for the detective. It was all I could do not to phone Charley with the news. Better to wait. I'm not good at waiting, but I had to. When I got home I took out the atlas and looked at all the places where Angel could be. All those big cities and little towns across America. All those farms and ranches in between. I let out a big sigh and said another prayer. That night I didn't fall asleep until two in the morning.

When I woke up I phoned Lacey right away, in case she had heard anything. She told me to relax. I told her I'd try. Then Darryl phoned and asked me what was new. I told him "nothing." He said yeah nothing new ever happens to him either, except when they get in some new chain saws at the store.

25 Donna

"I call it cowboy crème brulee…"

You know when you order a magazine subscription, how the magazine never comes until you stop thinking about it? Well, just keep that in mind while I tell you about Celia Moon's latest recipe. A couple of weeks after Lacey phoned the detective we still had no news. I was at Stella's with the twins, Mel and Harm. Celia had invited us there to show us something. Lacey was invited too, but she was working late and we started without her.

When we were all settled, Celia went into the kitchen and came back with a platter of desserts.

"What's that?" Harm said.

"Looks like custard," Mel said.

Celia smiled. "This is not just any custard."

She served the custard cups and we all screamed at once. Each of the desserts had a reclining letter J on the surface.

"The Lazy J!" Harm said. "You've branded the desserts!"

"That is so clever," Mel said.

"You've outdone yourself this time," I chimed in.

"I call it cowboy crème brulee," Celia said. "See the caramel glaze on top."

"I love it," Harm said. "How did you do that?"

"I just had a friend make me a little branding iron," Celia said. "That part was easy. Coming up with the idea was the creative part."

We all took our spoons and dove in, cracking the hard, glossy glaze. The custard beneath the glaze was a taste of heaven. We were careful to eat around the lazy Js in the middle, saving that part for last. Harm decided to save her lazy J to show her mom and dad. Chance and Audrey would get a kick out of it.

Midway through the dessert, Harm told Celia that she had to have the recipe. I wanted it too, and a copy to send to my mom. Celia brought us paper and pencils so we could write it down.

"I have a confession to make," Celia said. "I owe part of the credit to Thomas Jefferson."

"*The* Thomas Jefferson?" Harm said.

"Yeah, that guy," Celia said. "I was reading in one of my cookbooks about how Thomas Jefferson's cook made burnt cream with a red-hot metal brand. It was like a poker and they called it a salamander. Anyway, as soon as I saw that word 'brand' I knew had to brand the crème brulee. The first brand I thought of was the Lazy J."

"Cool," Harm said. "Let's have the recipe." She was hot to know it and didn't have any more time for history lessons.

"Okay," Celia said, "here goes. You take two cups of heavy cream and heat it till it's almost simmering. Then stir together eight large egg yolks or three large eggs, and half a cup of sugar. Stir in the cream. Strain it all through a fine-mesh sieve into a bowl."

"How do you spell sieve?" Harm asked.

"Hush, Harm," Mel said, "you can look it up later. Go on, Celia."

"Next," Celia said, "stir in three quarters teaspoon of vanilla. Pour the mixture into six or eight 4- to 6-ounch custard cups and place in a water bath."

"You put them in the bath tub?" Harm said. Mel gave her a look.

Celia forged ahead with the recipe. "Then you set the pan in the oven and set the oven at 250 degrees Fahrenheit."

"Good, I don't do Celsius," Harm said. Mel had to laugh at that one, although she tried not to.

"Bake until the custards are set," Celia said, "but still a little quivery in the center when you shake them. That will take about an hour, up to an hour and a half. Then take the custards from the water bath and let them cool at room temperature. Be sure to cover each one with plastic wrap and put them in the fridge for at least eight hours, or up to two days."

"I couldn't wait two days!" Harm said.

"Before you serve them, blot any liquid on the surface with paper towels. Then you caramelize the surface. That part you better call me when you're ready. It's a little tricky. You put two-thirds cup of sugar in a small, heavy saucepan. Then drizzle a quarter cup of water evenly over the top. Put the mixture over medium heat and swirl the pan gently by the handle until a clear syrup forms. Increase the heat to high and bring it to a rolling boil. Cover the pan and boil for two minutes."

"Slow down," Harm said, "I'm getting writer's cramp."

"Next," Celia said, a little slower now, "uncover the pan and cook the syrup till it begins to darken. Swirl the pan by the handle once again and cook the syrup till it turns deep amber. Dip the bottom of the pan in cold water for two seconds to stop the cooking. Then spoon a tablespoon of the hot caramel over one of the custards and cover it evenly. Then glaze the other custards quickly. Then put them in the fridge for at least 30 minutes or up to six hours."

"That's all? Simple," Harm said. "Or we can just ask you to make it."

"How about the branding part?" I asked Celia.

"That's easy," she said. "Heat the brand your normal way."

"Outdoors over a wood fire?" Harm said.

"If that's your normal way," Celia said. "Apply the red-hot brand to the middle of the glaze on each custard and you're done. Cowboy crème brulee."

"Finally," Harm said. "Thanks, Celia. I'm going to give this recipe to my mom to make."

"I knew that was coming," Mel said.

Just then the door opened and Lacey Anderson walked in. She had that look that told me she knew something and was busting to tell it.

"What's up?" I said.

"I heard from the detective."

"What detective?" Harm said.

"Never mind," I said. "And?"

"He found her!"

"Found who?" Harm said.

"That's great!" I said. "Wow."

"Wow is right," Lacey said.

"So tell me, where is she?"

"Alaska," Lacey said.

"Who's in Alaska?" Harm said, louder this time.

"Angel," Lacey said.

"Is she married?" I said.

"No, she's still single."

"All right!" I said. "Is she coming back to Reno?"

"I don't know," Lacey said. "The detective just gave me the information. We have to contact her now."

"What are we waiting for?"

"I wanted to talk to you first. Shall we give the information to Charley?"

"That would spoil the surprise," I said. "Let's bring her back. Do you have a phone number?"

"Right here," Lacey said, pointing to her handbag. "Oh, Celia, sorry I'm late. What did I miss?"

"Cowboy crème brulee," Celia said, "but I saved you one."

"She can eat it later," I said. "We have a phone call to make. Can we use your phone? It's long distance. Alaska. We'll pay for the call."

"Wow, calling Alaska," Harm said. "This is exciting. Will someone please tell me *why* we're calling Alaska?"

"Angel's there," I said.

"Great!" Harm said. "Who's Angel?"

26 Donna

"North to Alaska…"

You would think that someone named Angel would be ready to fly anywhere. Especially if that anywhere was back to Reno to see her long lost love, Charley Meyers. You would think that. Lacey and I had just assumed that Angel would drop everything in Alaska and rush back to Charley. I would, in her place. Lacey said that she would too. It wasn't as if she was married and had a house full of kids.

Lacey made the phone call at Stella's, but I had my ear right next to the phone, trying to hear what Angel was saying. Angel had a sweet voice, and if she was anything like that voice you could see why Charley loved her. Celia, Mel, and Harm were close by. Harm had that look she does so well, like "Would somebody please just tell me what's going on?"

It was a long call, and Lacey's face went from bright and hopeful, to concerned and doubtful. The best I could make out, although I couldn't hear everything Angel said, was that of course she remembered Charley, and she was surprised that he was looking for her, and Lacey had to explain that he wasn't looking for her, but I cut in and said "No, but he misses you something fierce," and then Lacey had to explain whose voice that was and how it was my idea to do something about Charley's loneliness, and then I cut in to say that it was Lacey's idea to have her detective friend find her, and it was a good long time before Angel was able to get in another word.

Lacey finally asked Angel to fly down to Reno to surprise Charley, and then there was silence on the other end of the line. When Angel finally spoke she gave Lacey a long list of reasons why she couldn't come to Reno. A lot of it had to do with being older. She told Lacey she had gained a few pounds and had some wrinkles in her face now, and Lacey told her that Charley was twenty years older too. I cut in again to say that Charley still looked great and his wrinkles were all cute ones.

Angel talked about being busy at work, and having two dogs to take care of. Then Lacey asked her if she was involved with someone else, if that was the real reason she was reluctant to see Charley again. When Lacey said that we all moved closer to the phone, although I couldn't get much closer than I already was. Angel said that she was seeing a guy at the moment. I liked that "at the moment" part, because it didn't sound too permanent. Then Lacey told her there was no harm in just seeing Charley again, like two old friends. "But not too old," I said into the phone. Angel said she was flattered, but she didn't think it was such a good idea. She said something about bad timing. I tried to grab the phone at that point, but Lacey held onto it. I was ready to sweet talk Angel, or yell at her, or whatever it took to get her sorry self back to Reno and Charley. Lacey put her hand up to stop me though, and she told Angel to think about it, that she didn't have to decide right away, that it must have been a shock to hear about Charley after all those years. Then they said goodbye and that was it.

"Why didn't you let me talk to her?" I said. "You were hogging the phone."

"I didn't want to overwhelm her," Lacey said. "Let her get used to the idea."

"I would have told her to get her butt in gear and fly back to Charley."

"I know," Lacey said, "but I don't think that would have worked. She needs to decide for herself. Otherwise she's just following your orders."

"Well, I *am* the love cop."

"Love cop?" Harm said. Then she started laughing.

"Let's do it my way," Lacey said. "We can call her again tomorrow, after she's had time to sleep on the idea."

"What if she's sleeping with her boyfriend instead?" I said.

"Well, at least we planted the idea," Lacey said. "Just let time take its course."

"Oh right, like another twenty years for Angel and Charley. They'll be collecting social security before they see each other again."

"Not twenty years," Lacey said. "We'll call her tomorrow."

Lacey had more patience than me. I suggested that we call Angel before breakfast, to make sure she was home, but Lacey said no we should wait and call her in the evening, and I said what if she's out with her boyfriend, and Lacey said okay we could call her in the late afternoon, and I said what if she's out shopping, and then Lacey asked me if I'd rather call her in the middle of the night and I said what if she's sleeping and we wake her up and she's mad at us.

Finally we agreed to call her early in the evening. Then we had to figure out the time zones. Alaska was an hour earlier than Reno, which wasn't too bad, but I remember saying that if two people love each other, and belong together, they should at least be in the same time zone, and I quickly realized I had said the wrong thing, because Lacey got this sad look and said, "Cody," and that was all. Cody was on Iowa time. He was on Central time and Lacey was on Pacific time. Two hours difference.

I suggested that she call Cody if she missed him, but Lacey said she would wait for him to call her, and I could tell that she had made her mind up on that one and nothing I could say would change it, so I let it go. For now. I had my hands full anyway, trying to get Charley and Angel back together. You can only tackle so much stubbornness at one time.

So we waited till the next evening to call Angel again, and she was home, but she wasn't any closer to changing her mind. She ran through the same list of excuses, and even added a couple of new ones. After she mentioned her two dogs she threw in one about having to feed the neighbors' dog while they were away. Suddenly I had this view of Angel's neighborhood with a whole pack of dogs who were going to starve if she wasn't there to feed them, and probably some wild cats as well, and some birds that depended on her. She may not have been married and feeding a bunch of kids, but she had enough hungry mouths around.

The third day we called her she was out, and we left a message on her machine. The fourth day we phoned again, and she was home. Lacey asked her if she had been thinking about Charley, and she said yes but she still didn't think it was a good idea to see him again, and this time she did mention a couple of wild cats that came around for food. I grabbed the phone and said hi and asked Angel if she was also feeding a moose and a herd of caribou, and she laughed and said no, not yet. She had a good laugh. When I heard it I thought of Charley and how he needed to hear that laugh again, and I just became more determined than ever to get the two of them back together.

I thought we'd wear Angel down, but after the seventh call Lacey said that was enough. We should let it go. Angel was never coming back. We were at Lacey's apartment and I was standing at the window gazing out at the mountains. I think I was looking north, and I tried to imagine driving over those mountains, going northwest to Oregon, then Washington, up into Canada, and then all the way to Alaska. Driving right up to Angel's house, knocking on the door, loud, and when she came to the door just grabbing her and throwing her in my truck and bringing her back to Reno. Then I turned from the window and looked at Lacey.

"Let's just get her," I said, my eyes big.

"Excuse me?" Lacey said.

"You heard me. Let's get Angel and bring her back. We'll drive up in my truck. It'll be fun. And when we get to Anchorage we'll just knock on her door and throw her in the truck and bring her back to Charley."

"That's kidnapping," Lacey said.

"Whatever," I said. "There'll be two of us and only one of her."

"It's still kidnapping. Besides, she doesn't want to come back."

"She doesn't know what she wants. We know what she needs though."

"Do you always know what everybody needs?" Lacey said. She had her arms folded and was looking at me as if I were some weird psychic who could see into people's minds.

"Not always," I said. "This time I'm right, and you know I'm right."

"We can't kidnap her," Lacey said.

"It won't be kidnapping. She'll take one look at us, and know we mean business, and then she'll come peacefully."

"That's a long drive." She was starting to come around.

"It's worth it," I said.

"I can't be away from work that long," Lacey said.

"I'll go by myself then."

"Oh sure," Lacey said, "then she's not outnumbered. Hey, we don't have to drive. We'll just fly up."

"Good thinking," I said. "Much faster too. The sooner we get Angel and Charley back together the sooner I can start working on you and Cody."

"Slow down," Lacey said, "you're working overtime."

"Somebody has to," I said.

A few days later I was flying over those same mountains I had stared at from Lacey's window, going north to Alaska. I had a window seat. I didn't know the man who was sitting next to me. He was a businessman, and he was studying some report. It should have been Lacey sitting in that seat, but she had gotten a call the day before from her San Francisco office. Victor Kleindich, the weasel, told her she was needed there for a week, and she called me and told me she had no choice and she couldn't make the kidnapping trip with me after all. I told her that I would just have to handle it by myself, and she wished me luck, and that was that.

We flew over some big mountains on the way to Seattle, where I would be changing planes for Anchorage. They looked great in the early morning light. It would have been fun to drive through those mountains in my truck, talking to Lacey, singing with the radio, on a mission. But Lacey was in San Francisco, slaving away for Victor, and the mission was all mine.

I can be very persuasive when I have to be, and stubborn. Angel seemed just as stubborn though. I'd be on her home turf, and she'd have all those hungry animals around, and maybe her boyfriend stopping by. She'd have all the advantages, if it came down to a war of wills. Still I had one thing going for me that she didn't have. I was right. Angel and Charley belonged together, and if Charley had only realized that twenty years earlier I wouldn't have been on the way to Alaska right now. Even if I failed in my mission, a thought that I tried to chase out of my mind, at least I'd get to add Alaska to my list of states I've visited, along with California, Arizona, Utah, Wyoming, South Dakota, and Oregon.

Oh yes, add Washington to that list, and I think that one hour at the Seattle airport does count. I saw Mount Rainier from the air, with all that snow on top, and that was the highlight of the whole trip, as far as sightseeing goes. I made a note to talk Darryl into taking me to Seattle sometime. In the meantime I was jumping on another plane and getting closer to Angel and the big showdown. I closed my eyes to imagine the scene, and ran through what I planned to say, although I knew it all by heart now. The next thing I knew I was waking up and we were getting ready to land in Anchorage. At least I was rested. Any good stuff I had missed seeing I could see on the way back.

All I had was a carry-on, good for a couple of days in case it took me that long to knock some sense into Angel's head, so once we landed I just scooted out to the curb and got a taxi and gave the guy Angel's address. It turned out to be a long ride. Angel lived outside Anchorage, in a small house down a back road. It was getting toward late afternoon. I kept looking for hungry wild animals, because that way I would know we were getting close. I did see an orange cat run across the road in front of us, but that was it.

Then the driver stopped and I was there. I paid him and asked him to stay for a minute till I was inside. There was a truck in the driveway, which I was happy to see. I walked up to the door and pushed the doorbell. Then I took a deep breath. Time to do your thing, Donna. Suddenly all I could think of Charley Meyers back in Reno, sad and lonely, his whole future happiness depending on me. And then the door opened.

"Yes?" Angel said. It had to be her. She was just the way Charley had described her, and time hadn't been cruel to her at all.

"Angel?" I said. Just checking.

"Yes," she said, still puzzled.

"It's me, Donna Cooper. From Reno. We talked on the phone."

"Oh my God."

"I hope you don't mind me just showing up like this."

"Oh my God," Angel said again, her face lighting up. Then she opened the door wide and apologized for making me stand outside.

We sat in her living room on an old leather sofa that was very comfortable. Her whole house was comfortable, clean and warm, not at all stuffy like some homes. She asked me if I was thirsty, and I was. So there we were, drinking diet Cokes because that was mostly what she had, unless I wanted some Jack Daniel's, and I said no thank you to that.

"I can't believe you're here," Angel said.

"I can't believe it myself."

"It is a change from all those phone calls," she said.

"I hope we didn't bother you too much, calling every day."

"Well," Angel said, "actually I started looking forward to those calls. You and Lacey are like old friends by now." She laughed. "Of course, you both have just the one subject that you ever talk about."

"Charley Meyers," I said.

"Yep, that subject. Ancient history."

"Don't say that, Angel. He's not ancient yet. And neither are you. If he was ten years younger, or I was ten years older, I'd be after him myself. If I didn't have Darryl, that is."

"Your boyfriend?"

"Yep."

"Do you want something to eat?" Angel said. "You've had a long trip."

"I have some peanuts from the trip." I pulled out the small pack of peanuts from my bag.

"We can do better than that. Come in the kitchen with me."

Angel had lots of good snacks in the kitchen, and sandwich fixings. She made me a ham and cheese on rye, and then she grilled it on the stove, and put some chips and carrot sticks on the plate, and pulled out a couple more diet Cokes. We sat at the kitchen table, which is always a good place to have important conversations. We put our elbows on the table and just relaxed with each other. We were friends already. Whatever happened between Angel and Charley, I would always have this new friend.

Two big huskies wandered in and lay down at our feet. They were good looking animals. Angel introduced us. The male dog was named Reno and the female was Fallon. Good Nevada names both of them. They looked well fed and happy. I got the feeling that Angel loved them a lot more than her current boyfriend, and that they would be around much longer than the guy.

"Angel," I heard myself saying, "Charley is lost without you."

"After all these years? I'm sure he's found a lot of other women."

"Angel, listen to me. You're still the one. He may laugh and carry on like everything's fine, but I look at him when he doesn't know I'm looking. He made a big mistake letting you get away."

"Why doesn't he come up here and tell me himself?"

"Well, it's like this. We haven't told him where you are."

"Why not?" Angel said.

"I don't know. Maybe because he needs somebody else to take charge of his life. Or maybe because I just like surprises, and I want to see his face when you walk in the door."

"Donna, we've been through all the reasons why I can't go back to Reno."

"I know, and most of them involve hungry animals. You don't talk much about your boyfriend."

"There's not much to say about him," Angel said. "He's okay, but it's a fading romance. Fading fast actually."

"Well then, the timing is good. Just fly back to Reno with me and see Charley. Give it a chance."

"I don't know," Angel said. That was music to my ears. "I don't know" is just one step from "maybe," and that's just one step from "okay, why not."

"You know," I said. "Your heart knows. Listen to your heart." Angel looked at me without saying a word. Then she stood up and walked to the back window. I didn't say anything. That's rare for me, I know, but it was time for a little quiet. Whatever was going on in her mind as she stared out that window I'll never know. I sat there and scratched Fallon's head. She smiled up at me, her tongue out. Dogs are simple. They've got things figured out.

Angel finally turned and walked slowly back to the kitchen table. She put her elbows on the table and rested her chin in her hands. I stopped scratching Fallon and leaned forward. I looked into Angel's dark eyes, and she stared back at me.

"Well," she said.

That was all she had to say. It was like a poem, or a symphony. I knew that she had listened to her heart. I knew that she would finally, finally say yes. I don't know what came over me but suddenly the tears were sliding down my face and Angel was grabbing Kleenex from the counter and then I stood up and we hugged. I was speechless.

"Thank you," Angel said, wiping a tear from my face.

"Oh no, thank you."

"No really," she said, "thank you." Then she laughed. "Damn, you're stubborn."

"Not as stubborn as you and Charley."

"Why did you care so strongly?" Angel said. "You didn't even know me."

"I know Charley, and I know when I'm right. You'd better start packing. We can fly back tomorrow. I have two open tickets that Lacey bought."

"Whoa, that's too fast. Give me a week. I have to make arrangements for Reno and Fallon, and the other animals. Have to fix up my boyfriend with someone new, so I can break it off easily. I know just the woman too. Then there's my job. They'll have to line up another bartender."

"Is that what you do? I never knew."

"Yep, good money in that. Good enough anyway. And I get to hear everybody's story."

"So you need a week?" I said. "Promise me you won't change your mind."

"Promise."

"Otherwise I'll just have to come back and kidnap you."

"I think you would."

"I know I would. Lacey and I talked about doing it." We laughed. My tears had stopped. Angel should have been the one crying, but I guess I'm more emotional than she is.

We made all our plans. She invited me to stay with her and fly back the following week, but I needed to get back to Reno and she needed time to settle all her job issues, and animal issues, and boyfriend issues.

Angel drove me to the airport the next morning. We talked all the way, and laughed easily. I kept thinking of Charley back in Reno. He had no idea. Something wonderful was coming his way in just a few days.

On the flight back to Seattle I stayed awake the whole way. I saw a lot of stuff from the plane that I'd missed the day before. Then on the flight from Seattle to Reno I saw more of the same stuff I'd seen on the way up, only in reverse order. When Reno finally came into view I watched the town grow larger outside the window. It was good to be home.

27 Donna

"An angelic visitor..."

One week and several long distance phone calls later, Lacey and I drove out to the Reno airport. We had a plane to meet. We got there half an hour early, which is a record for me. I'm always rushing at the last minute. Lacey played a couple of poker machines while we waited. With the kind of luck we had been having I fully expected her to hit a jackpot. She didn't, but she did win a few dollars. This day wasn't about Lacey and me, anyway. It was about a cowboy and cowgirl who were about to get a second chance.

When I was in Anchorage, Angel had filled me in on the twenty years she had been away from Reno. She had spent a few years on her sister's farm in Washington, then moved to Seattle and worked as a bartender for a year, and from there went to Anchorage. She had lived in Anchorage, Juneau, Ketchikan, and Anchorage again. Yes she had met a lot of men, but no she had never married any of them. She thought of Charley Meyers now and then. She always thought of him as married and having a herd of kids.

The whole week I was back in Reno I stayed away from Parker's, trying to avoid Charley. Even if I could avoid telling him about Angel, I was afraid that he'd see some big news in my face. I did call the store and find out when he'd be there. We planned to whisk Angel directly from the airport to downtown Reno and in the front door at Parker's. You might think that someone who had been away for twenty years could wait another day, or an hour or two, but I was tired of waiting. Angel was anxious to see Charley again too. As for Charley, he was clueless. Angelic appearances are always a big deal in the Bible, and such an event in Reno would be even more startling.

Lacey and I stood in the baggage claim area, watching the faces of the passengers from the Alaska Airways jet walking up to the carousel. We looked and looked, but nobody even resembling Angel was in the crowd. I looked at Lacey and she looked at me, afraid to say anything. Then I saw a straggler. She had long dark hair underneath a cowgirl's hat, and she spotted me at the same time I saw her.

"Angel," I called to her.

"Donna," she said, as we walked towards each other. Angel had a small carry-on bag, which I took from her. The three of us hugged. I was reminded of how sweet and beautiful she was. Charley had not been exaggerating at all, not a bit.

While waiting for her luggage we talked a bit about her trip. Then Angel let out a big sigh. "Twenty years," she said. "I can't believe I've been away that long."

"Well, lots of things have changed, that's for sure," I said.

"Bound to," Angel said.

"Except for one thing," I said. "One thing hasn't changed in all that time."

"What's that?"

"Charley Meyers," I said. "Everybody says he's still the same."

"That's good," Angel said. "I liked him the way he was."

"He still loves you," I said. "Maybe more than ever."

"Donna, I know. You've only told me that a hundred times." Angel and Lacey both laughed.

"And I'm telling you again, so you don't forget."

"Thanks," Angel said. "You two are amazing."

"Sometimes," I said. "Sometimes we are."

The drive from the airport to downtown Reno is a short one. I looked over at Angel a few times on the way in. Her face was glowing. She was a little nervous too. You could tell by the way her fingers drummed on the armrest. The closer we got to Parker's the faster she drummed.

I found a place on the street to park the truck and we walked a block to the store. Angel stopped us before we opened the front door. She checked her reflection in the front window of Parker's, took a deep breath, and then nodded her head. I was reminded for a moment of the bull riders, how they nod their head when they're ready for the chute door to open to start their wild ride.

Lacey held the door open and we let Angel walk in first. Charley was in the back, but he was walking up towards the front counter. When he saw Angel standing there he just froze in his tracks. I've heard that expression all my life, but I'll never be able to hear it again without thinking about Charley Meyers that day. He literally froze. Like a statue, or like someone caught in a bad blizzard in the middle of the winter. He was frozen solid in his tracks. It remained for Angel to thaw him out and bring him to life.

Angel took charge. She walked up to Charley, put her hands gently on his shoulders, and looked into his eyes. She moved one hand to his cheek and stroked it gently. Then, like a slow motion scene in a movie, she put her arms around him and held him close to her heart. I don't mind telling you that I cried when I saw that. Lacey too. We were a mess. Both of us were out of tissues, so we just stood there bawling. Big tears rolled down our faces and by our mouths. We were both licking them away, catching as many as we could. Finally Lacey tapped me on the shoulder and nodded toward the door. She was right. Charley and Angel needed to be alone. We stood outside guarding the entrance, our arms folded. I'm afraid we scared away a few customers that day.

⭐

For two weeks we enjoyed having Angel back in Reno. We got to know her better, although she spent most of her time with Charley. We took them both riding at the Lazy J, so Harm finally got her questions answered about

Angel. Celia cooked up some more cowboy crème brulee. This time my brother Rooster got in on the dessert at Stella's. We all went to hear Teri Autrey and her new band. Charley and Angel were good dancers. There was one heavenly fall day when we all piled into trucks and ran a caravan around Lake Tahoe.

And then it was over. On a cold, overcast morning, Lacey and I stood again in the Reno airport, hugging Angel and wishing her a good trip back to Alaska. Then we hugged Charley Meyers. Then we watched Angel take Charley by the hand and lead him to the gate. She was returning home with a two-legged souvenir of her Reno trip. I gave Angel and Charley my best wave. Then they were gone.

Lacey did her best to comfort me. This time she had tissues in her purse, a big supply. I needed most of it.

"I can't believe he's gone," I said as we walked slowly through the airport. "I've lost my best friend."

"I thought I was your best friend," Lacey said.

"My best cowboy friend."

"He'll come back to visit. You'll see him again. And Angel."

"I know if I see him I'll see Angel. Those two are joined at the hip now."

"But it's what you wanted, isn't it?" Lacey said.

"I know, darn it. I just assumed they'd settle in Reno. I can't walk into Parker's any more because that's where I'll miss him most."

"You know, Donna, if you keep crying you're going to get me started."

We crossed the road that separates the airport from the garage. I looked back at a plane taking off. I couldn't tell if it was Charley's plane. It probably wasn't, but it didn't matter.

"Lacey," I said, "I think my life has gotten way too emotional."

"It's your own fault," Lacey said. That surprised me.

"My fault? Why?"

"You get involved with people, so it's inevitable."

"Maybe you're right. I just know I'm not going to make any more long distance calls for a while."

On the drive back to town Lacey and I were quiet. I blew my nose and felt a little better. I found some good cowboy music on the radio.

"I can't believe they had to wait twenty years to get back together," Lacey said. I know she was talking about Angel and Charley, but I believe she was thinking about Cody, away in Iowa, lost in the fields of corn somewhere. My work was not yet done. I wiped away the last of the tears with the back of my hand and drove on into town.

In spite of what I had told Lacey about not being able to walk into Parker's any more because I missed Charley, two days didn't go by before I returned to the store. It was because I missed Charley that I had to go there, to remember the good moments, and to see the place where Angel hugged him that day. I had to remind myself that this wasn't about me.

I'll always be glad I went back to Parker's that day. Not only did it help me understand why things had worked out the way they did, but I also found a treasure. I was standing by the front counter when I happened to catch sight of a composition book, sticking out beneath a stack of horse magazines. Sure enough, it was one of Charley's books. I found two others nearby, and just like that I had Charley's story.

From the moment Angel walked into Parker's, Charley had lost his mind totally. He had run off to Alaska with her and left his composition books behind. I figured I would return them to him, but not before I read them all myself. There were parts I hadn't seen before. On the first page of the first book, he had written in big block letters, "CHASING COWGIRLS," and drawn a rope around the words. Charley could write better than he drew, but you could still tell it was a rope. I grabbed a pen off the counter and did something I'd been wanting to do for months. I crossed out the word "COWGIRLS" and wrote in "COWBOYS."

Then I gathered up the three books and left the store. I knew that if Cody and Lacey's story was ever going to get told I couldn't wait for Charley Meyers. It might be another twenty years before he remembered what he had left behind in Reno. That cowboy had a bad habit of misplacing valuable items.

28 Donna

"The rat bastard ..."

One mission accomplished, and one remaining. I had managed to reunite Charley Meyers and Angel McHugh. With spectacular results, I don't mind saying. My next goal was the one I had put on hold while flying to Alaska and talking Angel into seeing Charley again. Lacey and Cody also belonged together. Any fool could see that, but something kept yanking them away from each other. If it wasn't Cody's uncle getting sick and pulling Cody back to Iowa, it was Victor Kleindich pulling Lacey back to San Francisco. He had done it twice now.

Lacey promised me it was just business, but I know that Victor took her out to fancy restaurants and was after her for more than some legal help. It was business, all right. Monkey business. At some point, with Cody far away and not calling her every day the way he should have, Lacey might follow the words of that old song my mom loves, the one about if you can't be with the one you love, then love the one you're with. It would be wrong, of course, but wrong things happen all the time.

I knew that San Francisco was Lacey's hometown. She could see her folks when she was there and have all the produce she wanted from her dad's business. But I didn't want her there. To me San Francisco only meant Victor, so I was glad that Lacey was back in Reno, where she belonged. Now if we could only get Cody back I'd be able to relax. Darryl could tell I was edgy. When I told him why, he just shrugged and said that people had to live their own lives. I didn't want to argue with him but I know that's not true. If you leave some people to stumble along through life they'll end up like Charley, regretting a mistake made twenty years ago and not doing a dang thing about it.

A couple days after Angel and Charley flew off to Alaska, I stopped by Lacey's office to surprise her and take her to lunch. It had been clouding up all morning and now the rain started. I ran up to the front door of the law firm, but just as I went to open it, someone in back of me beat me to it. I saw a man's hand with perfectly manicured nails, gleaming gold cufflinks, a starched white cuff, and the end of a sleeve that said expensive Italian suit. I knew who it was, but I didn't want to turn around. Maybe if I ignored him, Victor Kleindich would vanish, like some bad apparition.

"Allow me," Victor said, holding the door open for me.

"Age before beauty," I said. I put my hand on the door and waited.

"I insist," Victor said. I didn't budge.

"What are you doing here?" I said. "I thought you were in San Francisco."

"This is silly," he said. "We're both getting wet." With that he walked right in and I trailed behind. I'd won the showdown. I like rain, but then I wasn't wearing an expensive suit.

The next thing I knew Victor had disappeared into Lacey's office and closed the door. I walked back to the receptionist's desk and asked her to phone Lacey.

"What's he doing here?" I asked Lacey when she came on the phone.

"We have some work to do, then we're going to have a late lunch."

"I was going to ask you to have lunch with me," I said.

"Sorry," Lacey said, "maybe tomorrow?"

"I'll call you," I said. I handed the phone back to the receptionist. I could have waited around and invited myself to the lunch to keep an eye on Victor, but I was hungry and I didn't feel much like seeing him any more than I had to.

I walked to my truck in the rain and drove out Virginia Street to King's Hardware. Darryl was only too happy to take me to lunch, although I was on edge about Victor being back in town. Darryl didn't care for the guy either, but he was mainly busy with the chicken fried steak on his plate. When he wasn't talking about hardware or sports, he loved to talk about food. He said that when you eat chicken fried steak, or anything with gravy on it, you had to be careful to make the gravy last, because if you had some meat left, or biscuits, and the gravy was gone, it was a frustrating end to a meal. Darryl has some weird theories. I think he gets some of them from his buddy, Shorty. I guess the theories are not so weird, actually, but he gets way too obsessive over them. In my mind the happiness of my friend Lacey was much more important than whether Darryl had properly managed his gravy consumption during lunch.

After we finished I drove Darryl back to the store and then I drove out to the Lazy J to see Mel and Harm. I told them that Victor was back in town and how frustrating it was. Mel told me to hang in there, that Cody would be back some day, but I wasn't so sure. The rain was coming down cold and hard then. I had hoped to get in some riding, but the weather was too bad. Harm, who is sweet and cheerful in the worst of times, told me that the rain had to stop sometime and that the sun would come out and Cody would come riding back into their lives one of those sunny days. I wanted to believe that, but nothing turns out the way you plan it. Even with Charley and Angel, I'd done the right thing but I'd lost Charley to Alaska, and I was missing him even more than I thought I would.

I stayed at the Lazy J until the storm passed over. It was dusk by then and I just wanted to go home and curl up with a good book or a movie, or call my mom in Vegas. I was tired of watching out for everyone. What I needed was a vacation, even if I just stayed in my own apartment and let the world run itself for a while.

When I got home there was a message on my machine from Adrienne, the receptionist in Victor's office in San Francisco. I'd talked to her when

Lacey had been working there this last time, and we'd gotten along great on the phone. Adrienne had left her work phone and home phone numbers on the machine and said it was important. I called her at home and she was there. We talked for ten minutes. When I finally hung up I knew my vacation would have to wait. I put my boots back on and headed out the door. I was glad that Lacey lived in the same building. I couldn't wait to talk to her.

I was about to knock on Lacey's door when I heard some laughing inside. Lacey's laugh and a man's laugh. Not good. I knocked loudly. It was the same knock you hear on TV cop shows when they say "Police! Open up!"

Lacey opened the door and I saw past her to Victor, lying back on the sofa, his shoes off and his tie loosened, holding a glass of wine.

"Donna," Lacey said, "what's up?"

"I was about to ask you the same thing. Can I come in?"

"Of course," she said. "Sorry."

I walked in, feeling like the police making a bust. I stood there, my hands on my hips, surveying the scene.

"Victor and I were working late," Lacey said.

"I can see that. Working on a bottle of wine?"

"Would you like a glass?" Victor asked. He held up the bottle. It was close to empty.

"No thank you," I said. "I just need to talk to Lacey."

"Okay," Lacey said. "Want to go in the kitchen?"

"No, what I have to say I can say right here."

"Maybe I should go in the kitchen," Victor said. He began to stand up.

"No, sit down," I said. "You need to hear this too."

"Let's all sit down then," Lacey said. She went back to the sofa and sat next to Victor. She finished the wine in her glass and Victor quickly refilled it. Then he refilled his own. The last drop left the bottle as I walked closer and remained standing.

"I prefer to stand," I said. All the cop show clichés were racing through my head. "This won't take long."

"What's wrong?" Lacey said.

"Well ma'am," I said, in my most serious police voice, "we have reports from San Francisco about a certain perpetrator."

"Perpetrator?" Lacey repeated.

"Yes, ma'am," I said. "A Victor Kleindich."

"That would be me," Victor said. He didn't know what the hell was going on. He seemed to think it was all a big joke. Victor never took me seriously anyway.

"What's he done?" Lacey asked. "And why are you calling me *ma'am?*"

"You sound like a cop," Victor said. I ignored him. I was looking right at Lacey the whole time.

"Well, ma'am," I said, "I'm glad you're sitting down because I'm afraid I have some bad news."

"Oh?" Lacey said. Now she looked worried.

"Did someone kill me?" Victor said. He was still enjoying it like a joke.

"Not yet," I said. "They might want to, however, after I tell you what we found out." Victor still had that smug look of his. He lacked appreciation for rodeo queen types, and love cops, but he was about to be educated.

"Tell me," Lacey said, knowing I was serious.

"Do you know a woman in San Francisco named Adrienne?"

"Sure, the receptionist at the firm," Lacey said.

"Well," I said, "I received a phone call from her just a few minutes ago. She told me that this Victor Kleindich has been spending a lot of time with a certain young female lawyer there named Deborah." I glanced at Victor. He was sobering up fast. Lacey was staring at him now.

"It's just work," Victor said. "Don't pay any attention to rumors."

"Adrienne tells me it's not rumors," I said. "She said you've been taking that woman to dinner, giving her jewelry, and promising her she will be the first female partner at the firm."

"You promised me that!" Lacey said.

"Don't listen to her," Victor said.

"And you never gave me jewelry," she said, even louder now.

"Adrienne's a little bitch," Victor said, "you can't believe anything she says."

"She's my friend," Lacey said. "How dare you call her a bitch!"

At that point I decided to sit down in Lacey's recliner and take in the rest of the evening's entertainment in comfort. My work was done. Maybe the love cop would get her vacation after all.

Lacey was fantastic, so fiery and verbal. She had an excellent vocabulary, and not just words she had learned in law school. Hearing about Victor's behavior with Deborah had ignited her fire, but when Victor called Adrienne a bitch he had thrown gasoline on the fire. I tried to remember all the wonderful details of that scene to share with Teri and Celia, and Mel and Harm, and Charley and Angel the next time I talked to them. It didn't last long. Lacey told Victor to leave and that he'd better not mess with her at the firm or she'd tell the other partners everything, in person, and Deborah was welcome to him and his "slimy ways," as she put it.

I stayed with Lacey a while after Victor left. The funny thing was that she didn't talk about Victor that much. After she calmed down she started talking about Cody. Maybe it was the wine, or maybe it all the emotions of her scene with Victor, but Lacey ended up crying and I had to go into the bathroom and bring back a box of Kleenex.

"At least that snake Victor's gone," I said as Lacey destroyed some more tissues.

"The rat bastard," Lacey said, spitting out the words as if they were bad meat that she had paid too much for.

That made me laugh. Then Lacey laughed too. I've always liked that expression, as if "rat" or "bastard" were not strong enough by themselves. It's a charming combination.

29 Donna

"The cowboy who loves you so true..."

In the high desert country of northern Nevada, far from the lights of Las Vegas, each new season of the year brings a different beauty to the land. According to one cowboy named Charley Meyers, who over the years had watched the seasons change from his vantage points on horseback and in pickup trucks, God must have loved the desert because he created so much of it. Charley said that God must be especially fond of sagebrush, because he put it everywhere in the high desert. You'd think you'd get tired of it, he said, but you don't. For a cowboy there's nothing like the smell of sagebrush, Charley said, unless it's the smell of cattle in the morning.

A cowboy out riding by himself could always find some company, Charley said. There were plenty of lizards and snakes around, sunning on rocks in the morning or evening, and different raptors in the sky—hawks and eagles, falcons and ospreys. Each season was better than the last, Charley always said. By the time you grew tired of winter snow and cold, spring arrived, then you got to warm your blood like the reptiles in the summer sun. By the time you got tired of hot August days, fall began to take over and cool you down.

Cody West had arrived in Reno on an April day that was part winter and part spring, when there were snow flurries in the air but days were getting longer. Then, in June, rodeo week had arrived in town along with summer. And it was on one of those lizard baking days near the end of summer that Cody had received the phone call from Iowa and climbed into his Dodge pickup to begin the long drive back to the Midwest to help his Aunt Alice and Uncle Max.

That first night out, Cody had tried to reach Lacey in San Francisco, but Ellen told him that Lacey was back in Reno. He finally reached her at her Reno apartment. He could hear my voice in the background. He congratulated Lacey on her victory in San Francisco and admitted that the timing was terrible. Cody explained that he might have to stay in Iowa for a while, but that he would try to return as soon as he could. Lacey said she read the note that he had left with Charley and confessed that she had cried a bucket of tears. She said I had cheered her up. She asked Cody if he had ever heard of a drink called a Fighting Cowgirl. He said he hadn't, and when Lacey told him the ingredients, he said that sounded like strong medicine.

Cody told her he had realized that he didn't have any pictures of her and asked her to send him one. Lacey said she would if he would send her his picture. Cody laughed and said they were having a backwards kind of courtship. Lacey agreed, saying she felt like a picture bride sending her photograph to someone in another part of the country whom she hadn't met. She said they had started out at a cemetery, which is where most folks ended up. Then they had spent the night together on their first real date. Next they had gotten better acquainted and become friends. After that Cody had met her folks and had to stay in the guest room by himself. The next night they had gone out riding and ended up parking and necking like a couple of teenagers.

It was one mixed up relationship, all right. Cody pointed out that they had done all the usual things, just in a different order. And now they would be thousands of miles apart for a while. Lacey said she would still be in Reno when he came back, and asked him not to change. "Don't turn into an Iowa farmer on me" was the way she put it. Cody told her not to worry, "once a cowboy, always a cowboy."

★

For two or three weeks after that conversation, Lacey succeeded in not worrying. She had a lot of support and company from me, she had her renewed interest in her career, and she was riding at the Lazy J every chance she got, which was two or three times a week. She worked on her riding and roping skills, and she started taking photographs of the ranch and the high desert country. By the time the early fall days reached Reno, Lacey had sent Cody prints of more than a hundred of her photographs.

It started with one roll of film, to give him a picture of herself as she had promised. It developed into a whole series of photographs of cowboys and cowgirls, of ranch scenes and desertscapes. Lacey had taken a photography class years before in San Francisco, and she had the skill and the eye for this new hobby. Chance Johnson had asked for an enlargement of one of her photos of the Lazy J, taken in the early morning, with the ranch house in one corner and his land stretching out in the distance. He had it framed and hung it in his den, right above his desk.

Lacey sent Cody a few of the shots she had taken of Mel and Harm—one a portrait of the twins on horseback, the others action shots of Mel and Harm racing around barrels. Most of the photographs, however, were of the land. She shot just about everything she saw. She shot a whole roll of nothing but sagebrush, and one roll she shot in Virginia City, with some fine views of the town taken from the cemetery, and some close-ups of the tombstones that she and Cody had stopped to read back in May.

Cody had asked Lacey for a photograph of herself and me at the Eldorado, Lacey drinking a Fighting Cowgirl and me with my Coke. Lacey obliged by returning with me and asking the same cocktail waitress to take a picture of the two of us sitting in a booth and raising our tall drinks in the air. This would become Cody's favorite. Lacey's favorite photograph was one that Cody had sent her from Iowa. It showed the cowboy sitting on a fence, wearing his Wranglers and black roper boots and black cowboy hat, with some good-looking pigs in the foreground and a field of corn behind him. For the rest of her life, whenever she heard the word "Iowa," she would think of this photograph. For Lacey, this was Iowa. The only thing wrong with the picture was that Cody should have been back in Nevada, surrounded by sagebrush and cattle instead of corn and pigs. When she showed me the photograph I took a post-it note out of my bag, wrote "Just Visiting" on it, and stuck the note on the bottom of the picture. Lacey decided to leave the note on because it improved the picture considerably.

As the days became cooler, and September turned to October, Lacey's moratorium on worrying was in serious trouble. Cody had told her that his Uncle Max was recovering from the open-heart surgery, but that the recovery was a lot slower than they had hoped. In the meantime, Cody was helping Aunt Alice with all the physical work around their large house and yard, and cheering up his uncle. Cody had always been Uncle Max's favorite nephew, and it was Uncle Max who had given Cody his sense of humor. The two could always make each other laugh. Uncle Max kidded Cody about his cowboy clothes, and Cody kidded Uncle Max about everything, even his health.

Cody asked Uncle Max one day how he let himself get in such poor health, and Uncle Max had blamed it on his love of bacon, which he had eaten almost daily. Cody wondered how Aunt Alice had let him eat so much bacon, and Uncle Max had said that it wasn't Alice's fault, that he had mostly sneaked bacon when he was out of the house, especially when he was with friends and they ordered double bacon cheeseburgers. Uncle Max lamented the fact that his bacon eating days were over, but Cody said there were other good things he could eat, like yogurt and oatmeal. Uncle Max had grabbed a cushion at that point and thrown it at Cody, but Cody ducked just in time.

One day I tracked down Cody's number through the phone company. Soon I was talking to Cody himself, instead of hearing everything second hand from Lacey. He said he missed Charley and me, and, above all, Lacey, but he knew he'd be returning to Reno some day. It was just taking much longer than he had expected. He thought about asking Lacey to fly out to Iowa for a visit. For some reason, however, he never did ask her.

A funny thing happened while I was on the phone with Cody. Suddenly

I heard a woman's voice in the background calling him "Cody honey," and I knew it wasn't his aunt because he said she was out shopping. I should have asked him who that was, but I was afraid of the answer. Before we hung up, though, I did give him a good talk about not forgetting Lacey. I even considered jumping on a plane to Iowa and dragging Cody back to Reno. There were good arguments in favor of that, but equally good arguments on the other side.

After I hung up I said a little prayer that Cody and Lacey's relationship would survive all the recent interruptions. Then I said another prayer asking God to do something about the Iowa girlfriend, the "Cody honey" one.

I debated telling Lacey about my call to Cody, and finally decided not to. Lacey told me she was beginning to wonder if Cody was stuck in Iowa forever, even though he assured her he was not. She told me her imagination was playing tricks on her, that she saw Cody visiting old friends back in Iowa, maybe running into an old girlfriend and rekindling their relationship. Then she saw him settling down in some small Iowa town or packing away his cowboy clothes and becoming an Iowa farmer. She pictured him on a tractor, with a wife and a pack of kids nearby. I swallowed hard and tried to reassure her.

As the nights became colder, Lacey said she felt the need for someone nearby to keep her warm. I suggested she get a dog, but she told me that wasn't what she needed. To add to Lacey's uneasiness, she watched Darryl King and me growing closer, and this only made her more aware of her own situation. She phoned her parents and invited them to spend a few days in Reno, but they said they wanted to wait until Cody returned. Lacey was an only child, so this brought out some unfamiliar feelings in her, something resembling sibling rivalry.

Lacey tried a change of scenery. She talked Darryl and me into driving around Lake Tahoe with her one Saturday. It was a fine October day, the lake was sparkling, and I was my usual cheerful self, but someone was missing. When we stopped at a casino in South Lake Tahoe, Lacey dropped some money at a blackjack table before she realized her lucky cowboy wasn't there to change her luck.

Lacey talked Mel and Harm into teaching her barrel racing, and she discovered there was a lot to learn. The twins' horses were experienced racers, but they weren't used to Lacey in the saddle, so she began working with another quarter horse that Mel named Grazer because it always seemed the graze the barrels when it raced around them. Lacey got lots of practice in reaching down and steadying a rocking barrel. She liked Grazer. Mel said that horse could turn on a nickel and give you change.

So there was plenty of activity to occupy Lacey's time, not to mention all of her work at the firm, but as the nights grew colder she felt a growing chill in her heart. She was stronger in mind, stronger in spirit than she had been the day that Cody left town. She would survive, even if Cody never returned. But she would be different. She could feel the transformation, feel herself growing older and tougher, less vulnerable. Added to her worries now was the realization that her toughness came at a price. She felt as if she were piling layers of protection around her heart, as one would put on layers of clothing against the onset of winter. When spring came again, and she removed the layers, what would she find?

On the last Saturday in October, Lacey and I drove out to the Lazy J to ride with Mel and Harm. Lacey had suggested that they just ride—no ranch work, no barrel racing—just saddle up and ride on the land, to feel the sun and the wind, to watch the sky and the mountains, to just ride. No destination, no timetable, no obligations except to be free. Mel and Harm took to the idea, and so it was that after a lunch of barbecue sandwiches and iced tea at the ranch the four of us mounted up and rode off away from the ranch house.

We rode a while, well out of sight of the house, before stopping to rest the horses. "Look at us," I said, "just like those four outlaw women in that movie we saw last week."

"Except that they wore a lot more makeup," Mel said.

"And one had a really rotten boyfriend," Harm added.

"But aside from that," I continued, "just look at us. We could be back in those days, running from the law. Do you think a posse could catch up with us?"

"Not likely," Mel said. "And if they did they'd be sorry."

"Damn right," Harm said.

"And if we were innocent, Lacey could sue 'em for false arrest," I said.

"Are we innocent?" Lacey asked.

"I thought your attorney wasn't supposed to ask you that question," Mel said.

"Oh, I forgot," Lacey said. "That's all right, they'd never catch us anyway."

"Look at that cloud of dust over yonder," Harm said, "we'd better ride. Yah!" she urged her horse. The rest of us joined in and we were off and flying.

I wondered what Lacey was thinking. Maybe she felt cut off from her immediate past. Running with the Johnson Cooper Gang, she was back in the old West, staying one step ahead of the law, wild and free. Whatever happened to that cowboy she used to run with, she asked herself. Was he sitting in a jail somewhere, or spending time with some señorita down in New Mexico? She had heard a rumor that he had gone back to Iowa and was hiding out in the cornfields, or pretending to be a pig farmer. They'd had some good times together, but that was so long ago. Where was that cowboy? If he came back, would things be the same? Did she feel the same way about him? It was downright annoying to be pestered by questions that she didn't have the answers to.

Maybe Lacey found herself jumping ahead to the present and trying to predict the future. Lately she had been listening to Willie Nelson sing "My Heroes Have Always Been Cowboys" and paying closer attention to the words. The line about "old faded memories" stuck in her mind and wouldn't leave. Perhaps it was time to create some new memories. She looked at the mountains in the distance. They had ridden several miles and the mountains seemed no closer than when they had started. What's up there, she wondered. What's waiting for me?

Maybe she decided to create a few scenarios, so that when she made it to those mountains one day, she would not be surprised by what she found. Perhaps she couldn't control the future, but she didn't like the idea of it sneaking up on her.

In the first scenario, Lacey saw herself staying in Reno, doing the work she was doing now, riding when she could, doing pretty much the same things, only she would get older and better at them. Nothing else would change, except that the memories of a certain cowboy would fade into the past.

In the second scenario, which was a variation on the first one, Lacey saw herself the same way except that there was an added element. Maybe it was that new lawyer at the firm who had asked her out the week before. All she had to do was say yes the next time he asked, and see how it developed. She jumped ahead a few years and saw herself married to the guy, starting a family, settled down, riding less, working more.

She jumped quickly to a third scenario, which was far different from the first two. She saw herself growing increasingly restless and discontented, and finally moving back to San Francisco, or moving on to another part of the country, to start over again. Cody would be only a memory, and they might exchange Christmas cards for a few years, but that too would eventually end. Then she looked at her friends riding alongside her, breathed in the fresh air and the aroma of the sagebrush, and decided she didn't want to leave Reno.

Perhaps Lacey searched for another ending to her Reno chapter, an ending that was more like a beginning. She tried to think of her first few months in town as an initiation. She had been transformed from city girl to cowgirl during that period. Cody had been part of her initiation, maybe a phase she had to go through, maybe a test.

Whatever happened from here on, the past few months would be only a prelude. She knew she wanted to give it more time. She studied the mountains in the distance once more. They were there yesterday, and they would be there tomorrow, and the next day, and the next year. Just keep riding. The only way to know what they were like was to make the journey and experience them. Everything else was just picture postcards that you bought somewhere for a quarter or two and never bothered to send. They were stuck away in a drawer and you forgot about them because you had to be on your way. You had to make that journey.

The one scenario that she could not bring herself to dwell on was the one in which Cody came back and everything was as it had been before. Although I had urged her over and over to "have a little faith," she worried that happy endings like that were only found in romance novels and Hollywood movies. Her life was not a romance novel, it was too complex and unstructured and realistic. And it was not some screenplay where the hero wins the girl and love conquers all. What was supposed to happen, were they going to ride off into the sunset as the credits began to roll? How many times had her mom told her to "be realistic" and "don't let yourself get hurt?"

She had not heard anything from Cody in almost three weeks. Maybe he was already sitting on that tractor and planning to propose marriage to some Iowa girl whose daddy owned lots of corn and pigs. Charley had told her that he read somewhere that Buffalo Bill Cody had been born in Iowa, and maybe that's where Cody got his name. He might even be related to Buffalo Bill, Charley had said. If that were true, then the Cody name had simply gone through the cycle of journey and return. Maybe all the Codys in the world were destined to return to Iowa someday.

Late in the afternoon the four wild cowgirls pulled up their trusty steeds and looked back. Nobody following us. Time to ride back to the ranch house. The mountains to the east could wait another day. We turned and headed back west, as the sun began its final descent over Reno and the Sierras.

Mel, who might have been a scout in an earlier life, spotted it first. "Look up there," she said.

"I don't see anything," I said.

"Something's kicking up dust," Mel said.

"That's probably just a little whirlwind kicking up," Harm said.

"No, I don't think so," Mel said.

"Not enough dust for a whole posse," I said. "Maybe it's just one big old sheriff riding out to bring us to justice. I hope he's cute."

Lacey suddenly yelled "He-yah!" to Grazer, who took off at a full gallop ahead of the other three.

"What's with Lacey?" Mel asked.

"She must be lonelier than we thought," I said. "As soon as I started talking about cute sheriffs, she took off. Let's give her a head start. She's more eager to go to jail than the rest of us."

With her jump on the others, Lacey was the first to recognize that the dust Mel had seen was not a desert whirlwind but the result of a single horse and rider, and the mysterious horseman was riding straight for them. Lacey thought at first it could be Chance Johnson, someone who knew where they were and was riding out to join them or tell them dinner was ready or some chores were waiting. As the rider came closer, however, she suddenly recognized who it was by the way he rode.

Lacey urged Grazer to go faster, and the quarter horse took off as if they were being timed and he was racing from the final barrel to the finish line. All the mental exercises Lacey had been putting herself through that afternoon, all the annoying questions and big thoughts and speculation about the future, all of that was left in the dust. She was pure action now, totally involved in the present. As the distance between the two riders closed, Lacey reached for the rope she had brought along. She swung it above her head and then, when the moment was right, she threw it toward the mysterious horseman. It flew straight to its target and settled around the cowboy. Lacey pulled it tight and tied her end of the rope to her saddle horn. She climbed down from Grazer, who backed up to keep the rope taut.

Lacey ran up to the cowboy, who had managed to free himself of the rope and was just jumping down to the ground. "Gee, ma'am," he said, "you didn't have to rope me. I'm not going anywhere."

Lacey threw her arms around Cody, as if to hold him to that promise. "Cody, you came back," she said, without loosening her grip on the cowboy.

"Of course I came back," Cody said. Lacey let go and moved her hands up to put them on Cody's shoulders. Cody looked into her green eyes. "I told you I'd come back, I just didn't know when. Did you ever doubt it?"

Lacey decided not to answer that question. Instead she distracted him by moving her hands to the back of his neck and moving her face closer to his. Cody met her halfway. The kiss that followed was one of the great kisses of the Wild West. No one was timing it, but it did go on a considerably long time. If Charley had been there, he might have compared it to the reunion of a legendary outlaw and his cowgirl sweetheart, after the outlaw had escaped from a Kansas jail and ridden for three days to see her again.

By this time, the twins and I had caught up with Lacey and witnessed the final ten seconds of the kiss. When Cody and Lacey finally came up for air, I started applauding and cheering, and Mel and Harm joined me. "Welcome home, cowboy," I said.

Lacey gathered her rope and got back on top of Grazer. Cody climbed into his saddle, and the two of them rode up ahead. Just then the sky was beginning to light up with a brilliant display of sunset colors—shades of gold and red. We watched them ride back toward the ranch house. Then I looked over at Mel and Harm.

"I swear, it's just like a movie," I said as I wiped some tears from my cheek. "I'm sorry, but I'm a sucker for happy endings."

30 Donna

"Epilogue: letters from home…"

Cody West's blue pickup truck was his favorite possession. It had served him well during the most eventful six months of his life, beginning with that May day when he and Charley Meyers had gone out to Bob Morgan's place to buy it. He still enjoyed looking at the photograph that Bob took to preserve the occasion. As Charley had predicted, the old Dodge pickup made him half a cowboy, and the rest was just a matter of time and practice.

It was the truck that had transported Cody and Lacey to that romantic cemetery date in Virginia City. It was in that truck that he and Lacey had listened to so many great Western songs, humming and singing along. The old pickup had taken him over the Sierras to San Francisco back in August, to Lacey's arms and to his date with a hero's destiny on the fateful cable car ride. It had taken Cody and Lacey across the foggy Golden Gate Bridge to the beautiful wine country and the haunting ruins of Jack London's Wolf House. When his aunt and uncle needed him back in Iowa, the truck had rushed him safely back to Iowa. And when Uncle Max had improved enough for Cody to leave, it had carried him back to Reno and the cowgirl who had won his heart.

It was also a truck that was dirty most of the time. Although Cody had the best intentions of keeping it as clean and shining as was possible for an old pickup, there was always something more pressing that caused him to put off washing the truck. Cody could count on the fingers of one hand the number of times he had washed the truck, since the week he bought it and became so preoccupied with Lacey's company that he first put off washing it. Charley used to joke that he couldn't tell whether it was a blue truck or a black truck. He sometimes referred to it as Old Black and Blue, but Cody just called it "my truck."

Cody's truck, which was what everyone else called it, sat parked in front of his apartment building one Saturday morning in November, only two weeks after Cody had returned to restore Lacey's faith in happy endings. By coming back to Reno, he had also destroyed her theory about Cody completing the cycle of journey-and-return-to-Iowa that Buffalo Bill Cody had started. Cody was back, which meant that Cody's truck was back, and after the long drive from Iowa, and two weeks in Reno, the pickup was showing more dirt than blue paint.

Lacey, who had been spending every minute of her free time with her long lost cowboy, offered to help him wash it. And so it was that on a chilly November morning, Lacey and Cody were out with a hose and buckets and sponges, restoring the blue splendor to Cody's truck. Lacey had dressed appropriately for the occasion in faded jeans and a warm University of Nevada sweatshirt I had given her. She and her cowboy had hosed down the truck and were about to start in with the soapy sponges when a small postal truck pulled in with the Saturday mail. Cody walked over to the mailbox and returned with a small handful of mail. He sat down on the curb and began to open a manila envelope. He saw at once that it was from his aunt and uncle in Iowa, and he wanted to know how they were doing.

Lacey tossed her sponge in the bucket and called out, "Hey, cowboy, what's up?"

"It's from my Aunt Alice and Uncle Max," Cody said.

"Oh, I hope they're all right," Lacey said, and she went back to washing the truck.

When Cody opened the manila envelope he found a couple of folded sheets of stationery with his aunt's handwriting and a sealed envelope with "Alan Cody West" written across the front. He held it up to the light but couldn't see much, so he started reading his aunt's letter.

Dear Cody, it began. Aunt Alice had written *"Alan"* and then crossed it out and written *"Cody."*

I'm glad you had a safe trip back to Reno. Forgive me if I worry about you, but you're like a son to me and I wouldn't want anything bad to ever happen to you. Just keep away from wild women, and if you have to go into one of those casinos don't bet more than you can afford to lose. Max told me you usually win anyway. He thinks it's your cowboy hat that holds your luck, so he told me to remind you to wear it whenever you visit one of those places. If you hang around with wild women, though, you're on your own, and I wish you luck because you'll need it.

Thank you again for all your help. I don't know what I would have done if you hadn't been here. Mostly you kept your Uncle Max's spirits up. You have a way of talking to him that nobody else has. He's improved even more since you left, so don't you worry about us. We'll be fine. And you're welcome to come back and visit anytime. Next time bring that lawyer lady friend of yours. We'd love to meet her. Tell her to watch out for those big drinks, like the ones she and her friend were holding in that picture you showed us.

I'm enclosing a letter that's addressed to you. I was cleaning out the attic yesterday and I found it hidden away in an old trunk. It was with some old papers and things that we've had ever since your mother passed on. I've never wanted to throw anything of hers away, and I'm sorry I never saw this letter until just yesterday. I left it sealed, although Max said I should open it and photocopy it, in case it got lost in the mail. I just said a little prayer that God would watch over it, and if you're reading this then my prayer was answered.

Take care of yourself, Cody. (I'm still trying to get used to calling you "Cody.") Give us a call sometime and let us know how you're doing. I'll try not to worry about you. And I'll say a prayer for you every day.

Love,
Aunt Alice

Cody held the envelope containing his mother's letter to him and stared at it a long time before opening it. All of his memories of her came rushing back. It had been more than twenty years since he had seen her. The envelope had been sealed with a red wax seal, and Cody's fingers shook slightly as he slowly broke the seal. He found that breathing had become difficult, and he tried to compose himself before beginning to read his mother's words.

"My dear son,

I know I am getting weaker and I may not have a chance to tell you this when you're older and can understand it all. I'll give this to your Aunt Alice and she can give it to you when you're older.

People are always asking me why I chose "Cody" for your middle name. I just tell them I liked the sound of it, and they're satisfied with that. Sometimes they'll ask if you're named for Buffalo Bill Cody, and I just laugh and say no. Buffalo Bill was born in Iowa, but you're not related to him, as far as I know. Your dad named you "Alan," which is a good, strong name. I know that everyone calls you Alan, including me, but I've always thought of you as "Cody."

You may not remember all the times I took you to cowboy movies, when your father was still alive and you were just a little squirt, and then later after he passed on and it was just you and me at the movies. We'd walk home after a Saturday matinee and you would protect me from the bad guys, using your finger as a six-shooter. You were my little cowboy.

Once they brought back Red River, and we went to see it, and afterwards you told me you were going to be just like "the John Wayne guy" when you grew up, and I told you that you could be anything you wanted to be, if you just put your mind to it. And that's still true. Don't ever forget it.

What I wanted to tell you about was some things that happened before you were born. When I graduated from high school, like a lot of people I didn't know what I wanted to do with my life. I was working that summer as a waitress in a little cafe in town. It's not even there anymore. One fine day in June a young cowboy walked in the door and sat down at one of my tables. He ordered chili (funny how you remember things like that) and told me he was on his way back to Wyoming from Chicago. He was having some engine trouble with his truck and had left it at a garage down the street. They told him he'd have to wait a few days for the part they needed, so he asked me where was a good place to stay and what was there to do in town.

I gave him the name of a motel and told him there wasn't a whole lot to do but that I'd be glad to show him the sights if he waited till I got off work. I wasn't in the habit of running around with strangers, but this cowboy was so nice and looked so lonesome that I felt like helping him out. He had the kindest blue eyes I ever saw. I asked him what kind of cowboy he was and he told me rodeo cowboy, mostly bareback and saddle bronc. He said he tried to stay as far away from the bulls as possible. He said a rodeo cowboy had to be a little crazy, but too crazy could get you hurt.

After my lunch shift was over I drove him over to the motel so he could check in, then I took him for a tour of the town.

He took an interest in everything, but mostly I think he was interested in me. I had never had a fellow treat me so nicely. I felt like a queen. He had dinner at the cafe, and when my dinner shift was over, we drove around some more. We went to a movie. They were playing some Western movie—I can't remember which one anymore. I do remember that he pointed out different things about the movie cowboys, how they rode and how they dressed, and so on. Every time he spotted something that Hollywood had gotten wrong he would start laughing and shake his head. Looking back, I'd say that watching him was a lot more interesting than watching the movie.

The next day he hung around the cafe some more, and I got someone to take my dinner shift, so we had most of the day together. We drove out in the country a ways, and I started seeing everything through his eyes. Those cornfields that I had seen all my life, the way he described them it was like seeing them for the first time. He talked a lot about Wyoming and Montana and the Dakotas, how they were different. He made them sound like a part of heaven.

I remember he said that when God was finished with the rest of the country, and he got around to creating the West, he just let himself go. He didn't hold back anything, or care what anybody said. That's why you see all those strange and wonderful landscapes throughout the West, all those canyons and craggy mountains, wild rivers and wild animals. The way that cowboy talked he just took my breath away.

On the third day, after the part had come in at the garage, and his truck was ready for the trip to Wyoming, I was ready too. I can't remember whether he asked me to go with him, or I asked him to take me, but it just seemed the natural thing to do. I wanted to see the West, and I wanted to see more of that cowboy. I left a note behind for my folks, because I knew they would just scream if I asked their permission. I promised I'd call would just scream if I asked their permission. I promised I'd call and write them, and I did. I wasn't running away from them, or the town, or anything else. I was just running to something.

My cowboy and I had a wonderful summer together. We followed the trail from one rodeo to another. We got as far north as Calgary and as far west as Reno. He was a good saddle bronc rider, and a better bareback rider. You should have seen him in the arena. I never got tired of watching him compete. He won enough prize money to get us from one rodeo to the next. It was a romantic life. And the West was everything he had said it was. I saw God's imagination in so many things out there.

It was some kind of fairy tale story I was living that summer, but it didn't last. He always treated me like a queen, so it wasn't him. I don't know. I guess I was too young. I wasn't ready to choose any one life, or any one man. I'd get quiet, and by the time fall came around we were not as close. We never fought, that's the funny thing. We'd be going down the road, and I'd be staring out the window of the truck, and he'd ask me if I was all right, and I'd just smile at him and say I was okay, but he knew something was bothering me.

I tried to stay. I kept hoping that whatever was happening inside me would go away and things between us would be the same as before. But I just got quieter. One night in Cheyenne I started crying and told him I had to go back to Iowa, that I was no good for him anymore. He tried to talk me out of it, but he saw it was no use. The next morning he drove me down to the bus station and bought me a ticket to Iowa. When the bus pulled out I looked back and waved at him, and he smiled and waved back. I think I cried all the way back home.

I always thought that the timing was all wrong with us, that I should have met him several years later. We would have had a different ending. Two years after that I met your father. He was a good man, and I loved him very much. My heart broke in two the day he died. Just before you were born, when your father was still with us, we were still looking for a name for you. I asked your father to choose your first name and I would think of a middle name for you. If you had been a girl you would have been Sarah Annie. (Your father had taken me to a movie about Annie Oakley.)

Your dad finally chose "Alan" for you. I didn't think twice—you were going to be Alan Cody West. I never talked to anyone about my rodeo cowboy, and nobody ever knew that he was from Cody, Wyoming.

So now you know. I hope you'll understand all these things when you're older. It's taken me a long time to make sense of it all. I know you'll have a good life. Build on your dreams and make them come true. Think of me now and then.

All my love,
Your Mom

"Cody, you're shivering." It was Lacey. She sat down next to him on the curb. He looked at her and brushed some soapsuds off her cheek.

"You're crying," she said.

Cody sighed. "I'm all right," he said. He handed her the letter. "It's a letter from my mom. She wrote it before she died and my aunt just found it in her attic. Do you want to read it?"

"If you want me to," Lacey said.

"I want you to," Cody said. "It's a beautiful letter. I wish she were here. I know she'd like you." Cody stood up and walked a few steps away while Lacey read the letter.

Cody glanced at his truck. Lacey had gotten all the dirt off and it sparkled again. He remembered the first night after he bought it, going down during the night just to look at it in the moonlight. He thought about his mother at eighteen—riding in a pickup at night along some lonesome Wyoming road with her rodeo cowboy, watching the moon and the stars and thinking the big thoughts. Then he watched Lacey's face as she finished reading the letter.

When she had read the last line, Lacey carefully folded the letter and held it against her heart. She looked up at Cody, then walked over to him and put her arms around him. She held him close for a while, without saying a word. Then she put her lips next to his ear and whispered, "Thanks, cowboy."

When they had finished drying the truck, Lacey asked Cody to take her for a ride.

"I'll go anywhere with you," Cody said. "Where do you want to go?"

"Take me up to Virginia City," she said. "I think it's a good day for tumbleweeds. Let's ride along and sing cowboy songs until we're up in those mountains. Let's just keep going and going and never stop dreaming."

And that's exactly what they did.

In the high desert country of northern Nevada, far from the lights of Las Vegas, each new season brings its own beauty, and it own signs. According to one Reno cowboy named Charley Meyers, the one with the gravelly voice, you didn't have to check the calendar to know that winter was on the way. Charley said you could tell because in the morning the coffee and hotcakes tasted better.

Then there was me, the Reno cowgirl who dreamed of becoming a rodeo queen, the one with all that big blonde hair. I told Charley I could tell when winter was coming down the trail because the nights were growing colder and the cowboys were growing warmer. But that's another season, and that's another story.

THE END

MICHAEL LITTLE

is a native Texan who wandered off to Seattle, then ended up in Hawai'i, where he writes novels and short stories that take a comic look at romance and modern life. His research for *Queen of the Rodeo* and *Chasing Cowboys* included frequent trips to Reno and the Reno Rodeo, where he interviewed rodeo queens and watched crazy brave cowboys flying off wild horses and bulls.

www.michael-little.com
ourchiefweapon.blogspot.com

STEPHANIE CHANG, the book designer, is trying out her rodeo queen wave with anyone who will oblige. As Director and designer of Stephanie Chang Design Ink, she is fortunate her job involves "travel" to places as fascinating as the American West. She is honored to work with people as interesting as Donna Cooper and the very big Michael Little.

Please visit www.stephanieink.com.

Printed in the United States
148827LV00001B/1/P

9 780971 795655